THE SIGNAL LINE

THE
SIGNAL
LINE

BRENDAN
COLLEY

transit lounge

MELBOURNE, AUSTRALIA
www.transitlounge.com.au
First published 2022
Transit Lounge Publishing

Copyright ©2022 Brendan Colley

Cover design: Josh Durham/Design by Committee
Author Image: Sophie Reid/Concrete Cloud Photography
Typeset in Adobe Garamond Pro by Cannon Typesetting

Printed in Australia by McPherson's Printing Group

A catalogue record for this book is available from the
National Library of Australia: http://catalogue.nla.gov.au

ISBN: 978-1-925760-94-1

For Yvonne

CHAPTER ONE

As IT HAPPENED, I arrived in Tasmania on the same night as the ghost train.

In the airport I scanned the crowd for my brother, regretting my acceptance of his offer to pick me up. I spotted Wes across the floor, his eyes fixed on me as he spoke on his phone. My heart sank. His creased suit and bloodshot eyes, from drink and lack of sleep, said everything.

I trudged over with a small bag of belongings in one hand, and my most valuable possession in the other. When my mother had gifted me her viola for my thirteenth birthday, even my father had been surprised. Seventeen years on, it was more than an instrument for my dreams; it contained every important memory I had of her.

Wes's voice rose an octave as I neared him. 'Rome? Bullshit.'

I crouched down and fished my mobile from my bag.

'Who's the psych doctor on duty? Tell Martin I've got a translator.' Wes glanced down at me.

I felt a prickle of irritation. Our ten-year age gap may have meant something when I was living in Hobart, but we weren't going to pick up from where we left off.

'And tell him to tell Alice. I don't want a scene when I arrive. I'll front up to Henry in the morning – this is on me.'

I started a text message to Alessia, saying it was all a mistake, that within a minute of being back I was reminded of why I'd left.

'Yeah, fluent,' Wes said.

But it wasn't fair to worry her. Without Alessia I'd never have found the courage to return. I deleted the message.

Wes finished his call. 'Let's go.'

I grabbed my bag and viola, and followed him out. As the terminal doors swept open, we stepped into a tepid Tasmanian summer evening.

Wes led me over to an unmarked police car, parked out front, and went around to the driver's side. 'We have to swing by Royal Hobart Hospital,' he said, resting an arm on the roof. 'Marty's got his hands full with a situation that's about to blow.'

I slid my baggage onto the back seat. 'Perfect. I'll walk from there.'

'We may need you for translation. You're fluent, right?'

There was no way he was pulling me into this. 'What are you talking about?'

'A group of Italians got picked up at the old Hobart yard. Apparently they got off a train all panicked. Now Martin's —'

'Tassie doesn't have passenger trains.'

'No shit. Problem is, none of them speak English.'

An uncomfortable moment passed as we considered one another.

He raised a hand. 'I'm in a spot here, Geo. Will you do this for me?'

Everything that followed happened because in that moment I forgot my reasons and baulked. 'I don't know … I'm scratchy.'

He pulled the magnetic siren off the car roof. 'Scratchy will do just fine.'

#

Wes and I didn't talk on the fifteen-minute drive from the airport, although that in itself wasn't unusual. I sensed something was troubling him, and when we arrived at the Royal Hobart I waited back as he scanned the information board for *Psychological Medicine*. It was my first time at the hospital since Mum had passed, and I didn't need a reminder that the oncology clinic for outpatients was on level one.

We found B Block on the ground floor and followed a sign down a narrow corridor to the Department of Psychiatry. The posters on the walls alerted us to the change in clinical environments. *Warning: This is a Hospital Watch Area; NO EXCUSE FOR ABUSE; Verbal & Physical Abuse WILL NOT BE TOLERATED; If You Display Offensive Behaviour You Will Be Asked to Leave.*

A policewoman stood guard outside the ward. She tensed when she saw us approaching.

'Alice,' Wes said with a small nod.

Her hand motioned towards the radio mic clipped to her shirt. 'Martin's inside with them. I've been told not to let anyone through.'

'My brother just got in from Italy. We're hoping he can help with translation.'

Alice's gaze came to rest on me. I shifted uneasily.

'That's lucky,' she said.

Wes ran a hand over stubble shot through with grey. In the fluorescent light I couldn't tell if he'd just been on the job for a week or had completely stopped taking care of himself. In the three years I'd been away, it seemed my brother had aged a decade.

He was straining to see through the small window in the door. 'Has anyone managed to communicate with them?'

The've been pretty hysterical since we picked them up. One's heavily pregnant.'

Wes cleared his throat. 'Alice … help me out here.'

In that moment, I understood. Alice's instructions weren't that nobody should be let through, but that *Wes* shouldn't be let through. Embarrassed, I pulled my mobile from my pocket, searching for a distraction.

I glanced up to see Alice pushing open the door. 'Be good, okay?' she said to Wes. 'Border Force arrived five minutes ago.'

Wes swept into the ward, and I hurried after him. Confidence had returned to his step now he was free to do his job.

When we turned into the unit's processing area, I pulled up in surprise. The Italians were scattered about the room, their distressed chatter echoing off the walls. A handful sat in front-facing chairs, but the majority were gathered in small groups. The thing that struck me were the heavy coats, jackets, scarves and gloves. The youngest among them, the pregnant lady, sat alone.

On the opposite side of the room a doctor was in discussion with a uniformed man, *ABF* stamped across his shirt in yellow block letters: Australian Border Force. Standing with them was

Martin Bowden, Wes's partner and best mate since their general duty days.

A man in his sixties was speaking to a nurse a few feet from me and Wes. He held a fedora pressed to his chest. The nurse leaned in to catch his words but clearly didn't understand anything he was saying.

Wes approached them and addressed the nurse. 'I'm Detective Rosenberger. How many are there in the group?'

'Twenty-seven,' she said briskly.

'And none speak any English?'

'Not that we can tell. Communication's limited to hand gestures and drawings.'

The din behind us grew louder.

'Then why have they been brought to the psych ward?' Wes asked, narrowing his eyes. 'Maybe this is all just a misunderstanding.'

The nurse skewed a glance at the Italians huddled in the chairs. Her expression hardened. 'It's clear enough they're trying to tell us they got here by train.'

'You mean from Italy?'

She gave a curt nod.

I glanced at the man with the fedora, who was still standing with us, watching Wes with either bemusement or distrust.

'Could they have dementia?' Wes asked bluntly.

'Well, delusions in mid-to-late-stage Alzheimer's patients aren't uncommon, but I've never heard of a case of mass delusion brought on by dementia. And what about the pregnant woman?'

Wes huffed. 'They have to be delusional, though. Or they're being coerced somehow – maybe even drugged.'

She gestured to the Border Force officer. 'Then what's he doing here?'

Wes stared across the room but said nothing.

'It's morning in Rome,' she said. 'The weather app says it's six degrees. They're dressed for it, wouldn't you say? Their wallets contain euros, electronic identity cards, Italian health cards, driver's licences. Where are their passports? Their travel documents? Not one of them has a single Australian dollar.' She shrugged. 'Maybe they're telling the truth.'

'What about the train?' Wes said belligerently.

'Transcontinental rail isn't my field.' Her tone was acid. 'These people are disoriented, not insane.'

I whispered to Wes, 'Are you sure I need to be here, man?'

The nurse suddenly seemed suspicious of us. 'I'm sorry, who did you say you were?'

'I'm Detective Wes Rosenberger, and this is my brother, Geo. He speaks Italian, so he can clear everything up right now. Geo, ask this gentleman how they got here.'

The Italian man wore a faded suit, a size too big, over a frayed white shirt. His fedora was as weathered as he was, but he projected a certain dignity.

I cleared my throat. 'Ciao, mi chiamo Geo Rosenberger. Forgive my poor Italian. This is my brother, Detective Wes Rosenberger. Come ti chiami?'

'Giacomo Pedroni,' the man said.

'Di dove sei?' I asked.

The man replied in his native tongue. 'Inform your brother we are Italian citizens. Today we boarded a train in Orvieto bound for Rome. Please tell me where we are.'

I stared at him.

'What did he say?' Wes asked.

I shook my head. 'He's delusional.'

Wes frowned in annoyance. 'Tell me what he said, not what you think.'

I told him, then added, 'Now they're here. Giacomo wants to know where here is.'

'What are you waiting for? Let's see his reaction.'

'Are you crazy? I don't want to be responsible for giving him a heart attack.'

'Lucky we're in a hospital. Tell the man where he is.'

'It isn't my job.'

Wes rolled his eyes and said to Giacomo. 'Tasmania, Australia.'

Giacomo's expression fell. With slumped shoulders, he turned to his compatriots and waved them closer. 'Come around. Please. Per favore vieni qui.' A quietness settled in the room as those furthest away shifted to nearby chairs. Giacomo gave a resigned shrug. 'It is true. Siamo in Tasmania, Australia.'

The group erupted in shouts, everyone gesticulating wildly. A seated man laughed in disbelief.

Martin glanced in our direction, then shook his head and returned his attention to the doctor and the Border Force officer.

'They're sincere,' Wes said.

I let out a nervous laugh. 'If they're sincere —'

'Find out who he is,' Wes said sharply. 'Why are they letting him speak for them?'

I tapped Giacomo on the shoulder. 'Scusi, Giacomo. Spiegare … did you offer to speak on their behalf?'

'I am the mayor of the town from which we come.'

'I understood that,' Wes said. 'Ask him for his ticket.'

'Ten bucks he doesn't have one.'

'Ask him.'

I turned to Giacomo. 'Posso vedere il suo biglietto, per favore?'

'The conductor collected our tickets.'

'How convenient,' I said in English. 'The conductor collected their tickets.'

Giacomo must have sensed my scepticism. 'He collected everyone's ticket. It seemed strange at the time because in Italy the ticket is clicked, but I didn't question it. The conductor too seemed strange.'

'How so?'

'He spoke poor Italian. Your Italian is better, although that is being disrespectful to you. But this conductor ... era incomprensibile.'

'Get the train details,' Wes told me, as he reached into his jacket for his notebook and flipped it open. 'Number, platform, departure time, arrival time in Rome. Anything he can remember.'

Giacomo provided the information with the help of those who were regular commuters on the route.

'Six-thirteen Trenitalia per Roma termini,' a woman to the side said. Her arms were crossed over a hessian bag. 'My husband and I take it the first Monday of every month to visit our daughter's family.'

'Piattaforma tre,' the man next to her agreed.

'The first train of the day is not direct,' a man two rows back offered. 'You have to change in Orte.'

Swivelling around, the woman wagged her finger. 'Except this train did not stop.'

The man nodded. 'The train today was direct. From Orvieto to here – whatever here is.'

Wes scribbled everything down as I translated. 'Hobart,' he said.

'Whatever Hobart is,' the man sneered.

The pregnant lady cradled her belly and glanced across at me. 'The regular train has six carriages. This train had two. That is why I was concerned.'

Wes glanced at me. 'Why did she board the train if she felt uneasy about it?'

The lady responded to my translation. 'Everyone was getting on.' She shrugged. 'It was the correct time. I get on the train every week with these people.'

'I don't like it,' Wes muttered. 'Not one bit.' He underlined something in his notebook. 'At what point did they realise they were no longer in Italy?'

'You're not actually buying this?' I said under my breath.

'I'm interested in what they think.'

I repeated Wes's question to Giacomo.

He ran his hand over his fedora. 'When the door opened and the conductor ushered us out of the carriage – I knew then. I knew the platform was not an Italian platform. And I knew the train was not an ordinary train.'

'In what way?' Wes asked, in response to my translation. 'I mean the train, not the platform.'

When I put this to Giacomo, he said something I couldn't understand.

'Scomparso,' another man said, joining the conversation.

The woman behind him agreed. 'Digli.'

The man who had laughed earlier waved his hand as if to suggest the situation belied belief and was undeserving of discussion.

Giacomo tightened his grip on his hat. 'I knew it was not an ordinary train because when the doors closed, it rolled forward ... and vanished.'

Wes's hand froze on his pen. 'Did he say what I think he said?'

I hesitated.

Giacomo lifted the fedora to his head and adjusted the angle. 'Scomparso.'

Wes sighed and flipped his notebook shut just as Martin caught his attention and waved him over. 'Mi scusi,' Wes said, crossing the room.

Giacomo and I watched him join Martin, the doctor and the Border Force officer.

'They are trying to decide if we are an immigration situation or a psychiatric situation,' the mayor said. 'Tell me I am wrong.'

A wave of tiredness swept over me – a combination of jet lag and being in the same room as my brother for too long. 'You are not wrong.'

'They can see we are from Italy. But the situation is impossible. Tell me I am right.'

'You are right.'

'You speak in an interesting style. Sometimes basic. I understand you perfectly ... but basic. And sometimes natural. Perché?'

'I am presently living in Rome. My mother was Italian.'

Hearing that I had arrived from their country, the passengers behind Giacomo agitated to life; perhaps I could attend to their complaints.

A man with a thick moustache cried, 'We need food. We haven't eaten since this morning.'

The man next to him jumped to his feet. 'Ignore this fool. He ate an hour ago. My situation is critical – I have not yet had my espresso. Show me your machine. I am a barista, so I can relax the situation for everybody.'

A woman squeezed between the men and placed her hands on her hips. 'If you are the police, I want my phone call. You say this is Australia? Pfffft. What is your name? I know people. Make no mistake, when I speak to them I am blaming you.'

As the crowd echoed their agreement, Giacomo looked back to me. 'You returned to Australia when?'

'Sta sera,' I said.

'You arrived by plane?'

'Si.'

A faint cry drew our attention. The pregnant woman leaned back, fluid pooling beneath her chair. The nurse hurried over, followed by the doctor. Wes and Martin came over to where Giacomo and I were standing. None of the Italians stepped forward to support the young lady; it appeared she was travelling alone.

'Border Force is taking it,' Martin said to Wes. 'They're bringing in an expert to rule out psychosis and other psychological disturbances. Assuming everything checks off, the Italians will be repatriated.'

'Where will they stay?' I asked Martin.

'Here,' he answered. 'They have the beds.'

Wes nodded. 'It's a sequestered environment.'

I shook my head, watching as Giacomo left us to weave among the group. 'I'm no expert, but that man is in his right mind.'

Wes snorted. '*Now* you think they arrived by train?'

'That's not what I said.'

'We're late,' he said, and marched off.

As I turned to follow him, Martin put a hand to my arm. 'Call if you need anything.'

I took the card he offered, but I didn't know what he meant by it. 'Thanks.'

He ambled back over to the Border Force officer as the doctor and nurse helped the pregnant lady into a wheelchair.

#

Wes drove us away from the hospital up Elizabeth Street. I wound down the window so the rush of air would keep my eyelids from closing. My mind drifted to our family home, and how a real estate agent might pitch it.

Comfortable three-bedroom weatherboard in North Hobart. Living room and Dining Room, one bathroom and toilet. A fourth space perfect as a study, nursery or yoga room. Back-yard studio set up for an artist/musician, but easily repurposed into a workshop or shed. Walking distance to schools and cafés.

Who wouldn't want to live there?

My last memory of the house was slamming the front door behind me and swearing I'd never again step inside. But my brother and I weren't selling a memory, we were selling a dream.

'That was pretty fucked up back there,' Wes said.

The comment jolted me out of my musings. 'Yeah. Totally.' The trick was to get him to drop me off without coming inside. 'You can let me out at State. No need to drive around.' I said this casually, like it made no difference at all.

The State Cinema was located at the end of the restaurant strip in North Hobart, a short hop across from our place on Yardley Street.

'We need to cut you a key,' he said.

'It's okay. I still have mine.'

Wes shifted in his seat. 'He changed the locks after you left.'

I didn't say anything.

'In any case,' he added, 'you're having dinner at ours.'

'Huh?'

'Nic insisted.'

'I've been in transit for twenty-eight hours. All I want is a shower and my bed. I'm sure Nic will understand.'

'Max is dead. I should have told you right away.'

'What?'

'Not long after Dad. He was eleven, so … you know.'

I stared out the window.

'Some people die after the people they loved die,' Wes said. 'Same for dogs, I guess.'

Within a week of Mum's funeral I'd flown out of Tasmania. Six months later our father died of a broken heart. At least, that's what the doctor told Wes. Maybe the doctor elaborated, but Wes didn't; when he tracked me down to give me the news, he kept it to that.

A detective in the Tasmanian Police, our father had been shot in the leg when I was fourteen. The bullet shattered his femur, and after twelve weeks in hospital he returned home with a defective gait that remained with him for the rest of his life. He wasn't demoted to a desk job, he was promoted to a desk job. I still remember the ceremony where the lord mayor hung the medal around his neck and joked, 'A tough cop who took shit from nobody. The station officers are on notice.' Smiles and light laughter from the audience. But being pulled off the street was like a punishment to our father. Enter Max. 'To temper the fire,' Mum said to me. She was almost right: it did nothing to the fire, but from the moment Max raised his head out of the box, he and our father were inseparable.

With Max gone, that left Wes and me. And the only thing binding us together was that damned house on Yardley Street.

Hayden was waiting on the porch when we pulled into the driveway in New Town. I climbed out thinking to sweep him into a hug, but when I saw how much he'd grown I held out my hand instead. We shook awkwardly. 'You've turned into a man,' I said.

Hayden squinted at my hair. 'You're going grey.'

'A sign of maturity, pal.'

Nic appeared in the doorway with a smile. Sidestepping Wes, she came over to embrace me. 'We missed you, Geo. You must be tired. I suggested tomorrow, but Wes was adamant.'

I fought back a comment and followed everyone inside.

If not for Hayden and Godfrey, their four-year-old Boston terrier, I'd have been forgiven for thinking my time away was a dream and I'd been over for dinner the week before. It wasn't the chipped kitchenware or the bowl on the counter with the plastic fruit. It wasn't the boxy television on the mahogany unit in the living room. It wasn't our parents' old fridge, which had needed replacing even before I helped bring it across as a stop-gap measure. It wasn't Wes in his frayed black suit and loose-fitting tie, and Nic in the faded red dress she'd worn to my graduation. It was the tension between them we pretended not to notice.

Wes disappeared to the other end of the house, and I helped Nic and Hayden bring dinner to the dining table. Nic removed a pre-cooked chicken from a sealed bag and placed it on a cutting board. 'I would have preferred to have made something, but with rehearsals, cooking is a luxury I don't have at the moment.'

'It smells great, Mum,' Hayden said, filling our glasses with sparkling water.

'You're a darling.'

'You're playing again?' I asked.

'A quartet. Nothing major – some friends, with a little time on our hands.'

Wes walked into the dining room, buttoning up a shirt, his hair wet and combed back. He sat across from Nic. 'Wouldn't take much to put a chicken in the oven,' he said.

She refused to meet his gaze.

He tucked a paper serviette into his shirt. 'A sprinkle of salt and pepper, and a lemon. I'm just saying?'

'They're performing at MOFO,' Hayden said, spooning tabouleh onto his plate from a plastic container.

I looked at Nic. 'That's huge. When?'

MONA FOMA was a music and arts festival that staged a mixed bag of performances across Hobart every January.

'Tomorrow night in the annexe at St Mary's Cathedral,' Hayden said. 'I'm away with the orchestra, so I'm going to miss it.'

Nic eyed Wes. 'That reminds me … I need to talk to you about something.'

'Say it.'

She grimaced. 'Not now.'

Wes angled his fork at me. 'We're with family.'

In the pause that followed, I recognised in Nic what I'd been through years ago: a final-round tiredness from the constant sparring that came with being bound to my brother.

'I've paid for Hayden's excurs —'

'I'll sort it out tomorrow,' Wes said.

Nic passed the pack of serviettes to me. 'What about you, Geo? How are the auditions going?'

'They're still going,' Wes said, scraping the last of the potato salad onto his plate.

She glared at him.

15

'He's right,' I said. 'The process is so artificial … I struggle to produce my best music out of context and on cue. I'm getting better, though. Bit by bit I'm getting there.'

'You'll break through,' said Nic. 'You want it badly enough. It's only a matter of time.'

'How long are you back for?' Hayden asked.

'Good question, mate. As long as it takes to sell the house.'

The table fell silent. Wes laid down his utensils. 'Like fuck you are.'

'Take your dinner to your room,' Nic said to Hayden.

In a move that felt rehearsed, he left the table with his plate.

Wes glowered at me. 'You flew back to sell the house?'

I dabbed my mouth with the serviette.

'You flew back for nothing,' he said.

'I have a legal right.'

'It's our family home.'

His response left me unmoved. I was looking for reasons to lose a brother, not keep one. 'I need the money for the audition circuit.'

He laughed. 'You have no talent.'

'It's what Mum would have wanted.'

'Anyone who looks to their mother for a measure of their potential is a fool.'

'That's *my* problem. The house is *our* problem. If you can't buy me out, we'll sell. I've engaged a lawyer.'

Nic frowned at Wes. 'You haven't told him?'

He ignored her. 'I won't allow you to piss our home down the toilet.'

'It wasn't a home then, and it's not a home now.'

He slammed his fist onto the table, sending his plate smashing to the floor. 'We're not selling the fucking house.'

'Enough,' Nic said, her voice shaking.

I'd expected this reaction, but I was angry at myself for forcing the issue in front of Nic and Hayden. I pushed back my chair. 'I'll get my things from the car.'

'Wait outside,' Wes commanded, pointing at me.

'Give me the keys. I can walk.'

'Wait by the car.'

'I want you to leave now,' Nic said to Wes. I could see it took all her strength not to avert her gaze.

'Shit.' Wes threw down his serviette and strode out.

She leaned forward, her head in her hands.

'I'm sorry,' I said.

'Just go, Geo.'

#

I trailed Wes onto the porch of our house on Yardley Street. He unlocked the door and stepped inside.

My pulse quickened, an ice-cold tide of adrenalin washing through me. I'd never felt at ease here after Mum died, and the feeling hadn't changed with time. I peered into the hallway without crossing the threshold. The stale air that wafted out was paint-thick. Alessia and I had talked about how I needed to be in the right emotional space before I entered. She'd wanted us to do it together, with me conjuring an image of her standing beside me or slightly behind me. I was sure I needed to do it alone.

The last time I'd passed through this door was with our father drunkenly in tow, waving his cane at me. I shouted that I wasn't ever coming back. He shouted that if I changed my mind, forget it, I wasn't welcome back. The taxi driver didn't flinch at the obscenities hailing down on us. Now here I was, re-entering under the only condition possible: because the old man was dead.

Wes was fixing a whisky at the liquor cabinet when I came into the sitting room. He offered me a glass, and I declined. I cast my eyes around the room as he retreated to the leather recliner in the corner.

Dust motes rose from the carpet with every step. On the coffee table were two overflowing ashtrays, a discarded packet of beef jerky, and a spoon in a dried out bowl of cereal. Two empty bottles of Jack Daniel's, a lidless bottle of Chivas Regal, and the torn shell from a carton of cigarettes littered the floor.

Wes took a sip of his drink.

'You're living here?' I said, registering the situation.

He lit a cigarette.

Everything was explained in that moment: his dishevelled appearance; Nic avoiding his embrace; the quick change of clothes before dinner; the question of money over Hayden's excursion; my brother's insistence on driving me back to the house.

'You and Nic …?'

He waved a hand. 'I don't want to talk about it.'

'So we're staying here together?'

His eyes locked on mine, searching for a reaction. I slowly gathered my baggage and went to my room. I didn't make it past the door. Bed unmade, desk cluttered with sheet music paper, clothes strewn across the floor – it was exactly as I'd abandoned it three years before.

Returning to the sitting room, I placed my suitcase and viola in the corner. 'I'll bed down here tonight.'

'Sensible. It's cleaner.'

I slumped down on the sofa. 'You still offering that drink?'

He pulled himself to his feet. Our father had kept the liquor cabinet locked when we were growing up, and I was amused to see that Wes was continuing the tradition. He took a bottle from a selection of blended whiskies on the upper shelf. The champion was the lone bottle of Lark beneath them; the thousand-dollar single malt, a rare cask series, had been a gift to our father from his colleagues when he was discharged from hospital.

'We should crack open that Lark before I leave,' I said. 'The occasion calls for it, don't you think?'

Wes gave a twisted smile and handed me a generous serve of the McAllister. 'What are we drinking to?'

'The house, of course.'

He raised his glass. 'Fuck it. To the house.'

I drank to the toast. He flipped me his pack of cigarettes and went back to the recliner. I was about to express offense, then realised I would need to resurrect one or two habits if I was to survive this time. I lit up and inhaled weakly, not wanting to cough and draw a mocking comment.

He smiled. 'Taste good?'

'Tastes like poison.'

'Push through. The reward is worth it.'

'The reward is cancer.'

He spiralled a perfect blue ring across the room.

I sat forward and reached for the empty packet of beef jerky on the coffee table. 'If we're staying together, we need to —'

'Don't.' The force of his tone seemed to surprise even himself. My hand froze an inch from the packet. His voice relaxed. 'Leave it be.'

I leaned back into the sofa as he watched me with unblinking eyes. I gestured to the bottle of Chivas Regal on the carpet. He shook his head. I nodded at the cereal bowl.

'Negative,' he said.

'Is there anything I can clean away?'

He pointed at the ashtray we were sharing. 'You can empty this when it's full.' He indicated my drink. 'You can rinse that when you're done.' He cast his hand about the room. 'Everything else remains intact. Untouched. Is that clear?'

I knew then my brother would never agree to sell the house. 'Wes, is this shit our father's shit?'

'When I say untouched, I mean if you need to sneeze, go outside.'

'You're seriously telling me this stuff's been sitting here for two-and-a-half years?'

He lit another cigarette.

I got up from the sofa. 'I'm taking a shower.'

It was an anchor to the heart. Wes was as connected to our father's rubbish as I was to Mum's viola, and we guarded these memories with our lives. I couldn't say for certain, and I wasn't about to ask, but I suspected in the months following Mum's death our father had lived in the sitting room. Which was why Wes kept it as a shrine of sorts. Which was why he now slept in the recliner – where our father had slept. I didn't need to ask to know.

I emerged ten minutes later with a towel wrapped around my waist. Minus his shirt and trousers, and sporting a stained singlet, boxers and socks, Wes looked set for the night as he tapped away on his phone in the corner. I went over to the photographs on the mantel above the gas fireplace. It was the usual assortment of family portraits, but one in particular drew my attention: a picture of Audrey and me before my school formal.

'You broke her heart,' Wes said.

'I don't need you to tell me that.'

'I mean snapped it in two.'

The formal had been our first date. We looked so happy as we posed in the backyard, but I'd been nervous in the lead-up to the night. At the time, Audrey and I were members of the Tasmanian Youth Orchestra: she was the pianist, and I was one of the violists. But her real gift was her voice. Two years after that photograph, she won a scholarship to the Young Artist Program of Opera Australia. When I invited her to my formal, she said she'd go if I accompanied her to hers.

'She came looking for you,' Wes said. 'Dad told her you'd left.'

The thought of our father being the one to give her the news made me want to weep. There wasn't any excuse for what I'd done, but my need to escape him after Mum died had overridden all consideration for the important people in my life.

Wes took a drag. 'I don't understand how anyone leaves a person the way you did.'

'I didn't leave Audrey. I was running from our father.'

'Why do you keep saying it like that ... "our father"?'

'You want me to say "Dad"?'

'What the hell did he do to warrant —?'

'Don't pretend you don't know.'

'So he was a grumpy old bastard. He had his life wrenched from him. Show some fucking compassion.'

'How could you possibly understand?'

'You know what I think? It wasn't that he wasn't a good enough father – you weren't a strong enough son.'

'I don't care what you think. He and I weren't fixable. Just like you and I aren't fixable.'

'Fuck you.'

'That bullet changed him. You were already a man. We were raised by different people.'

Wes stubbed out his ciggie. 'I don't want to talk about it.'

'Fine. Add it to the other topics. I'm happy if we live in silence.'

He lit two more smokes and flicked one at me. It bounced off my palm and fell to the carpet. I scooped it up and placed it between my lips.

'How about that train?' he said.

'What?'

'Pretty fucked up, hey?'

'You think it's real?' I asked.

'I have no idea what I think.'

I shrugged. 'I think they think it's real.'

'So you think it's all in their heads.'

'I didn't say that.'

He passed me his phone and went to top up our glasses. The screen showed the Wikipedia page for Orvieto. The mayor was listed as Giacomo Pedroni. When I clicked on the hyperlink, a photo of the man at the hospital sprung into frame. 'It's him.'

Wes spoke with his back turned to me. 'They boarded a train that departs Orvieto at six fifty-eight every morning. It's a one-hour and seven-minute commute to Rome. They disembarked in the old Hobart Railyards at 5.26 p.m. and were picked up outside the Henry Jones Hotel at around 5.57 p.m. The time difference between Hobart and Rome is ten hours. That means the train rolled out of Orvieto and traversed space and time before coughing them up at the Railyards twenty-one minutes later.'

'Don't be flippant.'

'They're the facts of the situation.'

'How do you know what time they got off the train?'

He handed me a drink. 'There was a witness.'

'Seriously?'

'The former Hobart stationmaster. Says he saw the train materialise out of thin air. He thought he was hallucinating.'

'So it's true?'

'We'd like to have another pass at this Giacomo character.'

I shook my head. 'I have to set up the studio for rehearsing. I'm only back a month.'

'Rehearsing for what?'

'I've lined up an audition with the Melbourne Symphony Orchestra.'

'When?'

'Twenty-first of January.'

'That's two weeks away.'

'You know the preparation that goes into it.'

'I'm asking for thirty minutes, an hour tops. When the ABF get their translation people on the ground, we won't get within a mile of the place. In any case, we have to cut you a key.'

I said nothing for a bit. Finally, I turned to him. 'I'll do it if you're straight with me about two things.'

'Shoot.'

'How long have you been staying in the house?'

'Eight months.'

'Are you and Nic getting divorced?'

He took a long drag. 'We're working our way back together.'

We sat in silence after that, watching the grey plumes of smoke trail up to the ceiling.

CHAPTER TWO

ALICE STOOD WITH her arms crossed, blocking the door to the psych unit. 'I shouldn't have let you in last night.'

Wes tried to play it cool. 'There's clearly been a misunder —'

'I'm certainly not letting you in now.'

'I'm sorry if I put you in a difficult —'

'I have a job to do. Right now my job is to tell you to leave.'

Wes wasn't going to figure his way around this one. God, why was I putting myself through this? The week before I'd played three gigs in the Pigneto Quarter, and on Friday I had commuted to Mannheim for an audition. I could support my dream with music – I'd been doing it for three years.

The door behind Alice opened, and Inspector Henry Sutter, our father's former partner, stepped into the corridor. A burly man with a bald crown, he wasn't pleased to see us. 'Well, well ...' He shot Wes a look. 'I didn't realise we had a translator on our payroll.'

Henry was Wes's senior officer. I glanced at my brother in panic.

'I made him do it,' Wes said.

The inspector extended his hand to me. 'It's been a long time, young Geo.'

I flinched under the strain of his grip. 'Hello, Mr. Sutter.'

'Inspector Sutter,' Wes corrected me.

'Wesley here is bound by rank. Unfairly for him, his brother can address me however he wishes. I'll settle for Henry.'

'Thank you, Henry,' I said.

Wes grimaced.

'You went away,' Henry said. 'I recall your father mentioning something about that.'

'I've been in Europe the past few years. I got back yesterday.'

'Good for you. Travelling the sights, I presume. Did you get to Eastern Europe yet? Marvellous part of the world.'

'I've been to a few cities. But only for auditions.'

'Yes, I remember now. You're a violinist, like your mother.'

'A violist. Yes.'

'A violist. That's right. Good for you. See if you can win a spot in the Ljubljana orchestra. Impressive place – Prague without the people. At least that's what the travel book said. I've never been to Prague.' He looked at Wes, his tone serious. 'I don't know where we go from here. Every time I see you, the hole's a little deeper.'

If Wes was intimidated, he didn't show it. 'We have a witness.'

'This is a sweep-it-under-the-carpet situation. You need to stop digging.'

'It's been confirmed. The stationmaster —'

'Open your eyes, man!'

Wes went silent.

Henry's voice softened. 'It's past the point of it mattering that you're Luca's son.'

Alice's gaze was fixed on an undefined point in the distance. I had nowhere to look, and watched my brother's shoulders sag under the weight of the reprimand.

Henry turned to me. 'Your father was a top man, an outstanding police officer. Your brother spoke well at his funeral, don't you think?'

'I'll take your word for it, Henry.'

His expression creased. 'You weren't there?'

'I was in Lisbon. At least that's where I think I was.'

There was an awkward pause as he tried to piece it together. 'You were abroad?'

'I was preparing for an audition with the LSO. I think. It's a long time ago.'

'I see.' Henry glanced at Wes. 'Well, a good day to you both.' He walked off, his footsteps echoing down the corridor.

'Give me the key,' I said to Wes. 'We don't need to get it cut together.'

He turned away without a word. I followed behind, and when we came into the foyer a man with a hipster-length beard rushed at Wes, his mobile held out like a dictaphone. 'Detective, can you confirm that a group of illegals are presently being held in the psych unit?'

'Get that thing out of my face,' Wes snapped.

The man was undeterred. 'Can you confirm they're from Rome?'

Wes pushed past him.

'Is it true, Detective? Is it true they arrived in Hobart from Italy by train?'

Wes pulled up short. 'Who are you?'

'Matthew Griggs, reporter for *BorderlessTIMES*.'

'Where did you get your information?'

Matthew shoved the phone closer. 'So it's true?'

I thought Wes might strangle him. 'It wasn't Rome,' I said, 'it was Orvieto.'

Matthew switched his attention to me. 'Did they arrive by train?'

'Don't answer that,' Wes said curtly.

'Yes or no?'

Wes brushed up against him. 'Turn that thing off.'

'Easy now,' I said, sliding an arm between the men. I admired this reporter's pluck, but he was marching his face right into Wes's fist. I ushered my brother towards the exit and pointed Matthew away.

The reporter slipped his card into my hand, and as we passed through the automatic doors I heard him speak into his phone. 'The detective neither confirmed nor denied that a group of Italians on a train from Orvieto to Rome disembarked in the old Hobart yard.'

The situation shifted from comedic to plain weird when we arrived at the car to find a folded envelope beneath the windscreen-wipers. I slipped it out and read the handwritten message on the back.

'What is it?' Wes said.

I tossed the envelope across to him. 'Hobart became interesting while I was away.'

Wes snatched it up. His face reddened as he skimmed the note.

To the Detective of this vehicle, I am the proprietor of Phantom Time Books @ 148 Elizabeth Street. I have information of complete and absolute relevance to the case you're currently investigating (train, Italians etc.). Please visit with me urgently. C. Labuschagne, President of APRCTAS.

'Who the hell *are* these people?' Wes crumpled the envelope and tossed it to the footpath.

I went over and picked it up, just to annoy him. He shook his head and climbed in the car.

#

Wes slowed as we drove past Phantom Time Books. We found a parking space on the next block and walked back down.

'There's no reason to stay tied at the hip,' I said. 'I'll get the key cut while you do your thing here.'

He ignored me in favour of staring at the literature in the display window: *JFK and the Unspeakable; The Oz Files; Cosmic Ships; The 37th Parallel: America's UFO Highway; African Temples of the Anunnaki; The FBI Files on John Steinbeck.*

'What is this bullshit?' He flung the door open and entered.

A man sitting behind a counter constructed entirely of books was writing in a legal pad with a rubber-tipped pencil. With black hair scooped into a ponytail and wearing thick-rimmed glasses, he glanced up as the bell announced our entrance. I couldn't tell if he was an old-looking early thirties or a young-looking early forties.

'If neither of you is Detective Rosenberger, I'm closed,' he said.

I placed the South African accent immediately. My first six months in Rome was in a flat-share with a flautist from Cape Town.

Wes stepped down onto the landing. 'How do you know who I am?'

The South African slid the pencil behind his ear. 'Thank you for coming so promptly.'

'What's your name?'

'Labuschagne.' He pointed at me. 'Who's he?'

'Nobody. He's harmless.'

'The last time someone said that to me, I almost had my tongue ripped out by a poltergeist.'

'What do you want?' Wes asked.

'I need to see identification – badge, driver's licence, credit card, anything with a name on it.'

'Fuck identification. How did you know where I was parked fifteen minutes ago?'

'Identification confirmed.' Labuschagne came out from behind the counter. 'Tomorrow a Swede is arriving in Hobart from … well, Sweden. I don't mean to be flippant, but this bloke gets around. Last week he was in Singapore investigating sightings on their rail transit system. I'll be perfectly honest, the train for him is a personal matter. He'll have no interest in meeting you. But I'm convinced you'd be a good match. You can help him, which is what I want, and he can help you, which is what you need.'

Wes turned from the counter and walked further into the store. Labuschagne removed his glasses. Wes slipped a book from a shelf, gave it a once-over, replaced it.

The end aisle was blocked off by a sheet stapled to two book-shelf ends. Wes lifted it back: a mattress on a base of books, a gas stove, and a candle waxed to a saucer. He glanced at Labuschagne. 'You live here?'

Labuschagne crossed his arms.

Wes let go of the sheet and came back to the counter. 'If you don't start answering my questions I'll have you shut down before the day is out. What's your name?'

'C. Labuschagne.'

'What does the C stand for?'

'Christian.'

'South African?'

'Born, raised, schooled.'

'So you've naturalised?'

Labuschagne nodded.

Wes tapped the counter. 'And this is your shop?'

'Yes.'

'What about this other business ... this ACTP —?'

'APRCTAS.'

'Talk to me about that.'

'Anomalous Phenomena Research Commission of the Tasmanian Academy of Sciences. I'm its president.'

Wes grimaced. 'And what do you do in your capacity as president of this ... commission?'

'Investigate incidents occurring within the state of Tasmania that are considered to be anomalous.'

'I think he means UFOs,' I said, holding up a second-hand copy of *The Day After Roswell.*

Labuschagne shifted his focus to me. 'UFO sightings are one example. Others include paranormal activity, chemtrails, urban legends, the reptilian elite ... and ghost trains.'

I came down onto the landing. 'Are you suggesting the Italians boarded a ghost train?'

'A nineteenth-century locomotive empties a group of Europeans onto a platform at a decommissioned station in Tasmania, then vanishes. What's your explanation, Mr Nobody?'

'Jet lag.'

Wes pointed a finger at him. 'Don't ever contact me again.' He made for the exit.

Labuschagne called after him. 'The Swede lands in the morning. We'll be waiting for you at eleven.'

#

On the way home I stopped by Pearson Realty and spoke with one of their agents, Terry Munroe. He was very enthusiastic when I told him the address. We scheduled an appointment for the following morning.

Back at Yardley Street I fetched our father's car keys and went into the garage to see if there was any life in the old Ford Explorer. The stale cigar smell made me gag as I slid into the front seat. I brushed spider webs from the wheel and tried the ignition, but the engine didn't turn. I hoped to get up to Launceston at some point to have my viola serviced, but it looked like I'd be taking the bus.

Exchanging the car keys for Mum's studio keys, I went out back. As I'd said to Wes, I planned to use the studio over the next couple of weeks to rehearse for my MSO audition. This would give me a sense of closure; after the house was sorted, I'd be leaving for good.

Bucket and cloth in hand, I peered through the studio window. A thick film of dust had preserved the sparsely furnished space in the precise state Mum had left it. Three items told the story of her final week. On the wooden desk beneath the window was Lionel Tertis's autobiography, *My Viola and I*. When she'd started reading it again, I had known her time was near. Alongside the book was a ringbinder in which she'd kept meticulous notes on her students, of which I had been one. Across the floor a bergère chair was positioned at a slight angle to a music chair and stand.

I knew the score on the stand was *Morning Mood* for Viola, from *Peer Gynt* Suite No. 1. Mum had been working with me on the first of the four movements in the days before she passed.

If I wiped away the dust I'd be erasing my last perfect memory of her. I couldn't do it.

#

This was my first time in the annexe at St Mary's Cathedral, an intimate venue for a classical performance. When the players took their positions, the fold-up chairs were filled and a standing crowd had gathered at the back. The featured music was Mendelssohn's String Quartet No. 4 in E Minor. I thought the group held it together well. Nic played with wonderful expression, gaining confidence with each movement.

When the performance finished, I remained in my seat. The crowd slowly dispersed, and after a little while Nic came over. 'God, I was nervous. I hope it didn't show.'

'You were great, Nic. And precise, for someone who's been out for so long. I was impressed.'

'That means a lot. Thank you.'

'You looked happy. That's what struck me.'

'I forgot how it felt.'

'A deep joy. At least, that's my experience.'

'That's exactly it.' She smiled.

I suggested a drink, but she had to get back as Wes was dog-sitting Godfrey. She kindly dropped me off at State, and a few minutes later I faced the steps leading up to the porch.

There was nobody home. I only had to go inside and flick on the lights to bring the house to life, but that's not how it had always been. For many years an unlit house had meant Mum was in bed and our father was drinking in the sitting room in the dark. He wasn't waiting for me, but it was impossible to get from the front door to my bedroom without being drawn into his web. We enacted the scene so often, it was like we were reading from a script. I'd enter quietly, then the moment the door clicked shut he'd say, 'Where you been?' I'd turn into the living room to face him. With the lights off he was a shadow from the waist up, but I didn't need to see him to see the man. Behind a blue curtain of smoke the fingers of one hand curled around a whisky glass; the other cradled a cigarette. I would speak to his protruding legs. 'Nowhere. I'm tired. I'm going to bed.' But I wouldn't leave; the scene had to play out for the house to remain still. A ball of smoke would roll out of the void towards me, followed by a threat. 'If I was a few years younger I'd come over there and beat the shit out of you.' During the day I'd challenge him; in the evenings I was worried about disturbing Mum. The objective was to get to my room. 'I believe you.' He'd finish his drink with a gulp, an action that drew his top half into focus: a singlet revealing shoulders that once flagged a boxer's build; small black eyes pinned to a jaw-heavy face. We'd glare at each other, ill thoughts arrowing across the room in both directions. 'You didn't answer my question,' he'd say. I'd gesture in the direction of town. 'Rehearsals.' Other nights, gesturing in the same direction, 'Audrey.' Two variations, and to both he'd cough in scorn. 'You have no talent,' or, 'She sees something in you that doesn't exist.' I'd gaze through the blackness with contained hate. 'You're right.' On good nights the interaction fizzled out there, and I'd retreat to my room.

As I strode into the hallway I started turning on lights, more than what was warranted. But shutting out the darkness was like bandaging an amputation, so I grabbed my viola and escaped to the outdoor setting on the patio. A calm descended as I angled my head to the chin rest. Music was more than my dream, it was my medicine, and under a moonless sky I applied ointment to a wound with the second movement of Elgar's Serenade for Strings.

The piece ran for thirteen minutes. When I opened my eyes I was startled to find Wes watching from the back door. He came over with a bottle of Dalwhinnie and two glasses.

I placed my viola in its case. 'It's a pity you couldn't be there.'

'Walk Godfrey, feed Godfrey, change a light bulb, dispose of a broken tumble dryer ... What Nic wants and what I want are usually two different things.'

'Those are good actions. Keep your focus on them. At least, that's what I would do.'

He scoffed, and took the chair adjacent to mine.

Wes had given up the violin when he was seventeen. Since then he'd found it difficult to encourage anyone who played. That used to be just Nic and me, but for years now, Hayden had borne the brunt of it. I'd always hated to hear the excuses for why Wes couldn't attend his son's performances.

It wasn't that my brother had exchanged one dream for another, but that he'd abandoned a rare gift. We're all born with different levels of talent, and the same can be said for desire. If I had Wes's ability, or he my passion, we could choose our orchestra.

He poured two serves and passed me one. 'Why do you love playing so much?'

The question surprised me. 'Does anyone really choose what they love?'

'I don't know. Maybe.'

'I think I'd have found my way to the viola whether I had two parents like Mum, or two like our father.'

He took a sip. 'How did Nic go?'

'She played from her heart. I could tell.'

'I don't know how to make her happy anymore.'

I didn't know what to say, and not for the last time we lapsed into silence as we finished our drinks.

#

The next morning Wes and I pushed the Ford out of the garage to see if it would respond to a jump, but it didn't utter a word.

'How much for a new battery?' I asked.

'Couple of hundred bucks. Four or five if you include a full service, which it needs.'

I let out a low whistle. 'Forget it. It's a luxury I can't afford.'

He rolled up the leads and returned them to the boot of his Commodore. 'How about this? I'll pay to get it roadworthy so you can have some wheels. Before you leave we'll sell it. I'll take the costs for the service, and we'll split the difference.'

'You'd do that for me?' I sensed a shift in him the previous night, but was wary to trust it.

'I'll arrange to have it picked it up.'

'I don't know what to say.'

He waved it off. 'It's one less thing to deal with.'

'Time for a coffee?' I said.

He glanced at his watch. 'I probably shouldn't. They've got me working a desk, if you can believe it. I even have to clock in.' He was clearly rebelling against the thought as he spoke. 'Fuck it ... a coffee would be great.'

We made for the house, but before we reached the door a car pulled up out front. The signage on the side read *Pearson Realty*.

Wes shot me a look. I shrugged. 'It's just a valuation.'

With a broad smile, Terry Munroe trotted up the steps. 'My first appointment cancelled, so I took a chance and swung by.' He extended his hand to Wes. 'Terry.'

Wes crossed his arms. The colour drained from Terry's face.

I leaned over and shook his hand. 'This is my brother Wes. We're co-owners. He's a little bit reluctant, but we're definitely putting it on the market.'

Wes skewed a glance at me. 'You're unbelievable.'

Before Terry could back away I ushered him inside. 'What's your normal process? Do I give you a tour, or would you prefer to wander around on your own?'

'Yes … um … right.' His composure gathered, he raised a clipboard and clicked his pen. 'Show me around like you would a friend visiting for the first time.'

I guided him into the living room, while Wes retreated into the sitting room. At the door to our father's study, I paused. Terry stepped inside.

'Would work equally well as a nursery or yoga room,' I said.

'Good space,' he observed. 'Large office, small bedroom. I see what you mean.' He looked out the window. 'Derwent River glinting in the distance. Lovely.'

He made a positive remark about the living room, and I delivered him to the doorway of our parents' bedroom. From this vantage point I watched him scribble down notes as he traipsed around. By now he'd picked up there were certain parts of the house

I was unwilling to enter. Next up was my bedroom. He registered the bin on its side, with burnt embers of paper scattered about the carpet, but said nothing.

Wes was smoking in the recliner when we came into the sitting room. Terry raised a fist to his mouth to hold down his gag reflex. I grabbed his arm and led him through the kitchen into the backyard. The scent of gardenia brought relief, and after a quick tour of the garden we found ourselves at the studio. Terry tried the doorknob. I shrugged.

'Rustic,' he said, peering through the window.

'Easily repurposed into a workshop or shed,' I added.

'Alluring. Storied.' He got it. The house; its circumstances.

We wended our way back to the front door, and Terry tucked his clipboard under his arm. 'There are many things to recommend the property. Clearly the selling point is the location.'

I nodded. 'Walking distance to schools and cafés.'

'Inner Hobart attracts all types of interest: first-time buyers, families, investors. My suggestion would be to outlay a little to protect its value.'

Wes came into the hallway with his hands in his pockets.

'I hope you're not suggesting more than a deep clean?' I said.

'Painting the exterior will go a long way to ensure you get what the house deserves.'

Wes laughed. 'He's a starving musician. He can't afford a car service let alone a paint job.'

'How much?' I asked.

Terry's eyes darted between us. 'You'd need to get a quote. Most of the cost would be in the labour.'

I grimaced. 'Okay, well … how long for the valuation?'

'Early next week.'

Wes opened the door, and Terry slipped out. We watched him drive off.

'Should I put on the kettle?' I asked.

Wes stepped out onto the porch and shut the door quietly behind him.

#

As I crossed Brisbane Street I gleaned the faint sound of guitar and vocals from the mall a couple of blocks ahead. I was annoyed, as I'd hoped to get straight into a busking session, but my focus was swiftly drawn to the present when a hand yanked me through a door.

'What the —?'

'Thank you for coming on time,' Labuschagne said. 'Where's your boet?'

'What?'

'Your brother.'

'He's … I have no idea.'

'Never mind.' He nudged me into the bookstore.

I stumbled down onto the landing and came face to face with a serene-looking man leaning against a bookshelf. He couldn't have appeared more disinterested in meeting me.

'This is the lower ranked of the two,' Labuschagne said to him. And to me, 'This is the Swede. The ghost train hunter.'

'There's obviously been —' I started.

The Swede raised a hand and looked away. 'I don't work with anyone.'

Something about him made me stare. It wasn't his offish manner, and it wasn't the clothes – high-waisted broadfall trousers with suspenders – it was his aura, a presence. He was the kind of person who would have seemed more at home in a black-and-white silent film than present-day anywhere.

Labuschagne leaned forward and whispered to him, 'The passengers have been detained. They'll have information about the train's interior.'

'I have nothing to offer you,' I interjected.

'You were there,' Labuschagne said, shooting me a look. 'I know this for a fact. You communicated with them.'

'Where did you get your information?'

Ignoring me, he turned back to the Swede. 'You've been chasing the train for forty years. Now it's here, and you only know it's here because I contacted you. I want for you to intercept it in my territory. There are witnesses. They can assist you. This is important.'

It was disconcerting to hear a South African refer to Tasmania as his territory.

The Swede turned his gaze to me and my instrument case. 'Violin?'

'Viola.'

'Professional?'

I nodded.

'Play something.'

Even more than his candour I was impressed by his indifference to the situation in which we found ourselves. Yet there was more chance of me boarding a ghost train than playing classical music in a conspiracy bookstore. 'I'm sorry. I'm of no use to you.' I nodded out of respect, and turned away.

'Don't be like your brother,' Labuschagne called after me.

I didn't look back.

'You've been on your own too long,' I heard him say to the Swede. 'You'll never find it if you keep refusing help.'

#

The guitar singer I'd heard before was still playing when I got to Elizabeth Street Mall. From an empty bench I watched him finish a rendition of 'Better Be Home Soon'. There was something about him that reminded me of Alessia. When she busked, people were moved to clap and tap their feet. That's what I saw with this young musician; he played as if everyone who walked by wanted to hear his song, and in return a steady stream of coins dropped into his case.

As soon as the session ended, I wandered over. 'Nice set.'

'Thanks, mate. You switching in?'

'I was hoping to. I don't want to step on anyone's toes.'

'All yours.' He smiled, scooped up his case and walked off.

I dropped some coins into my viola case and, after a quick tune-check, slipped into 'Death of Juliet' from Prokofiev's *Romeo and Juliet*, my favourite piece to perform unaccompanied. With closed eyes I drifted into a space where the soul relaxes and music rises, and it wasn't long before I heard the happy tinkle of coins landing at my feet.

Five minutes later I lowered my bow and opened my eyes. The Swedish ghost train hunter stood staring less than two metres from me. I recoiled.

His expression softened. 'As I watch you play, it occurs to me you sound how I feel when I chase my train.'

His complete disregard for what others thought of him was intriguing. I could only dream of possessing the same casual self-belief.

'You arrived this morning?' I said.

He gestured to the Gladstone bag next to his feet.

'Where are you staying?' I asked.

The Swede sighed. 'Labuschagne offered for me to sleep on the floor in his bookstore. But I don't want to do that. Not because I do not like floors – I have spent more nights sleeping on park benches and floors than I have in beds. But if I stay with him I will be obligated. And with my train I cannot be obligated.'

'I have a spare room at my house.' I immediately wasn't sure why I'd suggested it – perhaps to help out someone on the road, like many had done for me, or perhaps to insert a buffer between me and Wes.

It was the Swede's turn to show surprise. 'That is very kind of you, but probably I must decline. You charge more than I can afford, I am sure.'

'Would you work for board?'

'If it fits around my train, I can work.'

'Can you paint?'

He smiled. 'I have painted more houses than I have travelled on trains.'

This was turning out to be the most productive busking session of my life. 'I need someone to paint the outside of my house.'

'Do you have materials?' When I shook my head, he said, 'Good. My experience will save you money. But I chase my train at night, and I research in the afternoons. You would be satisfied with two hours a morning?'

'Sure.'
He extended his hand.

#

The Swede placed his Gladstone bag in the corner of the sitting room, and settled into one of the sofas. He didn't ask to see his room and seemed unfazed by our father's rubbish scattered about. Sitting across from him, I watched as he retrieved a leather tobacco pouch from his jacket pocket and proceeded to roll a smoke. He exuded the same ethereal quality I'd noticed in the bookstore, as though his energy was contained, so that when he moved he didn't disturb the air. As silly as it might sound, I thought perhaps he'd taken on the characteristics of his ghost train.

As this impression of him came together in my mind, he lit up, and I realised it wasn't tobacco, it was a joint. He offered it to me.

'I don't know your name,' I said, taking a drag.

'Sten.'

I passed back the joint. 'Geo.'

'Like in the word "geography"?'

'Exactly like in "geography". It means "earth".'

'Sten means "stone".'

Earth and stone. Could there be any doubt?

Car lights swept through the window. 'That's my brother Wes. His name doesn't mean anything. Ignore him.'

The front door opened, and Wes rounded into the sitting room. He regarded Sten. 'What's going on?'

'This is Sten the Swedish ghost train hunter.'

Wes sniffed the air. 'Is that weed?'

'He's painting the house for board.'

'I only work mornings,' Sten said, taking a hit. 'I chase my train the rest of the time.'

'Does he know that … Do you know that I'm a police officer?'

For a second Sten was confused, but then he took the joint from his lips and offered it to my brother. 'Sorry. I forget my manners sometimes.'

Wes's face tightened. I tensed for the reaction. But something in him relaxed. 'Ah, fuck it.' He took the joint and slumped into the recliner, waving a finger in the air. 'There'll be no discussion of the train. Is that clear?'

'Good,' Sten said. 'I prefer to work alone.'

Wes took a hit, passed him the joint, then slid a fresh ashtray across the coffee table. 'Use this one, not the other two.' He glanced at me. 'Keep an eye on that.'

Sten tapped the cone into the ashtray. Wes watched him for a minute, before getting up to leave the room.

I took out my phone and messaged Alessia. *Doing fine. Start rehearsing Sunday. Call next week. Geo xxx.*

'Help yourself,' Sten said, pushing the pouch to me.

I sat forward and rolled one for myself. 'I've been thinking about what you said before.'

'What did I say?'

'That I looked how you felt when you chased your train.'

'It's true. That is what I thought.'

'My dream is to play for a major orchestra. Attending auditions feels like I'm chasing something.'

'Maybe our dreams are the same?'

I wanted them to be the same, but his pursuit was paired with an ease that had yet to mature in my own. 'I don't know. You seem very calm.'

He relit his joint and handed me the lighter. 'I am calm because I know with certainty that I will find my train, and I am not in a rush.'

'What will you do when you find it?'

'Board it. Of course.'

It was the matter-of-factness that moved me.

'I think they are the same,' he continued. 'The way you play your music – I think they are. But there is a simple test to know for sure.'

'Oh yeah?'

'Who is the most important person in your life? Don't tell me. But you have someone, I suppose.'

My mind flashed onto Alessia. 'I do.'

'Could you leave this person if there was a possibility of achieving your dream, and doing it alone was the difference between having it and not having it?'

This was the right question, but it implied a coldness that I found difficult to own up to. I'd already abandoned one person – but that had been to flee my father rather than chase after something.

'So you had the conviction to do so?' I said.

'My train moves too quickly. I have never been in one place long enough to have someone to leave.'

His response dismayed me.

'A light is flashing in the other room,' he said.

I glanced around to see a sporadic glow emanating from our father's study at the other end of the house. I got up and crossed the rooms to crack open the door and peer through. Dad's lamp, as Wes and I called it, was flickering wildly on the study desk. It was one of those lights with three levels of brightness, so that when you touched it once it was dim, twice it was bright, three times it was brightest; the fourth touch turned it off. Sten came to stand behind me, and we watched as the light came on by itself, slowly getting brighter. All at once it jumped to its brightest level before switching off. After a few seconds it came back on, flickering up and down between the levels, then fading out.

'What's going on?' Wes asked, walking out of the bathroom with a towel draped around his waist, steam swirling behind him.

'Dad's lamp is acting weirdly,' I said.

He looked into the study. 'It's off.'

'Wait for it.'

Within a few seconds the lamp came on and shot to its brightest level, and blacked out. Then it came on at its lowest level and grew gradually brighter.

'Damned electrics,' he said.

I shook my head. 'It's the globe.'

'Someone's trying to communicate with you,' Sten said, the joint dangling from his mouth.

Wes and I looked at him.

He shrugged. 'Ghosts and ghost trains are different. Otherwise I would ask what it wants.'

Wes chuckled, and turned away. 'Just unplug it.'

I retrieved the lamp and brought it into the sitting room. Sten came in behind me and went to his sofa. Wes poured three glasses of whisky at the liquor cabinet. I placed the lamp on the coffee table, careful not to displace our father's rubbish.

'Why do you call it "Dad's lamp"?' Sten asked.

'He got it from some antique shop. I forget where.' I asked Wes, 'Do you remember?'

'New Norfolk.'

'Yeah, that's right, a long time ago,' I said to Sten. 'Then it began its rounds. First, his bedside lamp. For a spell his reading lamp in here. And finally his study lamp.'

'It is definitely him,' Sten said.

Wes handed out the drinks. 'I don't want to talk about my father even more than I don't want to talk about —'

I leapt to my feet, whisky splashing to the carpet. 'Holy shit!'

The lamp flickered to its brightest level again, then switched rapidly between the three levels. The cord lay curled on the floor with the plug exposed.

Sten dragged on his joint. 'As I said ... he is here.'

Five minutes later we sat back in the living room minus the lamp, which had been relocated to Mum's studio. Wes and I had charged Sten with the responsibility of transporting it, and watched through the kitchen window as he'd carried it up the stony path, the globe flickering violently in protest. He had disappeared into the studio, then tracked back down while the windows behind him flashed like lightning.

'I wonder which of us he's trying to communicate with,' I pondered.

'There isn't a train, and there are no ghosts,' Wes said flatly.

Sten was lying back on the sofa with his eyes closed. After a beat, he said, 'I would prefer not to say.'

CHAPTER THREE

THE FOLLOWING MORNING I woke to find Sten poring over his research at the Laminex kitchen table. Square and compact, the kitchen wasn't suited to a table, and not least of all a four-seater. Yet somewhere along the way it was deemed necessary to give up the dining room for an additional sitting area, so that we had the choice to lounge with company, or in solitude. My mother and father maintained a routine of taking their meals in the kitchen; but I don't recall a time where we sat together as a family after my father's accident.

'Sleep okay?' I said to Sten, flicking on the kettle.

'Yes. Very comfortable.'

I'd offered him my room, but he'd said if the owners of the house were sleeping in chairs then he too would sleep in a chair. 'Besides, in my occupation it is more productive to exist on power naps.'

I glanced at the assortment of literature spread across the table, what I took to be the essential materials of a modern-day ghost train hunter: an illustrated map of Hobart, a Tasmanian roadmap, a second-hand book on the West Coast railways, a freshly purchased book on the state's bush tramways, and a handful of leather-bound journals. One journal was open to a page in which illegible notes had been scrawled, and another showed a rough pencil sketch of a Federation building with a track running past the front. In the corner of the table a quartz stone sat within the curl of a silver chain.

'Coffee?' I said.

'Thank you.'

I pulled down two mugs with the wraparound score of Beethoven's *Moonlight Sonata*. Old and chipped, they were a gift to my mother from one of her students.

'That schematic looks pretty dated,' I said to Sten.

'It is a 1942 map of the Hobart tramway system.'

'You do know most of those tracks have been removed?'

'It does not matter that a line may be out of use, or even no longer there. My train will appear at any point where there is or once was a track. Regardless of gauge.'

'Gauge? What's that?'

'The spacing of the rails.'

'Interesting.' I scooped coffee into a plunger and filled it with boiling water.

'Actually, the closest I came to boarding my train was Bellerive in 1987, and that line was only used until 1926.'

I frowned. 'So you've been to Tasmania before?'

'After forty years of chasing, there are few places my train has not taken me. Did Labuschagne tell you I met him in Durban?'

'Honestly, I don't know that guy at all. I was born in 1987. What month were you here?'

He flipped open one of the journals. 'July sixteen I arrived.' Turning to the back page, he said, 'August four is my final entry.

I made an interception. It almost killed me. I got my hand stuck in the door.' He shuddered. 'My train dragged me along the street. I was dead for sure if it didn't vanish. At the last moment it let go of me like a crocodile changing its mind. Cars hooting, people screaming. My arm was broken in three places.' He closed the journal. 'I try not to think about it.'

The sound of loud banging drew our attention, and I looked through the kitchen window to see Wes hammering a white sheet across the studio window. 'What's he doing?'

'I think your neighbour complained about the light. He and your brother were arguing over the fence.'

'We need to get rid of that lamp.'

'Can you show me where the Italians got off?' Sten said, referring to the map of Hobart.

I dropped a finger onto Evans Street. 'That's the old Hobart Railyards, where they disembarked.' I pointed out the Henry Jones Hotel on Hunter Street. 'That's where the police picked them up.'

Sten marked the Railyards with a cross and a date. 'It only matters where they got off.'

He scooped up the crystal quartz. Clasping its chain lightly between the fingers of his right hand, he suspended the crystal an inch above the open palm of his left hand. Within a couple of beats, a movement arose from within the stone, and I watched in wonder as it drifted into slow wide circles above his palm.

'My train won't appear there again.' He wiped the quartz with his shirt and pushed the journal with the sketch towards me. 'Do you know this place?'

'How did you make the stone move?'

'It's a technique. Anyone can do it.' He tapped the sketch. 'Is this not familiar to you?'

'I think it's the State Cinema. Did you draw that?'

'Please show me on the map.'

I tapped the location on Elizabeth Street, and Sten marked it. He went through the same routine with the crystal, which once again rotated above his palm. But the circles weren't as wide this time, and though the crystal was now circling clockwise, I was certain that previously its motion had been anticlockwise.

He wiped it with his shirt and slipped it into a velvet pouch. 'There is a chance my train will stop outside this State Cinema next.'

'I'd love to see the looks on people's faces if a train appeared from thin air on Elizabeth Street.'

'You are welcome to join me. I will probably go at eight.'

'I thought you preferred to work alone?'

'That is true. But you are also in a heavy pursuit of something. I feel our energies are the same.'

'I may take you up on that.'

Staking out Sten's train seemed a whole lot more appealing than passing the evening in the sitting room, glancing nervously at the window every time a car drove by. Wes and I might be brothers, but to Sten's point, our energies folded away from each other. I was working to chase something down, and Wes was fighting to keep something together. It didn't make for good company.

Wes blustered into the kitchen. 'Damned lamp kept Charlotte up all night.' Charlotte was the ten-year-old daughter of our neighbours Walter and Irene. Her second-floor bedroom looked onto our yard.

'Just put it in a cupboard?' I said. 'You know I'm using the studio to rehearse.'

'It's not coming back into the house.'

'Then get rid of it.' I was about to say I'd put it in the bin, but said, 'Sten will put it in the bin.'

'It's Dad's lamp. We're not throwing it away.' The doorbell rang. Wes swung around. 'For fuck sakes, Walter.'

'It's Nic and Hayden,' I said, 'not Walter.'

His expression softened. 'Nic and Hayden are here?'

'Hayden has a rehearsal. They're not coming in.' I grabbed my key off the counter and hurried out.

#

Nic and I sat in her Corolla across from the performing arts centre at The Hutchins School. Situated a hop-skip-and-jump south of Hobart's CBD, the Anglican school for boys was known for its music program. A number of cars dotted Nelson Road and the adjacent car park, with parents waiting idly for their children to finish rehearsals.

'Has Wes been going?' I asked.

'He sometimes drops Hayden off. But he still won't watch.'

I shook my head. 'Just like our father.'

'Wes told me about your boarder, that he's painting the house.'

'He's Swedish, so I'm guessing it'll be white.'

'Fortuitous,' she said, though her tone suggested otherwise.

'I'll have to busk my butt off to afford the paint.'

'Can I ask a question?'

I turned to her. 'Nic, after what you did for me you can ask me anything.'

'You don't owe me that.'

'What's on your mind?'

A teenage student carrying a cello case crossed in front of us and entered the music building.

'You need the money for auditions,' she said. 'That's why you want to sell.'

'It's impossible to stay on the audition circuit without reserves.'

'I get it – as a dream, I understand. I do.'

'But?'

'Knowing your family, I can't help but suspect there's something more going on.'

'There's always something more with my family.'

'Maybe you want to be cut loose from the only thing that ties you to Wes. From where I'm sitting, you look like someone who's testing how much family they have left.'

I shifted uncomfortably, the seatbelt I'd left buckled tight across my chest. The last thing I wanted to do was burden Nic with talk about Wes, even if she was a sympathetic ear. 'The money would definitely make things easier,' I said. 'And there'd be a satisfaction in seeing every dollar from my half of the inheritance go into a passion our father despised. But when it comes to Wes, I don't know … I try to remind myself it's not his fault, that one of us had to take after our father.'

She didn't say anything, and for a while we sat staring ahead through the windshield, each lost in our own thoughts. Unlike me, Nic didn't have the choice to just walk away.

'I think I'll see if I can catch some of Hayden's rehearsal,' I said, undoing my seatbelt.

'He'd like that,' she said.

I took the steps down to the campus two at a time, and found the entrance to the arts centre. It was a path I'd taken many times. Because I was a former member of four of the six Tasmanian

Youth Orchestra ensembles, the yellow and red brick building, with its shiny glass façade, was like a second home to me. I'd come here at least once a week from the age of seven until I'd begun my Master of Music at UTAS, and even then the connection hadn't been broken, as I'd continued in the role of conductor for the TYO Chamber Orchestra.

When I entered the hallway, I was overtaken by the drone of competing orchestral sounds from the two rehearsal rooms. The cellist I'd seen earlier was seated on the floor, chatting to a red-haired trombonist. They paid me no attention.

The first door was the rehearsal room for TYO 1. I peered through the window at an angle so as not to draw the attention of the conductor. The players were faced away from me, but I quickly located Hayden in the position of first chair. His demeanour was one of relaxed concentration. His attainment of the role of concertmaster by the age of fourteen was a testament to his talent; the only Hutchins student who'd done so at a younger age was his father. Wes and I were cursed, we both knew that. He had inherited Mum's talent, and I her passion. If Hayden possessed a heart for music, he was looking at a future with many choices.

The orchestra stopped playing, and Hayden rested his violin upright on his thigh.

'Good. But not too fast too soon,' a woman said. 'A little less cello and a little more double bass.'

I knew that voice. Mouth dry, I shifted across and peered further into the room. Audrey was directing the string section at the front. I jerked my head back.

I'd always known there was a possibility I would see her again, but not on this visit. I'd thought she was in Sydney. My first impulse was to walk away – she'd never know I was here. But this seemed cowardly somehow, and I didn't know if I could live with doing cowardly twice over.

'Okay, the horns from the beginning,' I heard her say. The horns sounded out a few mellow bars before the orchestra joined in. 'Good. The bassoons ... Is it possible to play a little more pianissimo? Will just the bassoons play, please?' The bassoons responded. 'Super. And with a bit more melody. Okay. Good.'

Audrey was conducting the fourth movement from *Peer Gynt* Suite No. 1, *In the Hall of the Mountain King*. It was from the same suite I'd been working through with Mum in the week before she had passed away. The coincidence was unsettling.

Ten minutes later the rehearsal wrapped up, and the players drifted out. Intercepting Hayden, I told him to tell Nic I'd make my own way home. I regretted the words as they left my mouth.

After the last of the players departed, I went inside. Audrey's back was to me as she gathered up her sheet music.

As long as I'd known her she'd worn her hair in a straight bob; but now it sat below her shoulders, tousled and angled in an edgier style. She was dressed differently too, in wide-legged black pants and a cropped knit top. A far cry from the torn jeans and oversized T-shirts of our university days.

For a moment I didn't say anything – there wasn't anything I could say to undo what I'd done.

'Hi,' I stammered, awkward.

Her head flew up.

I took a step forward. 'How have you been?'

There was a long pause before she asked, 'What are you doing here?'

'I came back to sell the house.'

A silence fell between us. I should have taken the cowardly exit.

'You're a wonderful conductor,' I said. 'Truly.'

'I have to go,' she said, voice unsteady.

'Sure. Of course.'

'I'm not doing this.' She snatched up her bag and made for the door, taking a wide berth.

'I should have called,' I said, but she didn't seem to hear me. I wasn't sure I wanted her to. It was three years ago to the month I'd left. Audrey had never reached out to me, and I'd made no attempt to contact her. As I listened to her footsteps echo down the hallway, I felt the full weight of my abandonment.

#

I watched Sten from the sitting room as he went through his preparations at the kitchen table. Wes lay snoring in the recliner, his shoes kicked off and shirt unbuttoned. Delicately balanced in his left hand sat an unfinished glass of whisky, which on any other day would have fixed my attention. But Sten was more fascinating to me than a drink on the verge of tumbling to the floor from a sleepy grip.

I'd been observing the Swede for over an hour, trying to figure out his process, and I'd narrowed it down to two primary actions: the twirling of the crystal above an open palm, and the less clear activity of sketching. The literature on the table was merely an instrument for these two actions.

Wes's mobile shuddered with a loud jingle, and the whisky splashed onto his lap. 'Shit,' he said, fumbling for the phone. 'Rosenberger?'

Sten showed no reaction from the kitchen.

'How much?' Wes slipped his shoes on. 'Okay, I'll bring it over.' His brow furrowed. 'I'm busy tomorrow. I can be there in ten.' He hung up, then tied his shoelaces. Grabbing the glass from the carpet, he poured himself a shot and threw it back in one gulp.

'You're not actually driving?' I said.

'What time is sunset?' Sten called from the kitchen.

It had just gone seven, and the light was a little way off from fading.

'Eightish,' Wes said.

Sten leant back in the chair and looked at me. 'I am expecting my train to arrive in the first hour. I will leave at seven forty-five.'

'I'm good to go,' I said.

Wes placed his glass on the liquor cabinet. 'Always *my* train ... never *the* train.' He glanced at me. 'There's a lesson in that, don't you think? Kinda like the difference between *Dad* and *our* father.'

'I thought there was to be no discussion of my train between you and me,' Sten commented.

'I'm speaking to *him*,' Wes said, and left the room.

I went to the bathroom to wash my face. When I came out I caught Wes on his knees in his bedroom, counting money above an open shoebox. He inserted a handful of notes into an envelope. Our eyes met briefly, but he didn't seem bothered I'd seen him.

After he drove off, I went into his room and pulled out the shoebox from beneath his bed. I was winded by what I found: eleven rolls of cash bound with elastic bands. In one of the rolls I counted a thousand dollars in twenty-dollar notes. I replaced the money and pushed the shoebox under the bed.

#

Sten and I sat beside each other on an open bus bench, watching the traffic drift by on Elizabeth Street. A steady flow of patrons veered into restaurants, wine bars and cafés along the North Hobart strip. To the right of us a good portion of that crowd funnelled into the historic State Cinema.

A chill set in as the last of the light disappeared, and I tucked my hands into my pockets. 'Decent audience for a ghost train,' I said.

Sten grunted.

'I'm not being flippant. The more witnesses the better, surely?'

'I dislike crowds,' he said.

'But if the train appears, people will record it. If it goes viral it will validate —'

His eyes closed and his head drooped forward. I thought he'd dozed off.

'Shouldn't you be watching the road?' I asked.

'If my train arrives, believe me, I will be alerted.'

'Fair enough.'

He straightened, and reached into his pocket for his tobacco pouch. 'It is your first time. I understand. But this is more like seeing a comet than catching a butterfly. Once every two or three years if I am lucky. I think I understand the difference between you and me.'

'How so?'

'Your comment about people witnessing my train ... you mean to confirm my dream, yes?'

'Sure. To validate it.'

'I cannot say it more clearly ... I am chasing my train for myself. When I board it, I do not care if anybody sees me. In fact, I would prefer if it happens when I am alone – in the blackest shadows of an abandoned platform.' He had a deft rolling technique, and I watched as he nudged a clump of tobacco across a sheet and pinched it closed.

'You'll have achieved something glorious,' I said, 'and no one will know.'

'I think you are overlaying your dream on mine. You want to reach your goal to prove something. Your talent, perhaps?' He placed the cigarette between his lips. 'I want to reach my train to reach my train.'

He was right, of course. I felt so much angst in what I was trying to accomplish.

He patted his pockets for his matches. 'Do not feel bad. You are very young. Twenty something, I suppose? Maybe thirty something. I don't know.'

'Thirty,' I said. 'Exactly.'

He waved a hand. 'You are a child. The realisation that you do not need permission to live your own life usually arrives at death.' He struck a match and drew the cigarette towards it.

I was about to ask his age but realised he was lighting a joint. I swiped a hand between his cupped fingers, sending the spliff flying from his mouth to the ground. He glared at me, alarmed. I was impressed I hadn't struck his face.

'You can't smoke weed in public,' I whispered.

'No?'

'No.'

He scooped up the joint.

I changed the subject. 'When your train appears, will it come from around the corner or simply materialise in front of us?'

'That is a good question. Always it appears as if it is coming from somewhere.'

'Interesting.'

'The train is moving across lines that are here, or were once here. Sometimes it sweeps around the bend into the station, lights bearing down. It stops. And it departs before disappearing in the distance. This is the full narrative. All three acts. Approach; presentation; departure. These are my names for it. Other times you only see the presentation. Or, as you say, it will materialise. But even if it materialises, it still comes from around the bend. For the people on it, my train is real and always moving.'

'You mean those who board it?'

'Those who disappeared with it. The ghost passengers. They never get off.'

'Ghost passengers?' The Italians claimed the train had only two carriages. Were these supposed ghosts sitting amongst them?

'I have compiled detailed profiles of each of them. It is not useful to my search, but it reminds me there is life on my train. That I am not chasing a machine.'

'Why didn't the Italians mention them?'

'The ghost passengers are sitting in the forward carriage. When the train stops, only the door to the back carriage opens. This carriage is empty – I do not know why. And like the Italians did, people can get on and off this carriage. And like the Italians said, the conductor can come across into it. The ghost passengers, however, do not.'

'They choose not to?'

He pointed a finger in the air. 'That is the question. I have put it together bit by bit, but there are still things I am trying to understand. All I know is I must get on the back carriage. And when I do, I will cross into the forward carriage.'

I was disheartened. 'But then you will become a ghost.'

'When I get on, I have no intention of getting off.'

Here, finally, Sten and I were the same. I knew if I earned a place on an orchestra I'd never lose it. I'd make higher demands of myself. Nobody would need to remind me of my luck.

'Do you have tobacco?' Sten asked.

I shook my head.

He popped the joint in his mouth. 'It is okay. I am not going to light it.'

A man with a scarf draped around his neck walked by, smoking a cigarette. I rose and asked if we could bum a couple. He was taken aback by the request, but obliged.

Sten took the joint from his mouth and dropped it into the man's pocket. 'For later,' he said, patting him on the chest. 'Thank you for your kindness.'

I was horrified. The man's eyebrows furrowed, but he nodded and walked on.

We lit our smokes and settled back on the bench to watch the ebb and flow of traffic.

'Do you know what I like most about you?' Sten asked.

We'd known each other for less than two days and already he had a favourite thing. 'I'd love to know.'

'You have not asked me why I want to board my train.'

'That's a good question.'

'It is the thing I like most about you. It means you accept it as a normal need. Like I accept your desire to play in an orchestra.'

'I like that you accept that about me.'

'There is a reason, of course. And now that I have said this, you will be curious to know it.' He gestured at the cinema window behind us. 'But for this moment we have something more pressing to face.'

I glanced over my shoulder and recoiled. Sitting at a table, pretending to read a book as he held it too high, was the South African bookseller and president of APRCTAS, one Christian Labuschagne.

'My god,' I said, 'he's staking us out.'

Sten smiled. 'This man is good. I was hoping for one or two days, but with him it is impossible.' He flashed three fingers at me. 'Three countries, and each time on the first night in that place.'

'But how?'

'It is not important. What is important is that every time he is there. The man knows his job. There is nothing else to say.'

I was annoyed, as mine was a special invitation. Granted, the conversation had been stilted to begin with, but I sensed we were edging into dialogue that promised for meaningful musician-to-ghost-train-hunter bonding. I was eager to uncover all our connections, and now the evening was ambushed. 'How can you not be angry?' I said.

Sten waved away the suggestion. 'But for him I would not be here. Let us be honest – I would be clearing snow from driveways in Stockholm.'

'How did he know where to find you this evening? If you say he bugged the house, I'm calling my brother.'

'You watched me using the crystal today?'

'I was going to ask you about that.'

'It is a dowsing technique. It helps to remove the guessing from predicting where my train will appear. It is not perfect, but it gets me closer. Labuschagne was the one who taught me how to do it. Twenty-four years ago, in 1994.'

'He found us with a crystal?'

'He uses his mother's pendant. She was a psychic.'

I peered at Labuschagne through the cinema window. 'Do you think that's how he knew about the Italians? And where to find my brother?'

'Possibly. He has many ways.'

Labuschagne caught me watching and jerked the book up to hide his face. The title was *Hobart Tramways*. I realised that if any patrons of the cinema came to suspect our motives, we might end up spending the night in the psych unit with the Italians.

'How old is he?' I asked Sten.

The Swede shrugged. 'He was young when I met him. A senior in high school. He saw me on a station platform in Durban. He approached me. At the time he was suspended because he had written a controversial essay. I will never forget it – I was sitting on a bench and he walked up to me. "I'm suspended from school because I wrote an essay connecting ufology to Christianity," he said. Then he told me his mother was a psychic and was proud of him. Of course, I liked him immediately. We spent five nights sitting together on different platforms, hunting my train. I was happy for the company. And he had many ideas. For me it was about patterns and data. But he showed me the technique that diviners use to find water. On the fourth night I saw my train using this method. I have been using it ever since.'

I shook my head. '1994. I was seven.'

'It was the year of the first democratic elections in South Africa. Thirteen years later I saw him in London at Waterloo Station. I was there for my ghost train; he was investigating rumours of a giant rat in one of the tunnels. It was my first night staking the train in London on that trip, just like it was my first night on a trip to KwaZulu-Natal ... just like it is my first night in Tasmania on this occasion.'

'If you've only met three times, how does he know where to contact you?'

'There are places. Forums on the internet, legitimate and not so legitimate.'

'The dark net?'

'I cannot say in detail. But there is a community of people, yes. Labuschagne sent me a message through one of these channels.'

'And here I thought *my* pursuit was radical.'

'It is a good omen for me. Those three times I came very close.'

We looked up to see Labuschagne standing before us with his hands out. 'Fancy meeting you two here. How lucky.'

'Sit,' Sten said, patting the space beside him.

Labuschagne pointed inside as if to suggest he was here for a film, then gave up the pretence and sat down. 'What were you talking about? It looked serious.'

'The train,' Sten said. 'The passengers. Chasing dreams. You.'

His eyes widened. 'You were talking about me?'

'I was telling Geo about the time you taught me how to dowse.'

I felt I needed to explain my presence, as it was Labuschagne who'd sought out Sten and directed him to Hobart. But now that Sten was here, he wanted nothing to do with the bookstore owner. And yet I – *Mr Nobody* – had been invited. 'He's staying at my house,' I said.

Labuschagne's face tightened. 'I know.'

'I mean, that's why —'

'I understand.'

Sten nodded at the book tucked beneath his arm. 'Tell us something about the Hobart tramways.'

Labuschagne perked up. 'Hobart was the first electric tramway system in the Southern Hemisphere.'

'I didn't know that,' I said.

'The service initially only operated double-decker trams. Which was problematic on the hillier routes.'

Sten folded his arms and closed his eyes.

Labuschagne flipped through the pages. 'Unsurprisingly, this street was the most heavily trafficked route. By 1950, 132 trams left the post office each weekday between 4 and 6 p.m.'

'These are good facts,' Sten said. 'But not useful. Like my profiles of the ghost passengers.'

Labuschagne snapped the book closed. 'Shouldn't you be watching the road?'

I chuckled. 'If a train appears, believe me, we will be alerted.'

Sten smiled but turned the conversation against me. 'Actually,' he said to Labuschagne, 'there is a problem at the house that is in your field.' He glanced at me. 'Tell him about the lamp.'

The blood drained from my face. I didn't mind watching Labuschagne edge into Sten's domain, but I didn't want this weirdo anywhere near my own paranormal issues.

Labuschagne's interest was businesslike. 'Apprise me.'

'It's nothing. Forget it.'

Sten held out a hand to him. 'You think my train is strange? This is an unplugged lamp giving off light.'

I pointed at the street. 'We need to focus. The train could appear at any moment.'

'This is what I do,' Labuschagne pressed. 'I have everything you need, the perfect blend of experience and equipment.'

It took all of my composure not to walk away. I'd returned to Hobart to sell a house and play music, and perhaps reach one or two resolutions in my life. But here I was on night four, ghost train hunting and resisting the advances of a paranormal investigator.

'Your choice,' Labuschagne said, and leaned back against the window.

We watched the traffic, waiting with fading belief for Sten's train to appear.

#

The following morning, a Sunday, Sten and I stood outside the kitchen with cups of coffee clutched at our chests, appraising the exterior walls. The weather had turned overnight, and our breath clouded the air as we spoke. After spending a good forty minutes inspecting the house, Sten had called me out to give me a breakdown of the situation. 'It is not in bad condition,' he said. 'Before I examined it, I thought it would need more work. The only question is whether you want a proper job or a fast job.'

'What's the difference? I mean, I'm guessing the difference is money.'

'Really, the difference is time. The secret is the preparation. Good preparation costs little money but takes a lot of time. Then it is a choice of one coat or two coats. Two is twice the time. But you are not paying me for my time, so it is not really about money.'

Wes emerged from the kitchen, wearing only jeans, and proceeded to fill a watering can from the tap by the back door.

'How long do you normally stay in one place?' I asked Sten.

'It is impossible to predict. But this is the point exactly. One moment I will be here, the next I will be gone. You will wonder about me, but nobody will be able to tell you. I may be on my train, or I may be in the next country.'

'What's the shortest you've stayed anywhere?'

He thought for a moment. 'Five days. Cairo, 2003.'

I needed the sale. If we put the house on the market and it went quickly, a light paint job might suffice. But because of Wes, selling the house was looking to be a slow burn.

'I suggest doing it properly,' Sten said. 'It is better to do it properly or not at all. Even if I only finish the preparation. It will then be easy for you to paint the house. Two coats in one week.' He saw my expression and added, 'Or you can hire a painter, which won't be so expensive. Two coats in four days. Not a problem.'

'I trust your opinion. What do we need for the preparation?'

'I'm not driving you to Bunnings,' Wes said, overwatering a plant that was withered and dead. 'If you were thinking of asking.'

'Nic's taking us,' I said. We were still a couple of days away from getting back the Ford Explorer from its service.

He raised the spout. 'Nic's coming over?'

I turned my back to him. 'What do we need?' I asked Sten.

'First I must clean the walls. For this a ladder, a broom, a cloth and an old paintbrush. You have these already, I suppose?'

'I'll check under the house. Our father was handy, so I'm guessing yes.'

'After that I will wash the walls – soap, two buckets, more cloths.'

'Should I make a list?'

'We will make a list after. Drop sheets, masking tape … a lot of masking tape.' He walked over to a part of the weatherboard where the paint was peeling and pulled off a flake. 'Sandpaper. I can do it by hand, but that will take longer. An electric sander will save a lot of time.'

'I'll be raising the money as we go along. We'll cost everything and prioritise.'

Wes was back at the tap, refilling the can. 'Normally I wouldn't care because I oppose the end goal, but as we're not selling you're basically painting it for me. Dad had a sander. It's on the shelving behind the door under the house. You'll just need sanding sheets.'

'Good,' Sten said. 'We will also need filler and blades. Bucketloads of filler. There are many areas to smoothen. It would be impossible to get too much.'

'How many hours for the preparation?'

'For one person … maybe twenty hours? I don't know. I am a fast worker.'

That was one-and-a-half weeks at our agreed rate. I wanted him to board his train, but it would be a gift if he could at least finish the preparation and the first coat. I'd deal with the rest later. 'Let's do it.'

After we checked under the house to confirm the materials on hand, we went into the kitchen to make a list. I emptied the cash from my wallet onto the counter: $340 and a scattering of gold and silver coins.

'This is everything you have?' Sten asked.

I nodded.

'Including on which to live?'

'I have money in Italy I can't touch – an amount that will get me anywhere in Europe for my next audition. But for here in Tasmania, this is it.'

He considered me with the same admiration as when he'd seen Labuschagne the previous evening. 'Our dreams are exactly the same.'

#

Sten approached the Bunnings staff member at the welcoming booth and was pointed towards the paints section. Nic and I trailed behind him as he pushed a trolley along the aisles of the warehouse floor. At the paints counter, a female staff member skimmed through his list, then came around to help him gather the materials.

Happy to leave Sten to manage the purchase, Nic and I waited in a side aisle.

'Do you not wonder about him?' she asked.

'How do you mean?'

'I don't know … He appeared from nowhere.'

'You think there's a security risk?'

She made a face. 'No. Nothing like that. But you have to admit it's strange. He arrived from where – Sweden? – to chase a ghost train. Now he's painting the house.'

'When you say it like that, I mean …' I shook my head. 'I believe it's destiny. The more I'm around him the more clearly I see my future self. I think I've drawn him into my life to teach me something.'

'Good or bad?'

'I'm still figuring that out.'

'I can see the attraction, I suppose.'

'You want to know his real talent?'

'What?'

'Neutralising Wes.'

'How do you mean?'

'Sten has no regard for what people think of him. Most people would say that about themselves, but it's a lie. And you're right, there's something a little left field there. I think that's what makes Wes uncomfortable. He gets off on affecting how people feel, but

Sten doesn't feel anything. It's actually funny to watch. Around him Wes forgets to be an arsehole.'

'That's a trick I wish I could learn.'

We watched Sten tally up the materials as the Bunnings staff member went to fetch a calculator.

Nic held out an envelope to me.

'What's this?' I asked.

'Take it.'

I looked inside and saw four fifty-dollar notes. 'The money Wes gave you last night?'

'He needs to contribute.'

I tried to hand it back. 'You need this more than I do. I can't take this, Nic.'

'For Wes the house is a pause from his life with Hayden and me. We need for him to move on so we can move on.'

I felt a sadness hearing this.

She crossed her arms. 'Wes draws out his whole salary and then drip-feeds it to me. It's quite pathetic. I used to sit at the computer on payday, waiting for the money to land so I could transfer out expenses. I don't bother anymore. He does it for access.'

'You have no intention of reconciling, do you?'

Her voice faltered. 'I'm waiting for the right moment.'

Wes's nature made it difficult to empathise with him, but there was something heartbreaking in knowing the people he loved no longer wanted to be with him.

'You know where he keeps it?' I asked her. 'The money, I mean.'

'I really don't care.'

'In a shoebox under his bed.'

She laughed. 'My life is a cliché.'

The Bunnings staff member disappeared down one of the aisles, and I approached Sten and slipped the envelope into his hand. He glanced at the contents, his expression unchanged. When the staff member returned he collected twenty litres of primer, and had her put together four 250-millilitre samples of different white shades.

'He's one mistake away from losing his job,' Nic said to me.

'I've noticed things aren't good at work.'

'Everything changed after your father passed. It's not just our marriage at risk.'

'I think he's drinking on the job.'

'That's how it started. Turning up to the station in no condition to drive. Now he finishes his shift and heads out to the street. He's fabricating situations to resolve. Marty tells me everything. Wes is trying to win back credibility, but it's only making things worse.'

'Martin gave me his card at the hospital. I didn't know what he meant by it.'

'Save that number to your phone. You'll need it.'

'I've walked into the perfect storm, haven't I? This isn't just a dispute over an inheritance. The house is the only thing he has left.'

'Do you think he'd be different if he hadn't stopped playing the violin?'

Her question surprised me. 'You mean if he'd pursued a career in music?'

'It's a stupid thought.' She shook her head. 'Forget I asked.'

Sten thanked the Bunnings staff member, and Nic and I followed him to the checkout.

'Have dinner with us tomorrow night,' she said. 'And bring Sten. Maybe he'll help take the edge off Wes.'

CHAPTER FOUR

I SAT AT THE kitchen table with my viola on my lap, staring out the window at Mum's studio in the backyard. Sten worked quietly across from me, alternating between a book on Tasmania's bush tramways and crosschecking with his crystal. I was concerned the studio was becoming a 'thing'. This was supposed to be the easy part of the trip: a retreat from Wes as I prepared for my audition with the MSO, now less than two weeks away.

Perhaps sensing my hesitation, Sten said, 'You can practise here. It will not distract me.'

'Thanks. But if I don't play in the studio I'll regret it.'

'Can I tell you what I am picking up? I am picking up that when you leave this town, you are never coming back.' He was holding the crystal above a black-and-white photo of the Cataract Gorge Sewer Tramway. It circled anticlockwise.

'You're right. I'm never coming back.'

'Why is the studio important for you?'

'Mum was a violist with the Tasmanian Symphony Orchestra. It's where she rehearsed and gave lessons.'

He wiped the crystal with his shirt. 'I am picking up that there is more. But you don't have to say.'

I wasn't sure if it was a perception or intuition. 'When Mum was diagnosed I moved back into the house. We lost her twelve months later.'

'I'm sorry.'

'Our father wasn't in any condition to be her carer. Drink, professional frustration … it's another story. But having recently graduated, I decided to take a gap year. Mum was against the idea, but by the time she'd outlined her objections to me in a letter I'd already moved in. Why I'm telling you this is it explains the studio. We fell into a routine that produced some of my favourite memories. On her good days she'd nominate a piece of music, and I'd rehearse it before her from the first note. It was a wonderful shared experience, but it also took my sightreading skills to another level, an essential component of auditions.'

'She was preparing you.'

'I was oblivious. In my mind I'd pressed the pause button on my career, in order to be a faithful son. It was the most important education of my life.'

'I cannot think of a greater gift from a parent.'

'She'd listen from her leather chair and conduct me through every stage towards mastery. Some of the pieces took weeks. And the music she selected …' I opened a folder that contained the repertoire list for the MSO audition. 'Beethoven's Symphony No. 5, Berlioz's Roman Carnival Overture, Mendelssohn's Scherzo from *A Midsummer Night's Dream*, Walton and Bartók's viola concertos, Ravel's Suite No. 2 from *Daphnis et Chloé*, Hindemith's *Der Schwanendreher*, Shostakovich's Symphony No. 5, Strauss's *Don Juan*, Stamitz's Viola Concerto …' I shook my head. 'These are the common repetitions of repertoire for the viola. If you're on the audition circuit and you're well versed in them, it's simply a matter of learning the additional excerpts.'

'She was equipping you with the tools you needed.'

'There I was thinking, *I'm taking care of Mum*, and she was taking care of my dream.'

Sten squeezed my shoulder. 'She was doing her job. She did a fine job.'

I took a sharp breath. 'So you see. I have to play in the studio.'

'It is clear that you have no choice. And you will play there. Maybe not today. But it will be.'

'I believe you.'

'Can I tell you what I suggest? I suggest tomorrow, or the next day – without thinking or planning – picking up your instrument and marching in. Do not touch anything. Do not think about anything. Stand in the space and play. In this way you will preserve the memory and honour the dream. After that it will be easy.'

This was the encouragement I needed, and I ran my sleeve across my face. Sten scooped up his crystal from the table.

'Do you know where it's going next?' I asked.

'My train is moving north today. Not *north*-north, not Launceston, but in that direction. In any case, I do not have transport, so I will not chase it.'

'I think I'll head into town for a busking session. I need to break this mood, but I also need to rehearse. I may as well try to make some cash while I'm at it.'

'Are you going now?'

'I think so. I'll be back around five-thirty. It's only a twenty-minute walk to Nic's place from here.'

'Maybe I will come with you. I would like to speak to the stationmaster at the old Hobart yard.'

'Perfect. We'll catch a bus from town when we're done.'

#

Hayden's eyes went straight to Sten as he opened the door. There was a pause, and then, very matter-of-fact, very Hayden-like, he said, 'So you're the ghost train hunter.'

Light music and the smell of oven cooking wafted out, and I thought I heard a faint thread of laughter. In contrast to my first night in Hobart, the atmosphere was inviting.

'That is correct,' Sten said. 'Hunter of ghost trains. In Swedish we say spöktåg jägare.'

Hayden extended his hand. 'I can't say for sure, but I suspect by the end of tonight you'll be the most interesting person I've met. Don't be flattered. I'm fourteen, so it'll be temporary.'

He swivelled around and disappeared inside. Sten followed behind with a delighted expression. I was happy for him. On the bus ride over he'd spoken of his nervousness at attending a 'social dinner'. It had been a long time, he'd said. I'd told him that in spite of my brother's prickly personality, the family were down-to-earth people. He had shown me the bottle of wine he'd bought. 'Do you think it is sufficient? It is very cheap.' I'd said he was worrying for nothing, and that it was perfectly suitable.

Wes was setting the table as we came into the dining room. He broke into a smile. 'Welcome. Welcome.'

'Sten's possibly the most interesting person I've met,' Hayden said. 'I don't know for sure, but my feeling is strong.'

I glanced across the room into the kitchen, and it felt like someone reached into my lungs and yanked out a fistful of air. Audrey was leaning against the counter, talking to Nic. An arm across her midriff, her free hand holding a glass of wine. She stopped speaking when she saw me.

'Oh,' was all I could muster.

'Hello, Geo,' she said.

Nic swept by her to greet us. 'I'm so glad you came,' she said to Sten. She kissed me on the cheek. 'Hello, dear.'

Sten handed Wes the bottle of wine. Wes thanked him, and proceeded to fill the glasses on the table with sparkling water. I could tell Sten doubted his choice, but before I could whisper in his ear that my brother was making a fake effort to show Nic his drinking was under control, Hayden diverted our attention. 'My dad said you came to Hobart to get on a ghost train?'

'That is true.'

'Are you trying to board any ghost train, or is it one train specifically?'

'One train,' Sten said. 'But that is an excellent question.'

'Have you seen it before?'

'I have. Yes. A number of times.'

We were standing around the dining table. Audrey had resumed her conversation with Nic, who was removing a baking dish from the oven.

'When was the last time?' Hayden asked Sten.

'Last week.'

'In Tasmania?'

'Orvieto. In Italy. Some people confuse it with Oviedo in Spain. I have seen it there too.'

I snapped back to the conversation. 'You saw the Italians getting on the train?'

'I ran onto the platform as it pulled away.'

Wes stopped pouring.

Sten shrugged. 'This is my life. I chase it every day. Sometimes I miss it by a week. Other times by a minute. Last week I missed it by a minute.'

'How did you know?' Hayden asked.

Wes frowned. 'You're asking personal questions, champ.'

'I am happy to talk about it,' Sten said. 'Your questions are interesting to me. But it is up to your father.'

Hayden turned to Wes, his eyes pleading. Wes didn't object.

'How did I know it was the ghost train?' Sten said.

Shaking his head, Hayden asked, 'How did you know it was going to be there? On that platform, at that time?'

I was loving Hayden's questions as much as I was loving Sten's relaxed manner in dealing with them. But more than anything I was loving Wes's discomfort with the fact his fourteen-year-old was bonding with a ghost train hunter who had been thrust into our lives via a conspiracy bookstore paranormal investigator.

What I wasn't loving was Audrey's presence. Why had Nic invited her? For us to make peace, or under some weird assumption we might rekindle something? Or had Audrey prompted the neutral meeting venue? Was she looking for closure, perhaps? These were the questions flashing through my mind, but there was too much happening in the foreground to consider them properly.

'I have two techniques,' Sten said to Hayden. 'I can show you one if you like?'

'Dinner's served,' Nic said, bringing out the baking dish.

I moved a couple of glasses to make space around the trivet in the centre of the table.

'Thank you.'

Audrey followed behind with a large bowl of green salad. I rearranged a couple of glasses that didn't need rearranging. She set it down, and went to sit in the chair furthest from me.

Nic lifted the lid to reveal a lasagne. 'Home cooked,' she said, but Wes took no notice.

'It smells lovely,' Sten said. 'Thank you for the invitation. This is not usual for me.'

'Yes, thank you,' I said. 'I know how busy you are.'

'Why don't you sit over there?' Wes said to Audrey, indicating the chair across from me. 'I'm sure you two have a lot to talk about.'

'No. I'm fine here.'

There was an awkward pause as Wes came to my end of the table. I forced a smile as he pulled back the chair, struggling to hide my discomfort.

'Help yourself, please,' Nic said, handing the serving spoon to Audrey. She turned to Sten. 'How did you go with the house painting today?'

'Forget that, Mum,' Hayden said with excitement. 'Sten was about to show us how he knows where the ghost train appears.'

'Oh.'

I glanced at Audrey as I lifted a serving of salad onto my plate, but she wouldn't look across.

Sten reached into his pocket for his velvet pouch. 'It is not a science, but it is more accurate than guessing.' He slipped the crystal into his hand and said to Hayden, 'Tell me where you think the train will appear tonight.'

Hayden frowned. 'You mean a station? I don't know any.'

'Tell me a town. Any town in Tasmania. The first one that comes to your mind.'

'Burnie.'

Taking the clasp of the chain into his right hand, Sten held the crystal above his left palm. 'Will the ghost train appear in Burnie tonight?' The crystal started moving. He looked at Hayden. 'Can you see that it is turning anticlockwise?'

Hayden nodded.

'That means "no". Clockwise means "yes". If the circle is wide, it is a strong "yes".'

'That's clever,' Hayden said.

Wes said, 'That's the most ridiculous thing I've ever heard.'

Nic glared at him.

'I do not expect anyone to believe it,' Sten said. 'Normally I would not show my technique. But Hayden asked specifically, and his interest is genuine.'

Hayden glowed at the compliment.

'I believe it,' Audrey said.

'No, you don't,' Wes scoffed.

She thought for a moment. 'I believe consciousness is its own dimension, and that the energy of everything that's ever happened, and is going to happen, is stored there.' She shrugged. 'I can see how the crystal provides a path into that space.'

Sten regarded her. 'You are very wise. In some fields this path is called the signal line.'

'Don't make me laugh,' Wes said.

'I believe it too,' Hayden stated.

'It's okay for you to believe it, champ. At your age you're supposed to believe everything.'

Hayden lowered his head and pushed his fork through his lasagne.

'I also believe it,' Nic said.

'Now you're just ganging up.' Wes glanced at Audrey. 'If you truly believe it, ask the crystal if Geo had any intention of contacting you again. Ask —'

'Cut it out,' I said.

'Yeah, Dad. Play fair.'

Wes considered Hayden, and turned to Audrey. 'Sorry. I didn't mean it the way it came across. I was only —'

'I'll tell you why I believe it,' Nic said, laying down her fork. 'I believe Sten believes that what he's saying is true. And that's all that matters.'

The perception startled me, as this had been my response to Wes when he'd asked if I believed the story of the Orvieto mayor, Giacomo Pedroni.

Sten held up his hands. 'This is the most interesting social dinner I have attended. Only Labuschagne has shown more enthusiasm for my train.'

'Who's Labuschagne?' Hayden asked, pronouncing 'cha' as 'ga', rather than with the guttural fricative.

'Somebody you will never meet,' Wes said.

'But please, allow me to change the subject.' Sten turned to Audrey. 'What is your passion? I am curious to know.'

Sten, I was quickly learning, knew how to cut through the small-talk gibber and get straight to the dream.

Audrey dabbed her lips with her serviette. 'My passion is to sing opera.'

Sten clapped his hands. 'That is tremendous. Please sing for us.'

She regarded him in the same manner as I had when he'd

prodded me to play the viola in the conspiracy bookstore. 'I don't think so.'

'Of course you will,' Hayden said. 'I'll accompany you.'

'It's bad manners to force someone to do something they don't want to do,' Nic said.

Sten reached into his jacket pocket for his crystal. 'Shall we ask the crystal? A little fun. If it makes you uncomfortable, I will put it away.'

Audrey shrugged.

Sten held the crystal above his palm. 'Will Audrey sing for us tonight?'

The crystal immediately made clockwise circles.

'That's a "yes",' Hayden said.

Sten said to Audrey, 'Can I ask about the song you will sing?'

She nodded, clearly warming to the idea.

Turning to Hayden, Sten said, 'I need your help. I am a ghost train hunter. I don't know opera. Tell me the names of songs, and we will see how the crystal responds.'

Audrey fetched a pen from her bag hanging on the back of her chair, then scribbled something on an unused serviette. She folded it and passed it across the table to Nic.

Hayden stroked his chin. 'Hmm … I'm a violinist, so I think she'll sing what she knows I can accompany her on piano. Ask if she will sing *La bohème*?'

Sten said, 'Will Audrey sing *La bohème*?' The crystal moved in an anticlockwise direction.

'Schumann?' Hayden asked.

Sten posed the question, and again the response was negative.

'He's guiding it with his right hand,' Wes said.

Nic slapped his arm.

Hayden's eyes widened. 'Brahms.'

'Will Audrey sing to Brahms?' Sten asked.

The crystal swung clockwise.

Hayden's face lit up. 'Ask if she will sing "Wiegenlied".'

Audrey's jaw dropped. Sten asked the question, and the crystal swung clockwise.

Nic opened the serviette and gasped. She held it up so everyone could see what was written: *Wiegenlied*.

Hayden pumped his fist. 'Yes.'

'It's called "cold reading",' Wes said with a smirk.

'You feel foolish because you doubted,' Nic said.

He was defiant. 'It's a common technique practised by mentalists and psychics.'

I said to Sten, 'Ask if Wes will play the violin tonight.'

Before my brother could interject, Sten posed the question. The crystal swung broadly in an anticlockwise direction.

'Ask if he will play before I leave Tasmania,' I prodded.

'Okay, that's enough,' Wes said.

I felt no guilt at sticking a finger in his wound, but then in a tone that made me shudder, Audrey said, 'Ask if Geo had any intention of contacting me again.'

The table fell silent as everyone stared at the crystal suspended above Sten's palm. He glanced at me, as if seeking permission, but my gaze remained firmly on the crystal. After a beat it circled anticlockwise.

Nic was quick to break the tension. 'Why don't we retire to the living room?'

Hayden hurried off to fetch the sheet music for *Wiegenlied*. As everyone drifted away from the table, I intercepted Audrey. I knew we only had a few seconds. 'Audrey, why are you here?'

'It was a terrible idea. I realised it the moment you walked in.'

'Don't get me wrong, I'm glad to see you. But I wish we could talk —'

Her body tensed. 'I wanted to prove to myself I'm over you.'

Nic was watching from the living room, and when Audrey glanced over she smiled and beckoned us across. Audrey went through, and I followed behind.

After everyone settled, Audrey took her position beside Hayden at the upright piano. She placed a hand on the lid, and Hayden placed his fingers lightly on the keys. She nodded, and he played the opening notes. It was glorious, the music transporting us. He voice was enough to make a stranger fall in love with her. The Brahms piece didn't draw on her full range, but it committed her heart.

The others were equally entranced. It was a master performance. There was a brief silence after the final note faded, then an eruption of applause.

'Bravo,' Sten said, rising to his feet.

Audrey bowed, and acknowledged Hayden.

We had dessert in the living room, and nothing reached the heights of the dinner conversation and Audrey's recital. At the end of the evening Nic offered on our behalf to drop Audrey at home; this, I suspected, was so Wes wouldn't use the occasion to suggest staying over.

#

I sat in the back with Audrey as Wes drove us across town to South Hobart. I could sense him brooding. Sten, in the passenger seat, was chatty and animated – basically, very un-Sten. It was disconcerting.

'You have a wonderful family,' he said to no one in particular. 'Hayden is very interesting. He thinks I am interesting? He is much more interesting. Such curiosity. And talented. If he plays the piano like that?' Sten shook his head. 'I can only imagine the violin.'

'He's exceptional,' Audrey said.

Sten turned around. 'And you? A voice like … I don't have the words. Your talent is extreme.'

She blushed. 'You're too kind.'

He faced the front. 'To spend an evening with such people. I am the lucky one.'

We drove the rest of the way in silence, and I wondered how long this thief who'd stolen Sten's Sten-ness would be sticking around. I was more than relieved when we turned onto Macquarie Street and Sten put his crystal to work. His seriousness resurfaced.

We pulled up outside Audrey's parents' house, and I walked her to the door. After she stepped inside, she turned to face me.

'I'm glad you came,' I said.

'I always enjoy spending time with your family.' She smiled, and quietly closed the door.

Back in the car, Sten said, 'I am pushing the limit of my vocabulary, but I think the word is "wondrous". Yes … that's the word, to describe her voice.'

We needed to get him home and get a joint into his system asap.

#

When we arrived back at the house, a figure emerged from the shadows of the porch.

'What the fuck?' Wes said.

'It's me, Labuschagne.' His hands were raised, a cigarette dangling from his mouth. He seemed afraid that Wes might draw a weapon.

Sten showed the same reaction as when we'd found Labuschagne watching us at the State Cinema. 'Boy, this man is good,' he said.

Wes was livid. 'What are you doing here?'

Labuschagne nodded at the silver case by the door. 'I've come to help with your paranormal situation.'

My brother shot me a look. 'What have you told this prick?'

'Don't look at me. Have you not wondered how he found you at the Royal Hobart?'

'This man is at the top of his game,' Sten said.

Labuschagne lowered his arms. 'I can send the spirit on its way. This is my field.'

Wes pointed a finger at him. 'Shut it.'

Labuschagne's arms flew back up.

Wes was glaring at Sten and me. 'Can someone please tell me what the fuck's going on?'

'Let us in,' I said. 'It's been a long night.'

Wes's eyes darted from me to Sten, to Labuschagne. He was ready to brawl. But in the next instant his anger dissipated. Muttering an expletive under his breath, he opened the door and went inside. Sten followed him through, and I thought, *Why-oh-why has it taken me thirty years to realise I only need eccentric friends to disarm my brother?*

I gestured for Labuschagne to enter, and he gave a boyish grin as he picked up his silver case and stepped through the doorway.

Wes poured four whiskies and took one to the recliner. Sten slumped into his sofa, and I sat down across from him. Labuschagne stood by the liquor cabinet.

'You're all sleeping in here?' he said.

I pointed at the unoccupied armchair. 'If you're quick it's got your name on it.'

He placed his silver case in the corner next to my viola and Sten's Gladstone bag, and sat down.

'What's in the case?' Wes asked.

'The usual accoutrement for detecting paranormal activity.'

'You don't have to declare anything you don't want,' I said.

He shrugged. 'An electromagnetic field meter, a thermometer, a motion sensor, a recorder, a vibration detector, a spirit box, a listener. I have another case in the shop I didn't bring.'

I raised my glass. 'Impressive.'

Sten told Labuschagne about the questions asked of him that evening by Hayden, and the debate around dowsing. 'An experience as extraordinary as any ghost sighting. Truly.'

Labuschagne listened politely, but I could tell the lamp was front and centre of his mind.

'It's in my bedroom cupboard,' I said. 'Second door down from the bathroom.'

Wes frowned. 'I thought we'd agreed it wasn't coming back in the house?'

'One day you'll need to explain to me your definition of "agree". I'm rehearsing in the studio.'

Labuschagne pushed himself out of the armchair. 'Nonbelievers arguing over detail. Very telling. There's clearly a spirit afoot.'

Sten slipped his pouch out of his jacket, and very matter-of-fact, very Sten, said, 'We need medicine.'

Labuschagne went to fetch the lamp, but when he returned Wes pointed him away. 'Not in here.'

Labuschagne glanced at me. 'Please bring me my case.'

I followed him into the living room and placed his silver case beside the sofa. I retreated to observe from the doorway as he positioned the lamp on one of the side tables in the centre of the room. Unplugged, the cord lay curled on the carpet.

He took his time going through a sequence of actions I assumed to be his investigative process: he walked about the room, laying his hands on each of the four walls; he checked that the windows were secured; he closed his eyes and stood perfectly still, listening, thinking, feeling.

Sten sidled up to the doorway and handed me a joint. I took a drag and passed it back. A childlike naughtiness overtook me, and I flicked the main light on and off before retracting my hand. Sten's eyes widened. Labuschagne stiffened, and pointed his finger at the ceiling.

I smiled sheepishly, indicating the light switch. 'Sorry ... couldn't resist.'

Labuschagne gave me a stern look, then knelt down to place a hand on the floorboards.

'What's he doing?' I said.

'Checking for cold spots,' Sten said.

'How do you know?'

He shrugged. 'I spend my life waiting on platforms. I read a lot.'

Labuschagne said, 'I sense a presence. But it's faint.'

Sten discreetly took out his crystal and held it above his palm. It turned clockwise.

'Do you think it's the same presence that made the lamp come on?' I asked Labuschagne.

'Possibly,' he said, opening his silver case. 'It's too soon to say.'

Sten checked with the crystal, and this time it turned anti-clockwise. He shook his head.

We watched Labuschagne move on to the next phase of detection. It was the sort of method you'd expect to see on a ghost hunter reality show, except it was happening in my house. A couple of times I almost laughed, so absurd the actions seemed to me. I had to remind myself Labuschagne was testing for activity I'd witnessed with my own eyes. With a forensic thoroughness, he worked with different pieces of equipment to measure temperature, undetectable noise, frequencies, magnetic fields, and moisture. But as far as I could determine, nothing registered that he deemed worth recording.

By the time he laid down his thermal cam, Sten had returned to the sitting room. But Labuschagne had the stamina of a pack of wild dogs, and at this point resorted to the most basic of human tactics: begging. He sat across from the lamp and said, 'Is anyone here?'

The light didn't respond.

'If you are here and would like to communicate, please do so now.'

Nothing.

He glanced over, inviting me to ask the question, but I shook my head. 'I think I'm going to call it a night.'

'I'll continue, if that's okay?'

I nodded and retired to the sitting room. Wes was snoring lightly, and Sten too seemed to be asleep, but when I kicked off my shoes and slumped onto my sofa, he opened his eyes.

Exhausted, I drifted into a slumber with the metronomic tones of Labuschagne's voice resounding faintly from the living room.

'Is anyone here?'

'Is anyone here?'

'Is anyone here?'

CHAPTER FIVE

Terry from Pearson Realty called as Wes and I were driving out of the Woolworths in New Town. Wes had picked me up to do some shopping, as apart from coffee and milk, and a few old rags, the pantry and cleaning cupboards were empty.

At the end of the call, I hung up the phone. 'Four-sixty – the median value of what sold on Yardley Street last year. Terry's confident we'll fetch in the vicinity of that with the paint job Sten's doing.'

Wes lit a cigarette.

'Look. We're going to have to talk about it at some point. It doesn't matter what you say or how angry you get.' I shook my head. 'Do you really think I'd come all this way without having explored my options?'

He stared blankly ahead.

'I'm prepared to compromise,' I said. 'I appreciate you want to keep the house as much as I want to sell it. I'm not callous. This is mostly about money for me. If you want to live in it until you're in a position to buy me out, we'll get Terry to draw up a contract.

Four-twenty a week. You can set up a direct debit into my account for half that. Or if you'd prefer, take in a boarder and send me the full amount of their rent. We can work it out, but you need to come to the table.'

He took our father's hipflask out of the glove box. I watched open-mouthed as he twisted off the lid and took a swig. I'd seen our father do this before; one time in my late teens he'd had a swig at a traffic light in Moonah, and I had climbed out and walked home.

'Wes,' I said.

He returned the flask to the glove box without looking at me. The light changed, and the car eased forward. It was only when we turned onto Risdon Road that I registered where he was taking us.

I raised my hands. 'Don't do this.'

He drove through the gates of Cornelian Bay Cemetery and parked in one of the bays behind the office.

'You know I'm not going in,' I said.

He unbuckled his seatbelt. 'I'm not selling the house.'

A dangerous moment passed between us, before he opened the door and disappeared between the hedges that led into the cemetery grounds. I presumed our father's cremated remains were in an urn next to Mum's in the flowering garden on the Derwent River side. I drew three cigarettes from the pack in the console, and got out of the car.

#

An hour later, I arrived back at the house. Sten was at the kitchen table, going through his routine for that night's stakeout.

I'd worked myself into a mindset where I believed I had to make a statement. I wasn't angry; I was defiant. I respected Wes, but I needed him to know I didn't fear him. Strangely, I interpreted his choosing to park outside the cemetery office rather than driving through to the flowering garden as a sign that though equally defiant, he was respectful. Clearly, it was my move.

I checked the fridge and cupboards, and was relieved to see that Wes had dropped off the shopping. Before I had time to doubt my plan, I grabbed the roll of rubbish bag and asked Sten if I could bum a joint. He passed me his tobacco pouch, and I hastily rolled one. Ripping a bag from the roll, I stood in the doorway to the sitting room. Was I really going to do this, I wondered? It would be the most cutthroat play. *Fuck this shit. And fuck him.* I stepped into the room, joint dangling from my mouth, and proceeded to pick up our father's garbage.

Sten came into the room and tore a bag from the roll, and very casual-like, very Sten, began collecting rubbish. After we finished in the sitting room, we moved on to the living room, and from there worked our way back through the house. When Sten plugged in the vacuum cleaner, I slipped outside for a smoke. I didn't have the courage to see him run it around my bedroom, clearing up the burnt fragments of sheet music that littered the carpet. I wasn't ready to face the memory of that final night.

The only rooms we didn't touch were our father's study and Wes's bedroom. By the time we were done we had seven bags bursting to the seams. We put them out by the bins and came back into the kitchen. Sten patted me on the back, happy with our work. I was less enthusiastic – he didn't realise he'd helped me scoop up the broken pieces of my brother's heart and put it out as trash.

Sten left for his stakeout, and I used the newly purchased cleaning products to dust the house from ceiling to floor, and give every surface a spray and wipe. It wasn't a deep clean, but it was a respectable first draft.

Emotionally and physically drained, I took a bath in the dark with a fresh joint. The combination so relaxed me that when I climbed out thirty minutes later I completely doubted my actions. As much as I despised Wes for how he reflected the worst parts of our father, it wasn't my place to interfere with how he remembered him. It would be the equivalent of Wes throwing out Mum's viola.

I draped a towel around my waist and called Alessia. It was 10 a.m. in Rome, early for a musician. She answered after a few rings. 'Pronto?' she said in a groggy voice.

'I woke you. Sorry. I'll call back later.'

'Geo,' she said, switching to English, 'how are you?'

'I miss you.'

'I miss you too. I love you. Is everything okay?'

'Yes. No … actually, I've just done something stupid. I think. Now I'm regretting it. But I don't want to wake you.'

'I want to hear,' she said. 'But I need to go to the bathroom first.'

'Of course.'

The line went silent. Wes could walk in any moment. That was okay. If he came home now, fine, whatever, it was done. Fate had delivered the action, and fate would deliver the response. But I was hoping Alessia might offer some kind of confirmation to put me at ease.

She picked up the phone. 'I'm here.'

I explained the situation, and what Wes had done to put me in this mood. 'What do you think?'

'You have made a mistake.'

My heart sank. 'Really?'

'Yes.'

'What should I do?'

'For sure, you must replace everything.'

'Out of the garbage bags?'

'Yes. You must take everything out and put them back where they were.'

'But I don't know where everything goes.'

'That is not important. Do it as well as you can remember. And if you cannot remember, just put it out. If he loves you, he will understand. He will forgive you. You had no right. But now you must make a gesture.'

'I'm such an idiot.'

'Do it now. When you are finished, call me back.'

'Okay.'

'Call me back. But do it now.'

I got changed and went to work. I brought the seven garbage bags into the kitchen, and began replacing the items with a keen focus on the sitting room. There were some things – like the beef jerky packet and two bottles of Chivas Regal – that I replaced precisely; there were others, like the ashtrays and the cereal bowl, that I replaced approximately. But for the most part I was working in the dark. The fishing magazine more than likely went in the living room, but the box of tissues could go anywhere. Apart from my bedroom, which I didn't bother to restore, Wes knew the exact position of every item; but as Alessia impressed upon me, this was the extension of a forgiving hand.

It took me forty minutes to set everything out, and another twenty to finesse the pieces so they looked like rubbish rather than art installations.

I called Alessia. 'Done.'

I'd woken her again. 'Good. What time is it where you are?'

'Just after nine.'

'This is important. You must stay awake until he gets back.'

'That could be any time between now and tomorrow night.'

'It does not matter. You have put yourself in this situation. You must be there, and you must be awake when he opens the door. Be your normal self. He will immediately see that something is wrong, and he will understand – the whole story will come to him. But you must cross his energy as you would normally. Friendly, unfriendly, whatever is normal.'

'Probably aloof on the outside and sensitive on the inside.'

'Okay.'

'And then?'

'And then what will happen will happen.'

'He is going to go through the roof.'

'Perhaps. Or perhaps he will say nothing. But if you fall asleep, if he has time to see the situation on his own, then he will – what you said – go through the roof. If you are there, he might be – how do you say? Defused.'

'Like a bomb,' I said.

'Yes. Like a bomb.'

'Okay.'

'Okay. I am going back to sleep now.'

'Thank you.'

In the sitting room I settled into the armchair. I stared at the window for half an hour, watching for Wes's car lights. Nothing appeared. I got up to get a drink, but the liquor cabinet was locked. I was tempted to break it open and sweep the damage into the trouble already heading my way, then decided against this.

On a whim, in spite of Alessia's instructions, I grabbed my wallet and hurried down to the United on Federal Street for a pack of cigarettes. On the way back I picked up a cask of red wine from the bottle store behind the Winston, an alehouse and eatery at the top of the North Hobart strip, and breathed a sigh of relief when I came through the door to an empty house. I found a fresh ashtray, poured myself a drink and resumed my waiting position in the armchair. Ten minutes shy of midnight, headlights swept through the window.

I stubbed out my cigarette and took a deep breath. Wes entered the sitting room and saw immediately that something was awry.

'Hey,' I said. This was not what I normally would have said. Very un-Geo.

'You bought cigarettes?' Wes asked.

I threw the pack at him. 'Help yourself.' I was pleased I'd said it like that. It's precisely how I would have said it in a guilt-free exchange of dialogue with my brother. I'd have also thrown the pack. Totally Geo.

He slid out a smoke and lit up. Without question the story came to him. I'd cleaned up our father's shit, got guilty, and replaced it in the wrong places. Wes absorbed the full narrative as he worked the cigarette. I waited for him to go through the roof, but after what seemed like an eternity he said, 'Drink?'

I pointed at the cask wine. 'I'll stick with the red. Help yourself. It's deliciously fruity.' This was a phrase that didn't sit on even the outermost ranges of my vocabulary. Completely and utterly un-Geo.

He fetched an unwashed whisky glass and filled it with wine. That move told me Alessia understood Wes better than I did. We'd defused him like a bomb.

A half-hour later the front door opened, and Sten weaved into the sitting room.

'Hey,' I said. I was happy with this 'hey'. Sten was precisely the kind of person I'd say 'hey' to.

'Hello.' He was stoned. Scratching his cheek, he considered the mess strewn across the sitting room. I watched, anxiety pumping through my veins, as he went through the same process as Wes had. I was praying Sten wouldn't speak aloud the thought that had to be running through his mind: *Am I really this high? I cleaned the house already.* But he just shrugged, accepting the situation as his new reality, and flopped onto the sofa.

I exhaled, and we all three smoked in the semi-dark for an indeterminate part of the early morning.

#

I marched into Mum's studio armed with my viola and an empty mind, and promptly began playing Grieg's *Peer Gynt* Suite from the page at which the book on the music stand was open. Sten was right: the act of playing attached my dream to the memory, and finally I knew I could make it work. I'd rehearse among the dust, inspired by the memory and honouring the dream.

After lunch I turned my attention to the repertoire list for the MSO audition, and experienced difficulty with the faster outbursts in the first movement of Walton's Viola Concerto. My usual tactic – standing in the corner, facing the wall and slaving relentlessly at the music – didn't help to overcome the piece. By late afternoon I was fatigued and frustrated, and accepted I needed to carry the rehearsal into the evening.

I went down into the house to make a coffee, and found Sten in his usual place at the kitchen table. 'I enjoy the sound of your viola while I work,' he commented.

'I wish it felt as easy as you look when you prepare for your train.'

He held out the crystal. 'Perhaps you would like to ask something to calm your mind.'

The invitation surprised me, and I declined.

My hesitation didn't deter him. 'It is not a talent. Only a matter of believing.'

I relented. Taking the crystal, and carefully holding the clasps between the thumb and forefinger of my right hand, I suspended it an inch above my left palm. 'Like this?'

He nodded. 'Say "yes".'

I cleared my throat. 'Yes.'

There was no movement initially, then ever so faintly the crystal began turning in a clockwise direction.

'Oh.' I was astonished.

The circles rapidly disintegrated.

'Say "no".'

'No.'

I could feel the tension in the chain as the crystal set off in an anticlockwise direction. My circles were small and shy in comparison to Sten's, but I found it exhilarating to see the crystal reacting to my command.

Sten said, 'Say "I don't know".'

'I don't know.'

This time the crystal veered in an up-and-down motion along the length of my hand, a movement I hadn't seen before.

'Good. It is set. Now you can ask a question.'

I gazed at the crystal with serious attention. 'Will the ghost train appear in Tasmania tonight?'

The crystal started moving in an anticlockwise direction.

Sten nodded. 'That is the same response I got. Ask if it appeared last night.'

I posed the question, and the answer came back as *yes*.

'Ask it if my train appeared on the track passing through Campania.'

The answer was *yes*.

'Thank you,' Sten said. 'It was north, as I thought, but there was no way for me to get there. Now, ask your own question.'

'Will Sten go ghost train hunting tonight?'

Sten shook his head. 'No, I mean —'

But the crystal turned clockwise.

I looked at Sten. 'It's saying *yes*.'

'I have no plan to go tonight.'

'Maybe I did it wrong.'

'No, that is sometimes how it is. Ask another question. Not about me or the train – something about your own life.'

I stared at the crystal. 'Will Wes agree to sell the house?' For a beat the crystal didn't move, and my heart began to pound. But then it started circling above my palm. I exhaled. 'That's a *yes*.'

Sten smiled. 'Be more specific.'

I waited for the crystal to come to a standstill. 'Will Wes agree to sell the house before I leave?' The crystal turned in a clockwise direction. My heart leapt. With renewed confidence, I said, 'Will I win a place in the MSO?'

When the crystal started turning anticlockwise, Sten reached over and took it from me. 'Very good for your first attempt. But you have to be careful … You have to be sure it is giving you the truth, and not the answer you want to hear, or were expecting to hear.'

'It feels naughty, like knowing the questions to a test in advance.'

On the kitchen counter, my mobile rang.

'That is the third time,' Sten said, inserting the crystal into the velvet pouch. 'I didn't call you in because you were practising.'

It was Wes. 'Why haven't you been picking up? Are you at the house?'

'Yes.'

'Is Sten there?'

'Why?'

'Be ready to leave in five. There's a situation with the train.'

My eyes fixed on Sten. 'Where?'

The Swede clearly knew what we were talking about. My stomach lurched as Wes said the name of the town. I hung up.

'Campania?' Sten said.

I nodded.

#

Five minutes later Wes pulled up outside, his hand pressed to the horn. Sten and I hustled down to the car.

'What's in Campania?' I asked, buckling my seatbelt.

'A body.' Wes looked in the mirror at Sten. 'Hit by a train.'

'Jävla skit också! Jag visste det!' Sten uttered.

You didn't need Google Translate to figure out the sentiment.

Wes flipped a pack of cigarettes at me. 'Do us a favour and light us up.'

My plan to rehearse into the evening extinguished, I lit three cigarettes and passed them out. I turned to watch Sten silently ask the crystal a sequence of questions; its answers made him visibly distressed.

'How can you be sure this death has anything to do with Sten's train?' I said to Wes.

He took a drag, his eyes flicking to the rear-view mirror. 'Because the victim was mowed down on a stretch of rail that's been out of commission for twenty years.'

The hairs on my arms rose. 'Holy fuck. What does Martin think? Is he there?'

'Martin's wrapped up in something.'

I remembered Nic's remark about how Wes had been working cases unofficially in an attempt to earn back credibility. 'Please don't tell me you're using ...' I trailed off.

'Using what?'

'Nothing.'

'Jag visste det! Skit också!' Sten said.

If Wes's information was true, it proved Sten was pursuing something real and tangible. An astonishing revelation – I wanted to slap him on the back and congratulate him. I'd thought he was demonstrating the ultimate dream chaser's faith, but his objective was in fact more concrete than mine: the target of his goal had just felled a human.

We filled up at the Caltex on Brooker Avenue, and when Wes went to pay I slid into the driver's seat and told Sten to jump in the front.

When Wes returned, I said, 'Musical chairs.'

I thought he'd be difficult about it, but he climbed in the back without complaint. He tapped Sten on the shoulder. 'Pass me the flask in the glove box.'

I changed the radio station to Classic FM, and lucked onto my favourite piano piece, Chaconne in D Minor. Turning out onto Brooker Avenue, I threw the pack of cigarettes over my shoulder. 'Do us a favour and light us up.'

Wes grunted, but lit up a smoke and passed it forward. Not long after, he dozed off.

'Tell me about your other technique,' I said to Sten. 'You said you have two methods. I understand the crystal perfectly. I'm guessing the other one involves sketching?'

'With this other technique I am chasing visuals.'

'The sketches you make are what you visualise?'

'Yes.'

He took out his pouch and started rolling a joint. I didn't stop him; something about the smell of weed in Wes's unmarked police vehicle delighted me.

'When I say I "chasing visuals", what I mean is … I wipe my mind clean. It is called "blackboard". I imagine my target, which is the ghost train's next appearance, and I wait for a visual to appear. When it appears, usually some part of a scene, I draw it.'

'You just think of something, and *boom*,' I clicked my fingers, 'an image appears?'

'It is a technique. There are protocols. I close my eyes for one-and-a-half seconds and think about my target. I wait for the visual to arrive. After one-and-a-half seconds I open my eyes. Very quickly, I close them again. Only for one-and-a-half seconds, because after that the conscious mind takes control. I do this for three or four minutes, closing and opening, closing and opening, and bit by bit fragments of images appear on the blackboard that is my empty mind. These fragments are what I am chasing.'

'Like a trail of crumbs?'

'Yes. It is called the signal line.'

'The signal line? You used that term at dinner on Monday.'

'It is what your friend Audrey was speaking about. She is right, by the way.'

'She was talking about consciousness.'

He nodded. 'How consciousness has its own dimension, where everything that has happened or is going to happen exists. The crystal and my remote viewing technique track into this dimension along the signal line.' He licked the paper and pinched the joint closed. 'The most difficult thing is to stay on the signal line. You need to be in a half-awake, half-asleep state. The conscious mind is fighting to pull you back into a fully awake state. But if you are practised, if you remain focused, inch by inch you work along the line to reach the full situation. The whole picture. And it is the whole picture I am seeking to draw.'

'The signal line,' I echoed.

'After I have finished the sketch, I compare it to photos in books and on Google Images. I use the crystal to lead me to the match, and also to crosscheck. These two methods work very well together.'

'You said it's called "blackboard", and that there are protocols. Whose protocols?'

'Those of the CIA.'

'Really?'

'The United States government has invested a lot of money in extraordinary projects.'

'You mean psychic projects?'

'They were worried about the Russians. In 1998 I met a person in Hawaii who had been part of the Stargate Project, the final such project. I spent three months with him. He taught me everything I know about remote viewing. We still communicate.'

'Is that what the film *The Men Who Stare at Goats* is about?'

'If it is about the CIA and remote viewing, then yes.'

'It's a funny movie. What you're doing doesn't seem funny at all.'

'That is because it is my life.' He offered me the joint, and I declined. 'But it is the same for you. Music is your signal line. Every audition is a new situation; every time you practise you are chasing something. And you have to stay on the line. And piece by piece you work to arrive at the complete situation. To arrive on the stage.'

It was a good metaphor. 'I have a clear sense when I've got a lock on a piece of music. It feels like I've advanced another step closer to my dream. I just never had a name for it. The signal line. I like it.'

Sten puffed on his joint. 'Any person who has a dream has one. And any person who is serious about their dream knows when they are on the line, and when they are not.'

#

I slowed the car as we approached the rail crossing in Campania. We sidled past a uniformed officer speaking to two hippie back-packers beneath an oak tree. I pulled over and parked alongside a highway patrol car, the only other vehicle at the scene. Sten and I waited by the Commodore as Wes approached the trio.

About fifty metres along from the crossing, a policewoman was using barricade tape to cordon off a section of track.

'I remember this place,' Sten said. I thought he meant from one of his visuals, but he pointed at the oak. 'In July 1987 I slept for two nights under that tree. It is the coldest I have been, staking out my train.'

After a brief word with the policeman, Wes turned towards the track and beckoned for Sten and me to follow. As I trailed after my brother, I glanced over at the hippies. They looked concerned – or rather, the young man looked concerned. Wearing jeans rolled up at the ankles, he fidgeted and shifted as the officer spoke to him and his companion. The young woman was calm, bored even, twirling hair that was a mixture of colours, predominantly purple. Behind them a battered acoustic guitar rested against a backpack.

The policewoman approached us as we reached the cordoned-off area. Wes produced his badge and said something I didn't catch. She glanced at Sten and me, nodded, and turned back to the scene.

Wes slipped under the tape, with Sten quick to follow. Feeling the same trepidation as when my brother and I had met with the coroner on the morning of Mum's funeral, I was cautious. I remembered that day for all the wrong reasons. Wanting my lasting memory of Mum to be in spirit, I'd already decided not to view her body. But when Wes and I arrived at the funeral home, the director anticipated otherwise and immediately led us down a corridor to the room where she was kept. In the next moment I was standing over Mum's open coffin, her face pale, her eyes closed. This all flashed through my mind as I followed Wes into the crime scene. Sten was eager to see the remains; I not at all. But here I was in the perimeter of the scene, fumbling for any kind of mechanism that might help me through my second encounter with death.

The first piece of evidence I came across was a dismembered arm. The shirtsleeve covered the upper part of the limb, and where the arm had been severed the shirt was bloodied and congealed. I bent over and threw up violently.

Jerking up, I wiped my mouth and took a number of short forceful breaths. The policewoman glanced at Wes, but he pretended not to notice.

True to his name, Sten was like a stone. Showing no emotion, he progressed along the track at a steady pace, pausing every few metres to study what I presumed to be more body parts.

I remained where I was, figuring out my next move. About thirty metres of track had been cordoned off. I found it easy to imagine the physical damage from the force of the impact, and I didn't have the stomach to witness the scattered material.

'I'm going to wait by the car,' I said with another lungful of breath. Nobody paid me attention.

I turned quietly back, and when I arrived at the crossing I noticed that the uniformed policeman who'd been speaking to the hippies was now talking into a radio at his car. The young man was on his haunches, searching desperately through his backpack. The young woman casually rolled a smoke. I walked over. 'Can I bum one of those? I don't feel too well.'

'Who the fuck are you?' the man said.

The woman licked the paper and rolled it into a perfect cylinder. She held it out to me, expressionless.

'Thank you.' I lit up and took a deep drag, then pointed in the direction of the scene. 'One of those people is my brother. A detective. I'm Mr Nobody.'

The man muttered something in Spanish.

'Forgive him,' the woman said in a French accent as she rolled another smoke. 'He looks like someone who has seen a lot. He hasn't really. This is his first dead body.'

I raised an eyebrow. 'It's not your first?'

She looked at me and said nothing.

I noticed the accessory tied to a lock of her hair. 'Is that a bone?'

Twirling it in her hand, she said, 'I found it on a beach.'

'What kind of animal?' I said.

'A bird, I think.'

The man was pulling out the contents of his backpack, clearly anxious about some kind of contraband he wished to dispose of before the officer returned.

'What are your names?' I asked.

'I'm Camille. He's Paco. French and Spanish.'

'Geo,' I said. 'Tasmanian; son to an Italian mother.'

Paco peered up at her. 'Where did you put them?'

'We've done nothing wrong.'

He glanced at the officer sitting in the patrol car, talking into a radio speaker. 'It will cause suspicion.'

She rolled her eyes.

My eyes drifted back to the scene. If I hadn't been aware of the situation I'd have thought Sten was leading the investigation. Wes and the other officer were huddled around him, listening attentively as he explained something.

I said to Camille, 'How did you find the body?'

'We were setting up camp.'

'Here?' Twenty kilometres from the Midland Highway, Campania was a place tourists tended to bypass.

Paco rose to his feet. 'We hitched from Devonport. We arrived on the ferry this morning. We're going to Cygnet.'

'Berries?'

He nodded. Many backpackers came to Tasmania at this time of year for the soft-fruit picking season.

'We got a ride to Westbury, then to Campbell Town,' Camille said. 'From there a person dropped us here. For five hours we tried to hitch, but nobody stopped. So we decided to camp. That's when we found the body.'

'I see.'

'I knew we shouldn't have taken that fucking ride,' Paco said. 'It should have been Hobart or no thank you.'

'Calm down,' she said, handing him the tobacco pouch.

'We can drop you in Hobart,' I offered.

They stared at me.

'You would do that for us?' she said.

'Sure. We have space.'

'Step away from the witnesses,' the officer said, walking between us. 'What is this? Weed?'

'It's tobacco,' I said.

He glared at me, and I took a few paces back as he broke Camille's rollie in half and sniffed it. 'Open your backpacks.'

'Oh fuck,' Paco said. 'We're in such deep shit.'

'Shut up,' Camille said to him. To the officer, she said, 'Which one?'

'Both.'

I kept an eye on the track as I watched the officer impose his authority. Wes and the other police officer chatted as they watched Sten scour the bush outside the perimeter of the scene.

Paco and Camille interested me for entirely different reasons.

Here they were on their first day in Tasmania, bedding up against the trunk of a tree. And then what? One of them needed to relieve themselves and stumbled across a dismembered arm? I believed it. The situation would resonate with Alessia, I realised. Not because she was like them in a wandering hippie sense, but because she shared their impulsive spirit. She'd have been nudging me to offer them a room for the night.

Two unmarked police vehicles arrived on the scene in a hurry. Martin Bowden exited the lead car. Assessing the scene and spotting Wes, he made for the barricaded area. A man dressed in blue overalls emerged from the second vehicle. Very casual-like – very Sten, in fact – he went around to the boot and took out a forensics kit the size of Labuschagne's silver case.

Tension was developing with the backpackers. The policeman had found something in their possession he believed to be incriminating. Camille's arms were folded, like she couldn't care less. Paco pulled at his hair with both hands. 'Oh fuck! Oh fuck!' Spread before them on the ground were a variety of bones. Thoroughly decomposed, they looked as though they'd been boiled.

I wandered over. 'Everything okay?'

'Get back,' the officer instructed.

Paco whispered to Camille, 'I told you we shouldn't bring them. I told you.'

'These yours?' the officer asked her.

'Yes.'

'Where did you get them?'

'Side of the highway,' she said, unmoved.

The officer studied the bones. He knew he had nothing. 'So you just picked them up?'

'Yes.'

'For what purpose?'

'I haven't decided yet.' She pulled back her hair to show the small bird bone. 'Maybe my hair. Or maybe art.'

'This is deep shit,' Paco said.

In a matter-of-fact tone that made me want to applaud, she asked, 'What kind of animal is it?'

The officer frowned.

'Pademelon,' I said.

She turned to me. 'Paddy what?'

The officer pointed his finger. 'Return to your vehicle.'

'A small wallaby,' I said. 'A miniature kangaroo.'

Wes approached us. 'What's going on?'

'This is Paco and Camille,' I said. 'They're staying with us tonight.'

'What?'

'What?' Paco said.

Camille said, 'You are very kind.'

Wes studied the couple. 'Now hold on …' His brow furrowed. 'What the fuck's with these bones?'

'They were in one of the backpacks,' the officer said.

Wes bent down to take a closer look. 'You two are in such deep shit.'

'I told you!' Paco said to Camille. 'Why couldn't you just —?'

'You're not in shit,' I said. 'You discovered a body and now they're trying to make you feel guilty because they have nothing.'

'Shut the fuck up,' Wes said.

'Go to your vehicle,' the officer commanded.

I picked up the backpacks and the guitar, and lumbered across to the Commodore.

'Hey, where are you taking my guitar?' Paco called.

'What do you think you're doing?' Wes said.

'Shut up,' Camille said to Paco.

'Bring that back here!' the officer said.

I continued walking.

'Ah, shit,' Wes said.

CHAPTER SIX

WES WAS SILENT on the drive back to Hobart. He hadn't objected when I'd climbed behind the wheel, and he barely seemed to notice when Paco and Camille slid into the back with Sten. My brother was lost to his own thoughts, no doubt trying to figure how he might use his inside knowledge of the ghost train to reassert himself at work.

In the back middle seat Paco was chatty now that we were away from the scene. He spoke with a child's glee, sentences tumbling from his mouth with careless abandon. 'That was some heavy shit. I mean, fuck that shit ... a dead body?'

I glanced in the mirror. Paco's eyes darted from Sten to Camille. The Swede remained expressionless, and I knew what he was thinking: *I have missed an opportunity here.* Behind me Camille stared out the window at the passing landscape, with the soulful heaviness of someone who'd lived many lives. She was sucking a lollipop.

Paco nudged her with his elbow. 'Can you believe it? Twenty-two and my first dead body.' He caught my eye in the mirror.

'She's seen one already.' He looked back at her. 'One day you must tell me about that. But to see a dead body together on our first day in Tasmania – what an experience.' He shook his head. 'We will never forget it.'

Wes lit a smoke, and I held out my hand. He passed it to me and lit another. Paco's hand emerged between the two front seats. Wes peered down with a scowl that made me fearful he would rip Paco's hand off with his teeth. He grabbed the rear-view mirror and tilted it so he could see the young man.

Paco said, 'That train driver must be seriously traumatised.'

Wes sighed, lit a cigarette and dropped it into Paco's hand. Paco popped it into his mouth. I readjusted the mirror.

'I mean, we saw a dead body.' Paco shook his head. 'That makes me so pumped. But that driver ran a man down. That's a different kind of heaviness. And why didn't he stop? Unless it was suicide. He will need counselling for sure. Like they do in Japan.' Paco took a drag. 'Did you know Japan isn't the suicide capital of the world?' He glanced at Camille and Sten. 'It's true. It's Greenland. I was so surprised.'

I glanced at Wes, but he showed no reaction.

'This is the best day of my life,' Paco stated. 'Ferry ride, pademelon bones – I will look that animal up as soon as we get free wi-fi – car ride, camping, dead body, missing train, police ride. I mean, I'm only twenty-two.'

Camille's hand reached palm up between Wes and me. Wes's face tightened, but her calm entitlement seemed to disarm him, and he took the smoke from his mouth and dropped it into her hand. He lit himself another and passed the pack over his shoulder to Sten, who took it with a mournful lethargy.

For my entire life I'd conditioned myself to be extremely straight when dealing with Wes: defensive, braced for the outburst. Thus, he had me in his grip. But Labuschagne and Sten, and now Paco and Camille, remained true to themselves; they'd be damned if they adjusted for anyone. I didn't know if it was their self-assuredness or quirkiness or both, but Wes was unable to maintain his intensity in their presence, and I found that astonishing. Would Paco and Camille be open to helping Sten with the house painting in return for board? Paco had mentioned fruit picking, but they struck me as a pair whose plans were more of an idea than a purpose.

Camille took the lollipop out of her mouth, had a drag of her cigarette, and put the lollipop back in. 'Maybe the driver feels nothing. Maybe his only concern is to arrive on time, and anything that comes across his track must be sacrificed. Nothing should stop the train. There are more important things in life than life.'

I now knew I liked Camille as much as I liked Paco. In an age where the true individual had departed, here were two examples cutting their own path.

'You are right,' Paco said. 'It can't be both. The driver could be traumatised, or he could be thinking about his load. I'm truly excited. Death and trains and arriving on time. And my first body. I know what I'm doing tonight – I'm playing my guitar all night.' He slapped my shoulder. 'Thank you so much for the bed. In the morning we will do something. Anything. You have a garden? We can garden. Clean the house. Wash your car. Whatever you want. We are good workers.'

'My pleasure,' I said.

Wes took the hipflask out of the glove box and had a sip. Before a hand could reach forward he offered it over his shoulder. Sten had a sip, and gave it to Paco. Paco had a swig and handed it to Camille, who had a sip and passed it to the front.

'I hate highways,' she said. 'If I created a language with characters like kanji, the symbol for "highway" would be "soulless snake".'

She gave the impression of someone who'd been through many reincarnations, and was now bored by the act of living. The perfect yin to Paco's yang. Where he projected an innocence, she reflected a white-hot intensity. He would probably live to be the oldest person on earth, but the Camilles of this world – of which I was one – didn't last very long. We absorbed life's blows and kept them tucked in. We recognised the world's cruelty and the weight of that knowledge was too heavy to drum out a full lifespan.

I parked across from the Hobart Police Station on Argyle Street. Wes got out, motioning for Paco and Camille to follow him.

'What for?' Paco said, on edge again.

'Procedure. Bring your passports.'

'I thought we were clear?'

Camille was already out of the car and rummaging through her backpack. Sten and I leaned against the Commodore as the young couple fished out their passports and followed Wes across the road into the station.

I accepted the new situation, understanding it would compromise the preparations for my audition. In Rome I was so locked into my routine. I'd start every day at the same time and rehearse for the same number of hours. I'd take my first break at twelve for lunch, and my second at five for dinner, before concluding with an evening session. If there was a long run-in to an audition I'd fall into a pattern of eating the same things, drinking the same number of coffees, turning the light out at the same time. A day on perfect repeat, with one variable: the gradual climb in music quality. During these times I was impossible to be around, which is why I lived alone rather than in a house-share, or with Alessia.

I could have chosen to live away from Wes. I could have elected not to offer Sten a place to stay, and certainly not Labuschagne and the backpackers. Yet something was pulling me towards a chaotic scenario. These strangers provided a buffer to the most dangerous part of Wes's personality, and I needed them as much as I needed a bed under a roof.

Apparently reading my mind, Sten said, 'If you are serious about finishing the house painting, you might want to take on these backpackers under the same conditions you are employing me. We could finish the whole house in two weeks.'

'They could have my room,' I said with a shrug.

'Fifteen hours a week. They would have the afternoons and evenings for other work. It is just an idea.'

'It's a good idea.'

'Do not say anything tonight. Let me see how they work in the morning. It is no use if they are not good workers. But I have a feeling about them. They have the right energy.'

#

Back at the house I showed Paco and Camille to my bedroom, happy I'd cleaned it the night before. 'This is my old room.'

'Where will you sleep?' Camille asked.

'The three of us sleep in the sitting room. It's a long story. Make yourselves at home, just don't touch any rubbish lying around. That's a long story too.'

Paco beamed. 'A house with stories. People sleeping in rooms that are not bedrooms. Rubbish lying around. We are the lucky ones.'

'Thank you,' Camille said.

Paco hugged me and kissed my cheek.

I retired to the sitting room, where Wes and Sten were in their chairs. I flopped onto the sofa, and Wes flung the liquor cabinet key at me. 'Pour three doubles of something from the top shelf.' He turned to Sten. 'Roll three joints. When you're done you're going to tell me everything about your train.'

Sten considered him for a moment, and leant forward to open his tobacco pouch.

I uncapped the bottle of Glenfiddich. 'You should see the detail of his research in —'

Wes raised a hand. 'Let him roll. Then let him speak.'

I poured the drinks and set them down.

Camille came into the room. 'Is it okay if I use the kitchen?'

'Go ahead,' I said.

Sten shaped the joint in its paper. 'You are making an assumption that now you are ready to talk about my train, I am ready to talk about my train. But I am as unmotivated to talk as I was before.'

Wes frowned. 'You wouldn't want to obstruct an investigation.'

'I have little time for the police. There have been too many times where they have been the difference between me boarding and not boarding my train.'

In the kitchen Camille filled two large pots with water and placed them on the gas stove on high heat.

'How about this?' Wes said. 'How about I believe —?'

'I will tell you what I know because you have opened the door of your house to me. And to Paco and Camille.' Sten licked the paper and pinched the joint closed. 'And because you invited me to your other house to meet your wife and son. Two homes with all the important emotions: happy, sad, laughing, angry. Brothers here together. Brothers not wanting to be together. Their mother and father here in spirit.' He pointed the joint at the ceiling. 'Yes, they are here; I do not need Labuschagne's silver case to know. So thank you. For these things I will tell you about my train. Because believe me … otherwise I would not.'

He passed out the joints and lit his up. 'The most important point about my ghost train is that there is only one. When people speak about UFOs, they are speaking about different UFOs. Thousands of different sightings. Different crafts, different races of alien being. Whether or not you believe in UFOs, you would accept that there are different UFOs.

'But when people talk about ghost trains, they are talking about one train. They may not know this, but it is true. It is the same train. If you read the folklore, and I have read all of it, you would know the St Louis Light, the London Lord, the Russian Roller. But don't be fooled by Silverpilen – or Silver Arrow – the Stockholm metro legend.' He waved his joint at me. 'Sometimes it is just that; nothing more. Like with everything, there is always space for legend.' He turned back to Wes. 'The Phantom Funeral Train in Washington, DC, the one that shows itself on each anniversary of Abraham Lincoln's death.' He shook his head. 'It is the same train. People have made different stories out of it. If it is witnessed here, it will probably be called the Hobart Hotbox or something equally stupid. And it will become its own myth. But it is one train. This is why I call it my train. I am the only person who seems to recognise this … that one, single ghost train has appeared to thousands of people across the world for six decades.' He took a drag. 'And now it is in Tasmania.'

'Does it have passengers?' Wes asked.

'They are permanent passengers. Yes.'

'Ghost passengers?'

'I don't like to call them that … but yes. They never get off.'

'How can you be sure?'

Sten flicked the cone from his joint into the ashtray. 'Because when you speak to people who have witnessed the train – and I am a witness also – and you compare the details, it is the same train, with the same passengers. I have compiled profiles.'

'How many times have you seen it?'

'Eighteen.'

I was flabbergasted. Eighteen sightings in forty years. I doubted whether I'd have the fortitude to sustain the drive for my dream were I only to attend an audition once every two years.

'Why are you chasing it?' Wes asked.

This was the detail Sten had promised to share with me. His eyes flicked to me before he answered. 'My mother and father are on my train. I am trying to reunite with them.'

There was a beat as Wes and I digested the magnitude of the revelation.

'How …?' I stammered. 'How is that possible?'

'They boarded it when it was a normal train. And on that journey, before it reached its destination, it became a ghost. In that moment, the passengers who were on it also became ghosts.'

I asked, 'You've seen them?'

'My mother sits on the platform side. On those occasions I have seen my train, I have seen her. But she never looks out the window – she is staring ahead. Most of the passengers are staring ahead, caught in the moment at which point the train disappeared. They are moving. You can see them shifting, blinking. But their movements are on a loop. It is the same sequence every time.'

'Like a GIF,' I said.

He nodded. 'Except the loop is longer than that. One loop per station. Every time my train stops, the actions and expressions of the passengers are the same. There is a child, a young boy, and he is looking out the window. Whenever I catch sight of him it feels like he is watching me. He has a birthmark on his cheek. He is the one who breaks my heart, staring out the window at the passing world, his curiosity trapped.'

'Your father is sitting with her?' Wes asked.

Sten was about to answer when Paco walked in with his guitar and took a seat in the armchair. Barefoot and shirtless, he'd changed into knee-length denim shorts. An intricate tattoo of a dreamcatcher was tattooed across his right breast. He rested the guitar on his lap and ran a hand through his dripping wet hair.

'I didn't give you a towel,' I said, annoyed at myself.

'I wouldn't have used it anyway – I like the feeling of water drying on me.' He glanced over his shoulder into the kitchen. Camille was standing over two steaming pots. 'We haven't eaten since last night.'

Sten pushed the pouch of weed to him. Paco's eyes flickered with delight. 'May I roll one for Camille too?'

'Please do.'

She dropped the pot lid onto the kitchen floor, sending a *clang* through the house. 'Sorry,' she said.

Wes nodded at Sten. 'Please answer my question.'

His expression fell. 'No, my father is not sitting with my mother. You see … my father is the driver of the train.'

My jaw dropped.

Paco looked up. 'Are you talking about the train that smashed the body? Because if you are, that is seriously fucked up.'

Wes shot him a look, and he retreated into the kitchen to give one of the joints to Camille.

'I grew up in Stockholm,' Sten said. 'My father worked the Västra stambanan – the Western main line – from Stockholm to Göteborg … You know Göteborg?' he asked me.

'Sure, Gothenburg,' I said.

'This was his line. I was seven, and he would take me with him during the holidays. My mother was from Göteborg, and sometimes we would travel with my father and stay with her parents. And when he returned, we would travel back to Stockholm with him. On these occasions I would be allowed to sit with him in the cab for the early part of the evening. It was a night train, so it was very exciting. Naturally, my dream was to be a train driver. All boys want to be like their fathers.'

At this, Wes and I did well not to look at each other.

'Maybe this is not relevant to your story,' Paco said from the doorway, 'but I grew up in a co-op. My parents were very "out there". Our river valley in Beneficio had no houses – just shelters like tents and tipis. We called it a rainbow gathering. I say this because I didn't grow up wanting to be like my parents. To tell the truth, I ran away. But I inherited their spirit, and today I live exactly like them. I don't think it matters if you want to be like your parents or not; if you live long enough, you become them anyway.'

'That is an interesting idea,' Sten said. 'I am curious – what does "Paco" mean?'

'It's a nickname for Francisco. It means Frenchman.' He grinned and nodded towards the kitchen. 'Maybe it explains why I'm attracted to her. What does your name mean?'

'Stone.' Sten pointed at me. 'Geo means "earth".' He pointed at Wes. 'Wes doesn't mean anything.'

My brother reddened. 'It's short for Wesley, and it means "meadow". But can we please stay the fuck on task?'

Sten waved his joint in apology. 'So anyway, on this day – the day of the situation – my father was travelling to Göteborg, and my mother accompanied him. But I was to remain with my grandparents on my father's side, as it was during the school term. This was unusual, as my mother would never normally leave me. But her own mother was ill, and her father was older and unable to take care of her, so she was going to Göteborg to stay for a period. I was heartsore, and my grandparents took me to see them off. I waved goodbye, to my mother at the carriage window and my father at the cab. That was the last time I saw them.' He placed the joint in the ashtray. 'Do you have something to drink?'

Wes rose from the recliner. He topped up our three drinks and nodded at Paco. 'Fetch a glass if you'd like.'

'Thank you,' Paco said. 'And also for Camille. Thank you.'

'By the way,' Wes said to Sten, 'Nic's invited you to dinner on Friday. You were a hit with Hayden.'

'Ghost train hunter has more cache than detective or violist,' I said.

'That is my honour,' Sten said.

'Hold on,' Paco said from the doorway, 'you are a ghost train hunter?'

Nobody said anything. Sten relit his joint.

Paco raised his hands in wonderment. 'You're telling me …? This is too much. I am bursting with happiness.'

Wes glared at him.

Sten cleared his throat. 'The train never made it to Göteborg. It vanished. With all of its passengers, except for one.'

'A witness?' Wes said.

'A young man around his age.' Sten pointed at Paco. 'Later, when he spoke to the police, he said that as they were approaching Skövde, a town 350 kilometres from Stockholm … that is when the train started to rattle. He said it shook so terribly he was sure it was going to come off the rails. Baggage fell from the overhead racks, drink glasses went tumbling down the aisles. Those with companions huddled together, but this passenger, being alone, clambered into the enclosed vestibule. The train jolted wildly, and he made his decision. He opened the door and jumped before it entered a tunnel. He broke his leg as he landed, and tumbled down the bank. This decision saved his life. The train disappeared into the tunnel. It never came out the other side.'

'Fuck, fuck, fuck,' Paco said.

'There was a lot of coverage in the news – they called it the Flying Swede. There are records to prove it. This is the one I have been chasing my whole life. My train. My father's train.'

'Thank you,' Wes said.

Sten took a swig of his Scotch and forced a smile. 'So now you have it.'

'You should see the research,' I said to Wes. 'Journal entries, sketches, maps. This isn't his first time in Tasmania, you know.'

At first my comment seemed to irritate Wes, but then his expression changed. 'Actually, Sten, I'd be interested to see your notes.'

'They are on the table.'

We rose from our chairs and went into the kitchen.

'What year was it?' Wes asked.

'1987,' Sten said.

'The year I was born,' I commented.

'I mean originally.' Wes frowned. 'When did it disappear?'

'Oh, 1958,' Sten said.

We stood around the kitchen table and appraised the spread of literature. Camille glanced over her shoulder. I did a quick mental calculation and placed Sten at around sixty-six years old.

He was shuffling the papers and books. 'I have other case studies from other countries in my bag. This is only from my first visit to Tasmania.'

Wes turned a map around and ran a finger across the hand-written markings. He reached for one of the journals. 'May I?'

'Please,' Sten said.

Wes flipped through the pages.

Paco said to Camille, 'Smells good.'

She smiled as she turned a ladle through the pot.

'Is it okay if I read these over the next few days?' Wes said. 'Not to take away. I mean here, in the kitchen.'

'Of course. You have welcomed me into your two homes.'

Wes stepped away from the table and placed his glass in the sink. He glanced down into the pot, and his eyes widened. 'Are those bones?'

We all turned.

His face reddened. 'You're boiling pademelon bones in my mother's pots?'

Paco said, 'What does this pademelon creature look like? I'm so curious.'

I peeked into the pots. Sure enough, at the bottom were the pademelon bones from the backpack. I leaned over the sink and dry-retched.

'You said to make myself at home,' Camille said.

Wes glared at her. 'These are my Italian mother's pasta pots.'

I wiped my mouth with the kitchen towel.

Camille looked at me. 'You okay?'

'I'm fine,' I said, and immediately bent over the sink and dry-retched a second time.

Paco spied the contents in the pot. 'They look beautiful.'

'They're for art,' Camille said.

'They smell good,' Sten said. 'But please, can somebody explain to me what a pademelon is?'

Paco said, 'This is what I want to know.'

Wes was beside himself. 'What the fuck?! They're animal bones in a pasta pot.'

'Someone get me a drink,' I said.

'I will get it,' Paco said.

'Get your arse back in here,' Wes said, overtaking him. 'Nobody goes into my father's cabinet except for me.'

Camille had a sheepish look on her face.

'Don't worry,' I said to her. 'You didn't know.'

Sten leaned over the larger of the two pots and inhaled deeply. A look of pleasure creased his face.

Then Camille made a move that I was sure would remain in my memory forever. In a situation where most would have cowered, she untangled the small bird bone from her hair and casually dropped it into the pot.

Wes came into the kitchen and handed me a glass of Scotch. 'Tomorrow you both go,' he said, meaning Paco and Camille.

'Okay,' Camille said.

'We are grateful for your hospitality,' Paco said.

Wes turned back into the sitting room. Little did any of them know I had decided the pair were staying indefinitely, regardless of how well they worked with Sten.

#

As Sten had predicted, Paco and Camille were willing workers and more than able. They were happy with my proposal of fifteen hours per week in return for board, and determined to find bar work in the area for additional income.

I didn't bother telling Wes about this, but he figured it out soon enough when he picked Sten and me up for dinner at Nic's that Friday, and we emerged from the house with Paco and Camille in tow.

The evening passed without incident, although that's an unfair description as it went rather well in terms of the guests. Paco and Camille quickly endeared themselves to Hayden, but Wes was in a prickly mood. I could hardly blame him: only the day before, he'd given me the key to our father's car, fully serviced and roadworthy, and I'd repaid him by bringing two more people into the house. But these weren't ordinary people. They were true individuals, and it was to this I suspected Hayden responded. Paco was his usual passionate self; in the two days the couple had been staying with us, he hadn't veered from the personality he'd shown on the first evening. Camille was engaging and polite, nudging Paco occasionally as if to remind him to express ten per cent less enthusiasm in the company of others. Sten was Sten – very Sten – and overall the atmosphere was light and easy. However, the micro-family sensed a tension building in Wes, and whenever there was an offbeat comment or round of laughter, we cast a nervous glance in his direction.

After dinner Nic encouraged Hayden to recite 'Shenandoah' on the piano. I'd never heard him sing before, and accompanied by Nic, it was a moving rendition. Sten, Paco and Camille gave a standing ovation.

Paco was particularly enthused. 'It runs in the family?' he asked, looking at me, then towards Nic and Wes.

'My mother plays the cello,' Hayden said. 'My dad used to play violin, but he doesn't anymore. Geo's a violist.'

'A house of musicians,' Paco said, 'I'm so —'

'Watch the language,' I said.

He turned to Wes. 'Why not anymore? Once music is in you, you can never escape it.'

Wes shifted on the sofa.

'I've never seen him play,' Hayden said.

The news so distressed Paco that for a moment he was speechless. 'You must play for us now. I say this with urgent respect.'

Clearly sensing he'd overstepped the line, Camille rebuked him in French.

Paco wasn't having any of it. 'But this is family. An instrument. A song. This is life.'

'His violin is in the garage,' Hayden said.

It was crushing to know my brother's 1932 Melloni had been collecting dust in the garage for seventeen years.

'Not tonight,' Wes said.

'I will accompany you on my guitar,' Paco said. 'Choices and actions are simple – you only have to make one to do the other.'

'I must be going,' Sten said. 'I have a train to catch.'

Hayden was crestfallen. 'But it's so early.'

Wes turned to Nic. 'I'm happy to stay. Geo can take everyone back in the Commodore.'

Nic blanched.

'I've had too many,' I lied. 'I'm in no condition to drive.'

On the drive home Paco rode with Wes up front, going on about how 'transcendental' he felt. He'd brought his guitar – not with the expectation that he'd play, but because he took it with him everywhere – and he strummed it as we drove.

The music edged Wes towards a higher degree of irritation. He jerked the car to a halt on Yardley Street. After slamming the door behind him, he stormed up the steps before turning around on the porch. 'Stay out of my family. Do you understand? I'm trying to fix something here.'

Paco, Camille and Sten stood frozen behind me. I didn't say anything.

Wes looked away, looked back at me. 'You came home at the worst time, Geo.'

Only then did I notice the silver case by the door. Labuschagne stood at the end of the porch, looking alarmed by the confrontation into which he'd wandered.

'Ah, fuck,' Wes said, seeing him. He unlocked the door and stormed inside.

Everyone waited to take their cue from me.

'Where are you staking out the train tonight?' I asked Sten.

'Montrose.'

I glanced at the others. 'Anyone keen for a spot of ghost train hunting?'

'Fuck, yeah,' Paco said.

Camille shrugged. 'Sure.'

Labuschagne smiled broadly.

CHAPTER SEVEN

Sten, camille and Paco bundled into the back of my father's Ford. I got into the passenger seat and instructed a bemused Labuschagne to swing by the bottle shop behind the Winston before heading out to Montrose.

The Hobart line ran alongside New Town Road, and we followed it through the western suburbs of Moonah and Glenorchy before arriving at our destination fifteen minutes later. Labuschagne turned onto Riverway Road and edged across the track before pulling over.

A neatly trimmed patch of grass fronted the crossing. If you were walking past you'd be forgiven for missing it: there was barely space for five adults to stretch out. I raised an eyebrow at Sten. 'Really?'

'This is nice,' he said, walking up onto the bank. 'Compared to some platforms I have been to, this is lovely.'

Paco stepped onto the grass with his guitar. 'I've never been more pumped to play music in my life.' He flopped down and struck out a flamenco pattern.

Camille, Labuschagne and I followed suit. The night was perfect for it: a searching breeze, a partial moon, and a fistful of stars pounding a cloudless sky. The sound of traffic sweeping by on Main Street rose like organ notes in the background.

I slipped two bottles of wine out of their brown paper bags, and passed one to Camille and the other to Labuschagne. Camille opened her bottle, took a sip and handed it back. Labuschagne passed his straight on to Paco; I didn't know if this was because he was the designated driver, or if he wanted to remain sober for whatever investigation he had planned for the lamp when we returned to the house. Paco had a sip and passed it to Sten. I had a sip and gave it back to Camille. Sten took out his pouch and asked Paco to roll a few joints. Paco passed the pouch to me, and strummed a Latin guitar lick.

The music was gentle and melancholic. Paco wasn't technically proficient, but there was evidence of talent – and he was brave, unafraid of mistakes and, more importantly, attached to his instrument like most people were attached to their phones. He picked through a sequence of notes. 'I can't believe how lucky I am. A ghost train hunter, a violist, two gypsies …' He glanced at Labuschagne. 'I don't understand what you are president of, but it sounds fucking amazing.'

'Investigator of anomalous incidents,' Labuschagne said.

'Fucking amazing.'

'What does "anomalous" mean?' Camille asked.

'Unusual. Irregular.'

She lit up a joint. 'You mean like ghost trains?'

'Ghost trains are one example.'

'You mean like UFOs?'

'UFOs too.'

'I've been on a UFO.'

Labuschagne studied her. 'Abductee?'

'It is better for me not to speak about it.'

Paco thrashed out another flamenco riff. 'This is why I love being with her. Every day I learn something new. A UFO? Are you fucking serious? What a night to learn this detail.'

Labuschagne said to Camille, 'It's better for you not to speak about it because you can't remember, or because you can't speak about it?'

Thoroughly at ease with the conversation, I lit a joint. I supposed this was what it was like to be without a dream. Of course, we were here for Sten's dream. And Labuschagne was here to what …? Document the event of Sten chasing his dream? But Paco, Camille and I had come simply to hang out. Because life had dropped us on this patch of grass. I'd forgotten what it felt like to be inserted into moments determined by random social forces. Under normal conditions I'd have denied myself this experience because I possessed the discipline to shut myself in a room and rehearse. My dream required a tolerance for being alone, and I took satisfaction in submitting to that demand. But there was a certain pleasure in releasing oneself to opportunities such as this evening.

I was particularly loving how Labuschagne accepted the premise of Camille boarding a UFO simply because she stated it. I'd been brought up in a Catholic household where dinner conversation at its most contentious centred around school prayer or funding for the arts, so to find myself in the company of people talking about alien abduction was thoroughly exhilarating.

'I can't speak about it,' Camille said, a polite finality in her tone.

Labuschagne held up a hand. 'Clearly there is a line you cannot cross. My professional curiosity gets the better of me sometimes. One final question, and if you choose not to answer I'll treat the matter as closed. Can you not discuss it because it's personal, or because you were instructed not to discuss it?'

'I was instructed,' Camille said.

Labuschagne nodded.

For a minute the only sound was Paco's guitar against the hum of slow-moving traffic. I thought the conversation had ended, but Labuschagne made one final attempt. 'How binding do you think the instruction was?'

'It would invite an action.'

And with that the topic concluded.

'Why were you waiting for us tonight?' I said to Labuschagne.

'I was hoping to try a different technique with the spirit in the lamp. With your permission I'd like to forge contact through an ouija board.'

I squirmed at the suggestion.

'Ooh, I've always wanted to use an ouija board,' Paco said. 'Spirits would exchange blows over the order in which they'd get to communicate through me. My relaxedness flows from my soul to my extremities.'

He took a swig from the bottle and held it out to Sten, but the Swede's focus was down the track. He rose to his feet.

'What?' I said.

He raised a hand to quieten me. Labuschagne stood up too, took out his phone and opened the camera app.

We all strained our ears in the direction Sten was looking, and in the next moment we heard a faint chugging. My heart pounded. Without taking his eyes off the track, Sten retrieved the crystal from his jacket and held it above his palm. It turned rapidly in a clockwise direction. I clambered to my feet.

Paco's eyes were wild. 'I'm so pum —'

'Shhh!' I said.

A light appeared in the distance, and Sten did another check with the crystal. Without turning, he held out a finger. 'If this is my train, do not move. And do not interfere.'

A few moments later the train emerged into view. It was immediately apparent it wasn't stopping, and that it wasn't a ghost. The freight train swished by in an electrifying flash, its energy and noise enveloping us like a tornado. Almost as soon as it arrived it was gone.

Sten carried out a final test with the crystal. This was my first experience of rejection with the ghost train; I was crushed. But Sten took it calmly. He turned around. 'We can go. It's not coming here tonight.'

#

The lights were off when we arrived back at Yardley Street. I stuck my head into the sitting room and saw Wes snoring lightly in the recliner. Lifting a finger to my lips, I ushered everyone into the living room.

'Lamp?' Labuschagne said.

I fetched the lamp from my bedroom cupboard and placed it on the side table, which he'd again positioned in the centre of the room. He took out the ouija board and set it down on the floor.

Camille said to me, 'Your mother and father are both dead?'

'Yes.'

'I'm sorry.'

Paco was watching Labuschagne like a child watching a parent bring out their birthday cake. 'Shall we sit around it?'

Labuschagne addressed us solemnly. 'Does everyone here have a true interest in communicating with the spirit world? It's important you're honest and genuine. If you're not, it would be better if you left the room.'

'I'm interested,' Paco said.

'Sure,' Sten said.

Camille nodded.

Everyone glanced at me. I was standing a little way back with my hands in my trouser pockets. I shrugged. 'Why not?'

Labuschagne said, 'Geography, please fetch some candles and a drinking glass.'

I found three unused taper candles in the hallway cupboard, and went into the kitchen to wax them into saucers. I grabbed a glass out of the sink, and before returning peeked into the sitting room. Wes was awake, his face illuminated by his phone. We maintained eye contact for a moment, then I retreated into the living room and handed the candles and glass to Labuschagne. I whispered, 'By the way, it's Geo as *in* geography, not *short for* geography.'

Obviously irritated at the correction, he motioned for me to sit with the others across the board from him. Paco took a drag on a joint, and it was passed down the line from Sten, to Camille, to me.

Labuschagne positioned the three candles on the carpet around us so that if they'd been connected with straight lines we would have been sitting within the perimeter of a triangle. 'The wine is an offering for the spirit,' he said, pouring a small serve into the glass.

'If it's my father's spirit we're after, you should probably fill it.'

Labuschagne gave me a disapproving look, but discreetly topped up the glass. He said, 'We really shouldn't drink or smoke weed when we call on spirits, but you all seem like practised drinkers and smokers, so we'll just roll with it.' His expression hardened. 'There are rules. I'm the mediator – that means I'm the only one who asks the questions. Is that clear?' He cast an eye over us. Nobody protested. 'Good. When I speak, I encourage you to focus your energy on the communication. Try to sense the spirit. And if the planchette moves under my hand, do not challenge it.'

'What's the planchette?' I said.

Camille touched the moveable indicator that was used to point out the letters.

'I won't cheat,' Labuschagne said. 'You need to trust me. Cheating is disrespectful to the participants and any present spirits. Believe me when I say I know never to disrespect a spirit. If the planchette moves, I am being guided. If a spirit doesn't guide me, I'll feel no shame. We are seeking truth, not an experience.'

He looked at each of us in turn, and I must say he was believable. His speech certainly put me into a mindset that he might actually invoke a spirit, and I started getting nervous at the prospect of contact. I had a drag on the joint, and without thinking reached for the wine offering and had a swig. Labuschagne pretended not to notice, but I could tell my lack of discipline annoyed him.

In conclusion he said, 'The session isn't over until we say "goodbye" and close the board. This is very important. Please keep the right attitude until that point. Is everyone still comfortable to proceed?'

We nodded.

'Does anyone have any questions or objections?'

There were none.

'Good.'

The board consisted of two rows of letters in two arcs, one above the other: A–M and N–Z. Above the top arc were the words YES and NO. Below the bottom arc were the numbers 0–10, and below these numbers the word GOODBYE. Labuschagne placed his index fingers lightly on the body of the planchette and positioned it over the letter G, the most central of the characters. He closed his eyes. 'Would any benevolent spirits like to communicate?'

The planchette didn't move. Labuschagne's eyes remained closed, his head up. He seemed relaxed, ready to be guided should a spirit choose. I wasn't a sceptic, but I didn't want to be tricked. I glanced at Camille and noticed that she too was watching the planchette. She appeared calm, almost bemused, although I didn't know her well enough to have a read on her – perhaps she was expectant. Sten's eyes were closed, as were Paco's. But their expressions couldn't have been more different. Sten looked like he'd fallen asleep, the joint dangling from his mouth. Paco sat cross-legged with his hands on his knees, his back rigid, his head high; his eyes were tightly shut, and he had a huge grin on his face. The smell of incense wafted through the room. I only noticed this now, and presumed Camille had put the incense out while I'd gone to fetch the candles.

Labuschagne repeated the questions, but it seemed that no benevolent spirits were ready and available. I wondered whether the word 'benevolent' was the reason my father didn't respond. It wasn't a word he would instantly recognise himself by.

Labuschagne said, 'We are Labuschagne, Sten, Paco, Camille and Geo. Geo as *in* geography, not *short for* geography – an important distinction. We wish to speak with the spirit that has been communicating through the lamp. Are you here?'

The lamp gave the merest glimmer of a flicker. Camille and I looked at each other. Their eyes closed, Labuschagne, Paco and Sten had yet to notice.

Labuschagne said, 'Are there any benevolent spirits present that wish to communicate?'

This time the lamp flickered brightly with two distinct flashes.

I whispered to Labuschagne, 'The lamp.'

Everyone but Sten opened their eyes. The lamp, still unplugged, flickered again.

Remaining calm, Labuschagne looked down at his fingers. There was no movement with the planchette. 'Thank you,' he said. 'Can you tell us your name?'

The planchette didn't move, but this time the light flickered through the three levels of brightness before fizzing out.

Labuschagne said, 'Can you communicate through the ouija board?'

As he asked the question, a calmness seeped through my body. I felt an energy – neither negative nor positive – resonating to my core.

In the next instant Labuschagne's fingers began moving across the board to the letter T. After settling for about a second, the planchette moved again, this time to the letter H. As it moved a third time, Labuschagne whispered, 'Paper and pen.'

Without hesitation Camille left the room. She returned with a notebook and a pencil, the planchette having continued to sweep across the board in her absence.

'T–H–E–R–E–A–R,' Paco said to her.

She scribbled down the letters and watched the board. The planchette glided around to a metronomic beat as beads of sweat collected on Labuschagne's brow. Finally, the planchette stopped on the letter S.

We looked towards Camille, who scrutinised what she'd recorded. '"There are two of us."'

Labuschagne nodded. 'That makes sense.' He closed his eyes, his fingers on the planchette. 'Is the other spirit communicating through the lamp?'

The planchette slid onto the word YES.

'Are you the parents of Geography?' He shook his head. 'I mean, Geo, *short for* Geography?' He shook his head again, irritated by his mistakes. 'Are you the parents of Geo?'

The planchette remained on the word YES.

I felt a pull in my heart. I didn't want to believe it. I didn't know what I believed. I certainly wasn't constrained by my Catholic upbringing, but I knew I wasn't an atheist. Honestly, I was all over the map in terms of my beliefs, and now here I was, Labuschagne's fingers telling me my parents were in the room communicating with me, and whether or not it was true, it did something to me on an emotional level.

Labuschagne said, 'Is the father communicating through the lamp?'

Again, the planchette remained on the word YES.

To the surprise of us all, Camille broke protocol and assumed the role of mediator. 'What is Geo's father trying to say?'

Labuschagne's forehead scrunched, but the planchette began to move under his fingers and spelled out I–M–S–O.

Before it could go any further, I blurted out, 'Close it down. I don't want to hear any more.'

The planchette immediately slid down to rest over the word GOODBYE.

'Goodbye,' Labuschagne said. He opened his eyes and closed the board.

Sten looked around as if waking from a peaceful sleep.

Paco shook his head. 'That was wild.'

'We breached the spirit word,' Labuschagne said.

Camille was looking at me with a concerned expression.

After Labuschagne packed away the board, we remained in the living room, talking about the experience though not about the message. Nobody asked why I'd chosen to close the communication when I had. We chatted around this point, about the thrill in the existence of a spiritual world that was willing to communicate if approached with the right intentions.

After a period of time Labuschagne took out his silver case and used his gadgets to record different readings of the room. We stayed with him into the early hours.

#

I waited in the hallway of the Performing Arts Centre as the TYO players drifted out of the rehearsal room. Audrey was caught up chatting with the mother of the trombone player, and when their conversation ended I stepped inside. This time she smiled when she saw me.

'I came to see if I can give you a lift home. If you prefer not, I'll leave without a word.'

'It's okay.' She gathered her things, and we walked out together.

When I'd left Hobart, Audrey had been in the final months of a two-year training program for young artists with Opera Australia. I asked how things had progressed.

'I've been listed as a principal artist,' she said.

My face lit up.

'Don't get too excited. We're an ensemble of eighty. But the year before last I had a small breakthrough with the role of Mimi in *La bohème*.'

'That's fantastic, Audrey.' My voice sounded false, even to my own ears. I'd abandoned her, and there was nothing I could say to hide that.

'It's exciting, but it also means I've been living out of a suitcase for two years,' she added. 'When a gap opened in my schedule last month and I heard about this temporary gig, I took the first flight home. The regular conductor's in Austria for a workshop.'

'So when do you leave?'

'Next month I begin rehearsals for *The Rabbits*. In July I'm playing Susanna in *Figaro*.'

We had reached the car. 'You made it, Audrey.'

'I wouldn't quite define it like that. It still feels like I'm proving myself every time I step on stage.'

'I'm happy for you. Equations balance when good people get what they deserve.'

She smiled, and we climbed into the Ford.

'Do you remember the last time you drove me in this car?' she said.

'My school formal. How could I forget?'

'I was so nervous.'

'*I* was so nervous.'

We grinned at the memory, and I started up and turned into Churchill Street.

'Are you seeing anyone?' she asked.

'Yes.' I'd been expecting the question.

She was silent.

'Her name's Alessia. She's a violinist.'

Audrey stared ahead.

'Can I just say —?'

'Please don't.'

I focused on the road.

'I don't blame you, Geo. I understand. I think. There are many other things I don't understand, but let's not … let's just …'

'I'm sorry.'

A few minutes later, I pulled up outside her parents' house in South Hobart.

'I'm meeting a friend in town,' she said. 'I have time for a coffee.'

'That would be lovely.'

'I'll just drop my things inside.' There was an awkward pause. 'I think it would be best if you waited here.'

I nodded.

We went to Island Espresso, at the bottom of Elizabeth Street, and chatted on the sofa in the attic. She asked how the auditions were going, so I gave her the update. 'Basically, and I don't mean to be self-deprecating, I lack Wes's talent. I'm good – maybe better than good – but better than good doesn't cut it in the crowd I'm mixing with. I'm okay with that. It's taken time, but I've accepted it. What I lack in talent I make up with heart. I have enough heart to keep me in pursuit.'

'I'd take heart over talent every time.'

'I have no choice but to agree.'

We sipped our coffees.

She said, 'I don't mean to pry, but how are things with Nic and Wes?'

I sighed. 'I don't think they're going to make it.'

'Poor Hayden.'

'He'll be okay. He's one tough kid.'

'Nothing lasts forever.'

The comment saddened me. 'Music lasts,' I said.

'Yes. It does.'

She excused herself to meet her friend, and we both stood up.

'I'm glad you came to meet me,' she said.

'Me too.' I wanted to hug her, but hesitated.

'I should go,' she said.

She disappeared down the stairs. I remained standing in the attic, listening for the ring of the doorbell as she exited.

#

Back at the house I found Wes leaning against the kitchen counter, Scotch in hand. He lifted his finger to his lips when I came through.

Sten was seated at the table, describing aloud what he saw in his mind's eye as he sketched in a journal. 'It is a platform. At first I thought it was the edge of a field, but now I see it is raised. The platform is small, the length of a bus. It is made of concrete, but it is almost completely covered in grass. This is why I was confused – it splits a single track. The track on the left continues behind me. The track on the right sweeps away at a ninety-degree angle.'

Sten leaned back, and I saw that the journal page showed a triangle with a crudely drawn track dividing at the apex. At this point he began infusing life into the image, and I understood what he meant by inching along the signal line to reach the full picture.

'There are two people on the platform.' He drew the shapes of the figures sitting towards the front, their legs dangling over the side. 'Teenagers. A boy and girl. Eating from takeaway boxes.' Sten wasn't an artist, but he had a cartoonish grasp of form and perspective that made the scene apparent. His eyes opened, and there was a pause as he stared blankly ahead. 'I see it in the background now. My train. Advancing across a bridge over water. It is not a working platform, but it is a working track.'

As he drew the bridge, adding details, Wes said, 'That's the Bridgewater Bridge.'

I agreed. 'They're eating takeaways from the Bridgewater McDonald's.'

Sten seemed not to hear us. 'My train stops at the platform. The teenagers are surprised – I would say they are in fact shocked.' He scrunched his face. 'Now it is leaving. I have never seen my train stop for such a short period of time?' He turned the page in his journal, then retreated into his trance-like state. 'I see it travelling into the distance. It is not vanishing. This is strange. Now my perspective has changed, and I am at another platform. These stations must be close. I have never experienced this. Here it comes.' He drew a train approaching a platform. 'This looks like a freighting stop. It is operational, but because it is night there is nobody on the platform. Now my train is moving off. I see it trailing away. It vanishes. Finally, it vanishes.' He opened his eyes and exhaled. He was utterly spent.

Wes peered at the sketch. 'If the first location was Bridgewater, that second site must be the industrial estate in Brighton, the main transport hub for southern Tassie. I'm pretty sure you've drawn the sheds.'

As Sten held his crystal above his palm, it circled clockwise, and widely so. 'The crystal agrees. Brighton. I feel it strongly.' He looked at Wes. 'What did you say the other station was?'

'Bridgewater. I didn't realise there's a platform there.'

'How far between them?' Sten asked.

Wes shrugged. 'A couple of kilometres.'

The crystal confirmed that this was the case. After a bit more work it also confirmed the appearances would take place between nine and eleven that night. Sten slipped the crystal into its velvet pouch. 'I feel very confident about this.'

Wes shook his head. 'Compelling to watch, I'll give you that. But hard to comprehend how you put all your faith in the mechanism of a stone.'

'Eighteen sightings in forty years,' I stated.

'That's my point.' Wes looked at Sten. 'If your gift is real, why not use it to do good? Cold cases, for example. Missing people. I don't know ... Malaysian Airlines Flight 370. Information that would help people find closure.'

It was a valid question, but it didn't fluster Sten. 'Firstly, it is not a gift. Anyone can do it.' He pointed at me. 'Geo did it already.'

Wes arched an eyebrow.

I pulled a face. 'I asked a question. The crystal moved.'

'Try it, if you like.' Sten offered the crystal to Wes.

Looking uncertain, my brother held the crystal above his palm as he'd witnessed Sten do. I wondered whether he'd go straight to the core question or ask a tester. He appeared frozen, the crystal suspended above his palm, and I thought perhaps he couldn't think of anything.

Then the crystal circled in an anticlockwise direction. The movement seemed to agitate him.

'But he didn't say anything?' I said to Sten.

The Swede was smiling. 'He asked a question in his mind.'

Wes handed the crystal to Sten. 'This is bullshit.'

Sten turned to me. 'Will you go with me tonight? It is the strongest signal I have had for many months.'

'I'm sorry, Sten. I have to rehearse. My audition is on Thursday.'

His expression fell. 'I must get there.'

As he looked hopefully towards Wes, he was met with a similar response. 'We're relocating the Italians to Hadley's tonight.'

A Victorian-era building, the Hadley's Orient Hotel was walking distance from everywhere in the city centre.

'They've been declared sane?' I asked.

'We're awaiting temporary visas so we can fly them home.'

Sten was defiant. 'Then I will hitchhike. Unless there are buses.'

'Take the Ford,' I said.

He stared at me. 'You will lend me your car?'

'If you board the train I'll collect the car at Bridgewater. Leave the key on top of the front tyre on the driver's side.'

He shook his head in disbelief. 'You are the kindest people I know. You and your brother.'

#

That evening I had difficulty concentrating during my rehearsal. I settled upon the first and fourth movements of Mozart's Symphony No. 35, but my mind kept drifting as my hands went through the motions. Normally my concentration was a strength, but here I was struggling to lock on to the music, a disturbing trend, and I was more than concerned about my readiness for the audition.

Before calling it a night, I pushed on for another two hours. Occasionally a final drive beyond the point where the wall was hit could result in a breakthrough, but not this evening. I turned off the studio light and went back down into the house.

Wes was out, either with the Italians or fabricating situations to resolve. Sten was ghost train hunting, and Camille and Paco were working at their new part-time jobs.

There were a couple of unfinished joints on the coffee table. I lit one up, leaning back on the sofa that was my bed. I was just beginning to mellow when the door crashed open and Sten stamped into the sitting room. He threw my father's car keys onto the armchair and went into the kitchen. I watched him open his Gladstone bag and empty the contents onto the table, then open one of the journals and stare at the page. I checked the time: 10.20 p.m. Early for a ghost train hunter.

He shook his head. 'How could I miss it?'

He walked over to my father's liquor cabinet, but it was locked. He looked at me, and I nodded. When he pulled on the handles, the doors held firm. Knowing the latch was light-weight, he yanked harder, and this time the doors burst open.

'Anything except for the Lark on the bottom shelf,' I said.

He took out the bottle of Dalwhinnie and poured a shot into a glass. It was the first time he'd helped himself to anything since moving into the house. He drank it down in one gulp, then poured two tall glasses. He handed me one and held his up. 'To doubt.'

I didn't raise to it.

After taking a sip, he sat down. 'My friend, what is your worst fear when it comes to your dream?'

I thought for a moment. 'Being told to stop in an audition before I finish playing.'

'Tonight I was told to stop before the bow touched the strings.'

'What happened?'

He shook his head in disgust. 'I went to the first platform, Bridgewater. Nothing. I waited. I knew I should perhaps keep waiting, but I hedged my bet and went to the second platform, Brighton. The train didn't come. So I returned to Bridgewater. The train had come and gone from there. I raced back to Brighton, two minutes away. I arrived on the platform as the train disappeared in the distance.'

'Fuck.'

'"Fuck" is the only word that describes the depth of this failure.'

'Hold on. If you were at Brighton, how could you possibly know it had appeared at Bridgewater?'

'The teenagers on the platform.'

'Fuck.'

'I get close once every two years. That is my average. On those occasions the feeling I get is always the same. This is one of those times. I will wait another two years before I get another chance.'

'I'm sorry.'

He waved a hand. 'Let us smoke.'

He reached for the other unfinished joint, and lit it.

I said, 'I understand what you mean. When I prepare for auditions, I know when I'm close and have a real chance, and when the distance is as far as the horizon. For my audition next Thursday the feeling is the horizon.'

Sten raised his glass. 'To the nearness and farness of dreams.'

I raised mine. 'I'll drink to that.'

CHAPTER EIGHT

Alessia was the founding member of a popular quartet in Rome. After a chance meeting with me in Mum's home town of Brescia, the quartet had occasionally called on me to fill in for their violist, Federico. I'd met him a couple of times, but only later learned he was Alessia's ex-boyfriend. When he'd left for Sydney a year ago to join up with Cirque du Soleil, she'd invited me to be the quartet's regular violist. The timing had been good, as I'd tapped out my savings after two successive auditions in Reykjavik and The Hague. But although the steady income had been welcome, recently I'd become anxious about my obligations to the quartet. I believed that I should pursue my dream without restriction, and this was partly what had propelled me back to Hobart.

Not wanting to wake Sten on the sofa across from me, I quietly slipped outside to call Alessia. She picked up after a couple of rings.

'Less, it's me.'

'Geo. How are you?'

'Good. Fine.'

'How did it go with your brother? With the rubbish?'

'You were right. Defused like a bomb.'

'I am glad.'

'I don't know what I'd do without you.'

'Should I come there? It would be good to meet your family. I feel like it would be good. It would help me to know you completely.'

'You have the kindest heart. But there's nothing to know here. This isn't home for me anymore. When I get back we'll go someplace together, just the two of us.'

'I can arrange a trip. And I can visit Federico in Sydney while I'm there.'

As much as I'd love to have Alessia with me, I didn't have the resources to deal with Wes and also safeguard her from his energy. 'You'd be letting down Lisa and Elena. How's Marco doing?'

He was filling in for me while I was away, and keen to take my place should I bow out. Alessia was less enthused at that prospect. 'Marco is Marco.'

'I'm badly prepared for my audition on Thursday. There have been too many distractions.' The front door opened and closed. 'Hold on, someone's home.' Through the window I saw my brother walk into the sitting room. He didn't turn on the light and hadn't seen me outside. 'It's just Wes.'

'Is everything okay?'

'Everything's fine. There's something else I wanted to tell you – I bumped into Audrey.'

'Really?'

'I thought she was in Sydney. I went to watch Hayden rehearse with the Tasmanian Youth Orchestra last week, and she was the conductor. It upset her. But then I saw her again today, and things were a little better.'

'I am not surprised she was upset.'

'I know.'

I turned around and jumped up from the chair. 'Shit, it's happening again.'

A light flashed wildly in the living room.

'What is it?'

'Dad's lamp is on.'

'What lamp? Your father's lamp?'

'Yes. It started flickering on and off last week. We put it in the studio because it scared us. Now it's flickering again.'

The sitting room lights came on. Wes stood by the doorway, peering into the living room. Sten rose from the sofa.

'The light is off?' she said.

'It's not plugged in.'

'It's not plugged in and it's showing light? You are sure?'

'I need to go. I think it's our father trying to communicate with us. It's hard to believe, I know. I'll explain everything later.'

'It sounds very strange.'

'I wish you were here for this part. But I have to go.'

'What time is it?'

'After twelve-thirty. The light is out of control. I'm sorry, Less.'

'Can you call me tomorrow? At the same time.'

'Of course.'

'Promise me. We were talking before. And then the lamp.'

'I promise.'

I hung up and hurried inside, but immediately back-peddled out. Sten was carrying the flickering lamp before him, with Wes, Camille and Paco in tow. I hadn't realised everyone was home.

Sten looked calm, Wes looked irritated, Camille looked engaged. Paco looked like a child standing atop a water slide. He said, 'When people say, "Shit got real", this is the kind of shit they mean.'

'I'm calling Labuschagne,' I said.

'No, you're not,' Wes said.

Sten placed the lamp on the stone steps leading up to the studio. We stood back and watched it do its crazy light dance.

Camille glanced at me. 'The spirit won't stop until you listen to what it's trying to say.'

'Maybe it's speaking to him,' I said, gesturing at Wes.

'The word "spirit" makes me uncomfortable,' he said.

'Where is the phone?' Sten asked. 'I will call Labuschagne.'

I went to hand him my mobile, but Wes thrust an arm between us. 'Nobody's calling anyone.'

Sten shrugged. 'The man is so good he is probably already driving here.'

The light finally extinguished, and we stared at it expectantly. In the next moment my mobile rang. We all jumped.

'Yes?' I said, holding it to my ear.

'Geo, it's me again.' It was Alessia.

'What's wrong?'

'Nothing. I wanted to make sure everything is okay.'

The light flashed on again.

'Shit,' Wes said.

Paco grabbed Sten's arm, a mad grin on his face. 'Oh fuck.'

'This is not natural,' Camille said. 'Even for a spirit.'

'Who is there with you?' Alessia asked.

'Camille and Paco and Wes.'

'Who are Camille and Paco?'

'Two backpackers we picked up. They're helping Sten paint the house.'

'Who's Sten?'

So much had happened, I'd lost track of what she knew. 'He's a ghost train hunter from Sweden.'

'Ghost train hunter?'

'A ghost train arrived in Tasmania a couple of weeks ago, bringing a group of Italians. It sounds crazy, I know.'

'There is a ghost train in Tasmania?'

'This is my life right now.'

'And you saw Audrey?'

'Yes.' I looked around at the others. They were all staring at the lifeless lamp.

'And through this you're rehearsing?' Alessia said.

'It's been a struggle.'

'I am sure.'

'Less, everything's fine. There's just … there's just a freaking unplugged lamp flickering on and off. It's really messing with our minds.'

'I will let you go now,' she said.

'We'll chat tomorrow. I promise.'

She hung up. I slipped the phone into my pocket, regretting everything I'd just said.

Sten said, 'This is the second most interesting thing I have witnessed after the ghost train.'

'Put it back in the studio,' Wes said.

Sten peered at me, and I shrugged. He lifted it off the step, and we watched him carry it up the stony path to the studio.

'Fuck second most – this is the coolest experience I've ever had,' Paco said. 'Cooler than the northern lights. Cooler even than the time I went to an ayahuasca retreat in Costa Rica.'

#

Paco, Camille and I whiled away the morning smoking pot on the studio deck. In the window behind us Dad's lamp sat on the desk, silent and ominous. With the Derwent River shimmering over the rooftops in the distance, and Knocklofty Reserve a wedge of green to the right, there was no better aspect from which to enjoy Hobart.

We were chatting about nothing in particular until Paco complained about his job – not the work itself, but the act of working. He'd been taken on as a kitchen hand at the Winston. 'When we get paid we'll have $400,' he said to Camille. 'We can make it last for two weeks, longer if we eat once a day. We'll buy a guitar for you, and play all day and night.'

'I have to work,' Camille said. 'I need money to get to India.' She was bartending evenings at the Republic at the other end of the strip, a café-style pub that played live music every night.

Paco beamed. 'I fucking love India. I've never been there, but I already know it's my favourite country. Probably because of my experiences in Pondicherry in a previous life.'

'Karnataka – that's where I'm going,' Camille said. 'Bathing elephants is something I feel compelled to do.'

Paco said, 'Do you know shampoo was invented in India? It's true. It comes from the Sanskrit word "chämpo". I was so happy when I learned that.'

It fascinated me how people attached a monetary value to freedom. For Paco that figure was $400 for two weeks for two people living with discipline; an additional week if they could subsist on a starvation diet. Freedom for Paco was playing his guitar all day. For Camille it was a touch pricier: a ticket to India. Staying in motion was freedom for her. For me it was €2000: funds for two back-to-back auditions to anywhere in Europe, including the lead-up rehearsal time. Freedom for me was the ability to pursue my dream. For another it might be the outstanding debt on their mortgage, or a first division lottery win for across-the-board luxury. You needed a certain amount of money not to be held at its mercy, but after that you could never have enough – particularly if freedom was perceived as being money itself. I tried to keep my need for it in check, gravitating towards that band of artists who wanted just enough so they could spend the rest of their time doing what they loved.

Paco leaned over his guitar and improvised a Spanish lick. '"Fuck money" is my motto. I already have music. Fuck food, even.'

I smiled. 'You've nailed life, Paco. Truly. You might be the only person in the world who has.'

'And I'm only twenty-two,' he said. 'Can you believe it?'

'For the rest of us there's always the next thing. I play in a quartet, but I want to play in an orchestra. I make enough to survive, so why do I want more than the music I already have? If I get what I think I want, I'll just want something else.'

'It is natural to want the things we cannot get,' Camille said. 'This is the tension of living. I don't know anybody who is satisfied.'

Paco strummed hard. 'Yes, you do … me. I have my instrument, and I am here with you this morning. That makes me completely happy.' His joint dangled from his lips. 'The only thing I don't want is a job.'

A voice cut across the yard. 'It kept her up again.'

We turned to see a man's eyes and nose angled at us over the fence.

'Hello, Walter,' I said.

'She climbed into our bed at two. The light in your studio is terrifying her.'

'Who is he talking about?' Paco asked me.

'My daughter Charlotte,' Walter said, pointing at the second-floor window behind him. 'That's her bedroom. It's damn rude is what it is. For the love of god, take the bulb out of the fitting. It's not like I'm asking you to call an electrician.'

'Tell her to close the curtains,' Paco said.

'Pardon?'

'You heard me.'

Walter glared at me. 'Who is he?'

'The artist formerly known as Paco,' Paco said. 'Guitarist and painter of houses and pictures. I'll draw a portrait of you looking over the fence for twenty dollars.'

Walter sniffed the air. 'Is that weed?'

Oh hell, we were done.

Paco walked through the studio into the yard, and I followed after him to the fence.

'We don't want trouble over something as stupid as a light?' Paco said. He opened Sten's pouch to reveal a handful of pre-rolled joints. 'Maybe this will help make the problem go away.

You can tell your daughter, "It's only a light, don't worry. Go back to bed and enjoy sweet dreams."'

Walter's nostrils flared. 'Are you bribing me with weed?'

We were fucked. *Fucked.*

Paco raised the pouch higher. 'How many? Two? Three? Say a number.'

Walter's eyes lowered, and after a moment his expression broke. He glanced over his shoulder. 'Yeah, five should do the trick.'

As Paco held up the pouch, Walter hastily scooped up the joints and disappeared behind the fence. Paco winked at me, and we went back down into the house with Camille.

Wes was on the phone in the kitchen. 'Yes,' he said. 'Hmm … I see.' He held up a hand for us to be quiet. 'And that's official?' He pulled a face, as if the person at the other end had said something silly. 'And the unofficial … I mean, if you're saying that's the official …?' He caught my eye and made a writing gesture.

I grabbed a pen and an unopened letter from the counter.

'Can you repeat that?' He looked at me. 'Bill Bright.' I wrote it down, then Wes gave me a mobile number. 'Thank you. Yes. I understand. And thank you for returning my call.' He hung up. 'That was Stan Prior, the director of TasRail. Officially, there haven't ever been any ghost train sightings in Tasmania.' He tapped the name on the envelope. 'Unofficially, this man witnessed something a number of years ago.'

'Bill Bright?'

'He's in Sheffield.'

'The timing couldn't be better,' Wes said. 'SteamFest is currently running. Tomorrow's the last day.' He nodded at Sten, who was consumed in his research at the kitchen table. 'We're going.'

The festival displayed working steam machinery, including steam trains.

'I don't know,' I said. 'My audition's on Thursday.'

I'd never been this unprepared, but I wasn't willing to pull out. It wasn't in my nature to do so. Sure, I was practised in the pieces I had to perform, but to borrow from Sten, I wasn't on the signal line with this one.

'Forget it,' Wes said. 'We're way past that. You brought this situation into our house. You're coming.'

#

That evening the five of us lounged around the sitting room. Sten was prone on the sofa, his eyes closed and an unlit joint dangling from his mouth. Paco worked a rumba flamenca on his guitar, and Camille lay stretched across the carpet with her mobile.

The landline phone rang in the kitchen. Wes got up to take the call.

Camille turned to me. 'Perhaps if you have time you could pick up something for me in Sheffield?'

'Of course.' I was a little surprised, as it seemed an arbitrary location.

'There is a store there that sells second-hand goods. I've never been, but a friend we met in Byron Bay arrived in Devonport a few days ago. She is travelling along the West Coast, and she saw this in the store.' Camille passed me her phone. It showed a photo of an old ukulele, with a note Blu-Tacked to the body: *This ukulele shrieks in torment.* 'I must have it,' she said. 'I have been looking for an instrument for many months. This is the one. If I give you the money and it is still there, will you get it for me?'

'Sure.' I handed the phone back to her. 'I know that place – Arlo's Attic.'

'Thank you.' She lay back down on the carpet, but as an afterthought turned to me again. 'Too much money tricks you into thinking about the future. Tomorrow, next week, next year. I try to keep only what I need, when I need it. I don't want to lose my connection to right now. Playing music is one of the best things for connecting to the moment. That's why I need the ukulele. And anyway ... it shrieks in torment.'

Wes's voice rose in the kitchen. We all turned to look. Even Sten, who subsisted on a diet of power naps, opened his eyes.

'I'll bring it over —' Wes pressed. 'No. I can come now. It's not —' He slammed his fist against the wall. 'It's not ... fine, okay, tomorrow night. I can have dinner with you and Hayden. Why not ...? Whatever. I'm going to Sheffield. I'll drop it off on the way out.' He screwed up his face. 'With Geo and Sten. Fine ... okay. Goodbye.'

He replaced the receiver, and we glanced away. He came into the sitting room and dropped into the recliner.

I cast a casual eye in his direction. 'Everything okay?'

He ignored me and said to Sten, 'You okay for Sheffield?'

Sten nodded. 'I've been there.'

'When?'

'Nineteen eighty-seven. I checked my journal. I was coming back to Devonport from Queenstown. My train was presenting in a triangle along the West Coast: Smithton, Deloraine, Queenstown. The night before Sheffield, in Queenstown – the fifth of August – I came so close. I faced it like a matador facing a bull. It swept through me as if I was a red cloth. I will never forget it.'

#

We stopped at the McDonald's in Bridgewater for coffee, and when we returned to the car Wes threw the keys at Sten and told him he was driving. I took the passenger seat, and as we exited the roundabout onto the Midland Highway a male backpacker under the footbridge stuck out his thumb.

I pointed at him. 'Hey, maybe we should —?'

'Sten,' Wes said, 'if you so much as look in his direction I'll put a fucking bullet through your head.'

Sten drove by with his hands glued at a quarter-to-three.

Due to his refusal to go above eighty kilometres, it took us an hour-and-a-half to reach Campbell Town. A line of cars were backed up behind us for most of the journey, and at one point Wes gave the finger to a tailgating SUV. 'Put the siren on the roof, Sten. We'll see if this dickhead has any cahoonas.'

We grabbed another round of coffees at Zeps Café, and this time Wes threw me the keys. 'Nice driving, Sten. Geo can take it from here.'

Back on the Midland, Wes asked Sten, 'How's the search coming along?'

Sten glanced over his shoulder. 'For my train?'

'Yeah.'

'I always feel close. When I say my train might be in one of two places, I believe with absolute certainty it will arrive at one of these two destinations. So my task is simply to select the correct one. There is no consideration that it may arrive at neither of these locations. So how is it coming along …?' He shrugged. 'Fifty-fifty … like always.'

'And you're really going to board it?'

'Without hesitation.'

'What if someone like me got on?'

I glanced in the mirror.

Sten's brow furrowed. 'What do you mean?'

'Would it accept me? I can understand how it would accept you – you have family on the train. But I'd be like the Italians who boarded it in Orvieto. It'd just spit me out at the next stop, right? Probably Kyrgyzstan or somewhere equally random.'

What was Wes's angle? That he might also board the train if we intercepted it? The first thing that crossed my mind was I wouldn't be able to sell the house. I saw visions of myself waiting on abandoned platforms for the next forty years with a contract and pen in hand.

Sten said, 'This situation with the twenty-seven Italians, I tell you, it is strange.'

'How so?' I asked. 'I mean, aside from the obvious.'

'That they did not know something extraordinary was taking place. This is not a usual train. When your eyes see it, you know. You don't only realise it when you get off and nobody speaks your language.'

'They're an elderly group, aside from the pregnant woman. Maybe they knew but didn't have the confidence to own the situation.'

'Giacomo, the mayor, did say the conductor was strange,' I commented.

We all fell silent for a spell.

Sten said, 'I know when it is coming next. I have the same feeling as I did on Saturday. The crystal is very strong in its indication.'

'Oh yeah?' Wes said.

'Tomorrow night in New Norfolk. I am optimistic I'm going to board my train.'

'That's excellent,' I said. 'I hope you're on the signal line.'

'Would you like to witness it? You have been very good to me.'

'I'd love to, Sten. But I fly out to Melbourne first thing Thursday for my audition.'

He waved his hand. 'Your own dream must come first. I will invite Labuschagne. After all of these years he deserves the opportunity.'

I felt a twinge of jealousy.

Wes spoke from the back. 'Would you board the train if you saw it?'

I glanced in the mirror. 'You're asking me?'

'Yes.'

I returned my focus to the road. 'My viola is my platform.'

#

Two hours later we parked outside Fudge'n'Good Coffee in Sheffield. The shop walls on Main Street displayed life-size paintings that gave light to its nickname, Town of Murals. The tourists had arrived early for the final day of SteamFest, the street abuzz with an energy that complemented a watchful Mount Roland in the distance.

We wove our way through the crowds in search of the Information Centre. I'd never been to SteamFest, and I soon learned it featured working displays of vintage machinery, traction engines, cars, model railways, and military vehicles. But we were here for one reason: to speak with ghost train witness Bill Bright.

A lady at the Information Centre pointed us in the direction of Gerald Fisher, festival organiser, who ushered us to the locomotive shed. When we walked in, Bill was bent over the engine of a small locomotive. He was dressed in oil-stained bib-and-brace overalls, with a cloth and monkey wrench in each hand. Wes called out his name, and Bill's head popped up. I placed him in his late thirties.

Wes made our introductions, then added, 'Stan Prior said you were the man to speak to; we've come up from Hobart.'

Bill wiped his arm across his forehead. 'Must be serious to drive all this way?'

'The topic is delicate.'

Bill said nothing.

Wes went around to his side of the train. 'Did you hear about the body in Campania?'

'The one hit by a train?'

Wes nodded.

Bill dropped his rag onto his toolbox. 'Yeah, I read about it.'

Wes didn't need to tell him the train line there was decommissioned. 'It's back, Bill.' He nodded at Sten. 'He's been chasing it for forty years. Stared it down like a matador in Queenstown, 1987. Damned thing near swept through him like a bull.'

Bill glanced at Sten. His eyes skewed. 'No, it didn't.'

Wes frowned.

'1987. Queenstown.' Bill looked at him. 'It was me it swept through.'

Sten smiled.

Bill pointed at Sten. 'He was there. I remember. Me and my father, and him. I was eight.'

Sten said, 'You were very brave.'

The shift in dynamics seemed to catch Wes off guard, but before he could respond Bill glanced at his watch. 'I have to get this thing going. I'm the only driver today, and it runs every hour on a one-kilometre track. You can ride up front with me if you like.'

#

Twenty-five minutes later we rolled out of Sheffield in the cab with Bill Bright, the three carriages behind us packed with tourists.

'She's a Krauss locomotive,' Bill said. 'The only two-foot gauge passenger to operate in Tasmania.'

'I have been on many Krauss locomotives,' Sten said. 'The light railway engines are my favourite.'

'Let's talk about that night,' Wes said.

I thought Bill might deflect the conversation, but he seemed happy to get back on topic. 'Like I told you, I was eight. Dad worked that line for thirty-one years. On weekends he'd take me with him. I looked forward to those times like I looked forward to holidays.'

Sten showed no reaction, even though Bill may as well have been talking about the Swede's childhood.

'Your father?' We asked.

Bill shook his head. 'He passed four years ago. I'd ride with him in the cab until I got tired, then go back to the cabin to sleep. But on this night I was in the lead locomotive, and it must have been, I don't know ...' He looked at Sten. 'Nine-thirty?'

'Nine forty-two,' Sten said.

Bill nodded. 'It was an evening run without passengers. We were taking the train to Strahan where we were staying over.

The next day was the Strahan to Dubbil Barril run into the rainforest. So we're humming along when we see this light. I mean, this light … like a full moon yo-yoed down onto the track. Dad hit the brakes, and we screeched to a creeping roll. I tell you, the feeling in my stomach … If you were driving on an unlit road and a UFO appeared ahead of you, this is the feeling I'm talking about.'

'I could not describe it better,' Sten said.

Bill continued. 'So we're facing this light – a light seemingly from a train – and we had slowed, and it had slowed, and all at once we were both stopped. Squared off. I mean, how do you figure that as an eight-year-old?'

Surprised by this detail, I turned to Sten. 'Your train can break the rules of direction?'

Sten paid me no attention. 'Your father was calm.'

Bill looked at Wes, and jerked a thumb at Sten. 'He probably told you already … but he walked into the station in Queenstown a couple of days before, asking Dad if he could accompany him on some routes.'

'I told him I was looking for work experience,' Sten said. 'These days I tell the truth – I say I am hunting a ghost train.'

'Dad knew your reason was a lie. He suspected you were looking for something.'

'I am grateful to him for trusting me, or I would not have seen my train. It appeared on the third night, the first time you came with us.'

'It was a train, alright,' Bill said. 'But it was alien. I mean, it couldn't have been anything else. Only two trains worked that line, and the other one was undergoing repairs in Queenstown.'

'Describe what you saw,' Wes said.

'The thing I remember most is the steam rising from its chimney. This was thirty years ago, but I can picture it like it was yesterday. And above the train a large yellow moon, as if it was a reflection in the sky. The memory still terrifies me.'

Sten said, 'I was transfixed, and I had been hunting it for ten years. But you showed no fear. You were silent and alert.'

'What did your father do?' Wes asked.

'Just a moment.' We were entering a turn, and Bill shut down the throttle and increased the cut-off. As we exited the curve he opened the cylinder valves with a foot pedal, and set the cut-off low. He released the throttle to give some steam, moved the cut-off back up, and adjusted the throttle to its final position. 'Shut off the blower,' he said to Sten, who did as instructed. After another twenty seconds, Bill closed off the cylinder valves. He said to Wes, 'What were you asking?'

'What did your father do? After you faced the train.'

'He told me to stay in the cab, then climbed down with a torch. I watched him approach the side of the train.' Bill nodded at Sten. 'He went down too. It was difficult to see beyond the light, but I could hear my father or him rapping on the side of the cab.'

'It was your father,' Sten said. 'I was searching the carriages for an open door.'

'I heard Dad calling out to the driver. Then I heard him walking back along the carriages.' He glanced at Sten. 'I heard him or you rapping on more doors.'

'I was already at the back of my train. It was your father.'

Bill said, 'The train was impenetrable, or that's my impression. Because I could still hear Dad pounding on the steel.'

'There were no doors open because it wasn't a stop,' Sten said to Wes. He turned to Bill. 'Even though you showed no fear, you must have been scared.'

'What was scaring me was that the train was physical. I mean, it was extraordinary, but it was real. I knew it was extraordinary the second I saw it. It steamed like a train, and it sounded like a train. But it stared you down like an animal.'

'So what happened?' Wes asked.

Bill shook his head as though in disbelief at the memory. 'It jumped to life. The horn whistled, and it started moving forward – moving towards the train where I was sitting. Dad screamed in my direction. I remember that very clearly. He sprinted alongside the other train, but he was too far back. I heard him shouting for me to jump out of the cab. But I was frozen. Transfixed.' He looked at Sten. 'That was the moment I was transfixed. The train was coming … I mean, it was really coming. I saw the big wheels turning. And if it hit me …? I mean, nobody was going to die. It hardly had any speed. But still, I was eight, and my thoughts were extreme.'

'I agree with Sten,' Wes said. 'You were brave.'

Bill shook his head. 'I haven't spoken about this to anyone except my father.'

'You're explaining it well,' Wes said.

'I was sitting on the stool, watching it come at me. By that time Dad was in line with the driver's car, hammering at the door, screaming for it to stop.'

Bill didn't know what we knew, that the driver was Sten's father. I glanced at Sten, but he was expressionless.

'And a few metres from contact,' Bill continued, 'the train started to lose form. I mean, I don't know how else to describe it. You can call it a ghost train … You can call it whatever you want.

But I was watching Dad banging on the cab door, and I can tell you it wasn't a ghost. But in the next moment it started disappearing. It passed through me, swept through me.' He glanced at Sten. 'Like a bull through a red cloth.'

'Incredible,' I said.

Sten nodded. 'We were so close.'

Back at Sheffield, Sten went ahead of us to fetch some literature on the local railways from the Information Centre. When he was out of earshot, Bill said, 'I don't know your relationship with that man, but my father – when he spoke about him after he left – he said he didn't trust him. He just felt this Swede already knew the answers to the questions he was asking. Like he was looking for confirmation, not information.'

'You've been very forthright,' Wes said. 'Thank you.'

Bill shrugged. 'No difference to me if you're making the ghost train your business. I hope I never see it again.'

#

I walked into Arlo's Attic, an eerie little second-hand store on Main Street. Outside the entrance, palindromic phrases had been etched onto the paving with different coloured chalk: *Was it a car or a cat I saw?*; *UFO TOFU*; *Do Geese See God?*; *Murder for a jar of red rum*; *Nurse, I spy gypsies, run!*

The store was crammed with all sorts of wares, from antique books to coins and war memorabilia. I meandered through the aisles, pausing here and there to read the editorials on the sticky notes attached to the stock. Eventually I happened upon the target of my quest on the top shelf of the far wall. A number of sticky notes were pasted to the body: *A Pretty Crappy Ukulele*;

Don't Ignore Me!; *$20*; *This Ukulele Shrieks In Torment*. It was missing the first and fourth strings. I took it down to feel it in my hands. Camille was going to love it.

A round of coffees later, and after declining a photo with a llama shepherded by an authorised busker, we drove out of Sheffield.

The final comment by Bill Bright preyed on my mind. With Sten having drifted off to sleep in the back seat, I asked Wes what he was planning to do with all of the information.

'Look, I don't want to get into that right now.'

'I heard what Henry said.'

'It's –' He glanced at me. 'I'm putting together an explanation.'

'Yeah, well, I'm sure the whole department's trying to do that. The train killed a man.'

'Nobody's going to miss this person. That's the problem.'

'How do you mean?'

'Turns out we know him. He's done a bit of time; one of those names that always crops up.'

'Damn. What was he doing walking along the train line outside Campania?'

'Word is he was carrying debt with his dealer. My guess – he made a run for it.'

'To where ... Launceston? On foot?' It seemed a bit far-fetched.

'A scared person's capable of anything. Trust me.'

It cast a different light on the signal line: though an opportunity for Sten, the train seemed a death sentence for anyone else that crossed its path.

'It makes me mad,' Wes continued. 'The less a person matters, the less the truth matters.'

His response surprised me. 'But we know what happened here?'

'Who's "we"? You? Me? Sten?' He lit a cigarette and wound down the window.

'I think we can agree the Italians were deposited in Hobart by train. Their statements were consistent. If you had evidence to suggest otherwise, you would've told me. You don't need to be Sherlock Holmes to connect the dots between them getting off at the Railyards, and what happened in Campania.'

'There's an unwillingness to acknowledge ...' his voice trailed off.

'Then how are they explaining it? We're talking about a decommissioned line.'

'It's not worth getting worked up over.'

'Tell me. I deserve to know.'

His gaze fell on me as he paused. 'Hit and run,' he said.

'Hit and run? Are you fucking serious? The body was at least thirty metres along the track from the road.'

'This is what I'm up against.'

'But there are witnesses.'

His voice rose. 'To be clear, there are no witnesses.'

'The Hobart Stationmaster. You said so yourself.'

'Henry blocked us from getting him on record. By the time Marty and I got back to him he denied seeing anything.'

'What about the teenagers at Bridgewater? Sten said they saw it. Have you not spoken to them?'

'We ran a check on "teenagers" and came up with twelve thousand profiles.'

'Can you please refrain from being a dick right now.'

'Cut me some slack. I'm the one trying to put together an explanation here.'

'It's going to take a witnessed sighting. I mean … otherwise, how?'

'I know.'

'Otherwise, I mean —'

'I understand.'

We drove a little way in silence, and I asked, 'What's his name?'

'The druggie?'

'The victim.'

Our eyes met briefly.

'What difference does it make?' he said.

'It makes a difference.'

He took a drag on his cigarette. 'Wayne Barnes.'

'Thank you.'

\#

Wes wasn't pleased when I ignored the turn-off for Hobart and announced a detour into Launceston. I'd been planning to make a trip north to get my viola serviced, and the visit to Sheffield presented the perfect opportunity. Although there were excellent luthiers in Hobart, Jacob Weiss was the only person I trusted to handle the instrument. He hadn't made the viola I'd inherited from Mum, but he'd rescued it.

I parked in the bay outside the shop on Charles Street, and fetched my viola from the boot. Wes mumbled that he'd wait in Princes Square across the road, and Sten went with him. Our family's connection to Jacob was through Mum, and although Wes knew him well there was some leftover tension in the alliance.

Jacob was trimming the ends of the bass bar on a violin when I entered. He laid down his block plane and came out from behind his workbench. 'Geo ... Geo, how are you?'

We embraced. 'Good, Jacob. And you? How's Greta?'

He threw a hand in the air. 'Good. We're good. Getting older by the minute. Joints, eyes, liver ... body parts that didn't put up an argument for sixty years now highly combative. But the important bits ...' He held up his fingers and wriggled them. 'Surgeon steady.' He rapped on his chest. 'And the heart? Trampoline strong.' With a grin, he pointed at the stool on the customer side of the workbench. 'Sit. Sit.'

I placed the viola case on the bench and sat down.

He went around to the other side and took out the instrument. 'It's sad and beautiful to call it yours now.'

'I want you to know how much I appreciate you and Greta driving down for the funeral.'

'Your mother was a majestic violist. The most talented I've seen.'

I tried not to blink for fear I'd embarrass myself with tears.

'I was saddened to hear about your father,' he said. 'Unfortunately, we couldn't —'

'I didn't go either.'

He peered at me over his glasses. Perhaps recognising that one of us should change the subject, he examined the viola. 'It's in the same condition as I remember. You're taking care of it. Thank you.'

'It's as important to me as my heart.'

He smiled. 'A normal service, then?'

'I'd also like gut cord for the tailpiece.' Although gut cord had been the staple for centuries, these days players and violin-makers preferred nylon, braided wire and, recently, Kevlar. But I wanted gut cord for the warmth and tonal colour.

Jacob asked, 'Is it for a particular performance?'

'I'm auditioning for the MSO on Thursday.'

'Wonderful,' he said. 'Wonderful.' He crouched down to open a cupboard.

'I also have a friend's ukulele that needs restringing. I don't want to waste your time, but —'

'Bring it inside. Put it on the bench.'

I went to the car, but the doors were locked. Wes and Sten were stretched out on the grass in Princes Square.

My brother threw me the keys. 'How long?'

'Twenty minutes.' I started off, then turned around. 'Pop your head in and say hello, okay.'

His stared at the fountain.

By the time I returned to the shop, Jacob had removed the old strings and was on to the second new string. When I laid the ukulele on the bench, he glanced at it without slowing his hands.

'I picked it up in Sheffield,' I said.

'Arlo's Attic?'

I nodded.

After restringing the viola, he moved swiftly on to the guitar. 'I'll never forget the first time your mother came to me with the viola. Her eyes were red. She'd travelled up from Hobart. At the time I was the only luthier in the state. Three hours and she was still crying. It was like a scene from a film. The day itself was crying, rain streaming onto the street – and in walks this young lady, a smashed viola in her hand.'

I knew the story intimately, but Jacob told it as if it was his.

'She didn't have the case with her. The instrument was hanging so sadly at her side. But I saw immediately the neck was intact. This filled me with hope, even though she hadn't uttered a word. She was younger than you are now.'

'She came by train,' I said.

'I'll never forget it ... in the softest voice, she told me she'd be indebted to me forever if I could rescue this instrument that was as important to her as her soul.' He shook his head. 'How can a person remain unmoved by such a request? And I knew ... I knew I'd do everything in my power to restore it for her.'

'You did.'

'I may not have built it, but I feel more for this viola than any other instrument I've made.'

'Did she tell you how it was damaged?'

His brow furrowed. 'There was a line not to be crossed. That's the feeling I got. I respected the line.'

If everything with the house turned out as I hoped, I'd never see Jacob again. And because of his love and care for the viola over the past forty years, he deserved to know the complete story.

'There was a fellow violist at the TYO. His father was a professional musician. Austrian. A real taskmaster. He pushed his son hard. I mean, disciplined him – to the point that playing was no longer a joy for the son. Maybe it never was? But he had talent, there was no doubting that. And because he had talent, his father demanded perfection. This man never took pleasure in his son's playing. Never took pride in his development. He was solely concerned with the next level. He'd sit in the room while his son rehearsed. I don't know the exact details, but you can imagine the situation. Then one night there was a confrontation, and the son snapped. He broke his viola in front of his father. Self-defence?

To make a point? Who knows. Personally I believe it was so he never had to play again.'

There were tears in Jacob's eyes. 'I never realised.'

'The next day he showed it to my mother. He was eighteen, she was seventeen … This was three years before they got engaged. He was going to throw it away, but he wanted to show her first. Of all her reactions, he couldn't have predicted she'd get on a train and travel 200 kilometres to have it restored. To return it to him as a miracle. A new instrument without memory. But he wouldn't accept it. He never played again. This is how it came to be hers; and how it came to be mine.'

Wes never went into the workshop to say hello.

CHAPTER NINE

I<small>T WAS</small> 9 P.M. when I arrived back at the house after the day in Melbourne. I closed the front door and placed my viola on the cane chest in the hallway. Still in shock, the only thing I wanted was the one thing I didn't have: my own space.

Wes's car was outside, so I knew he was home. I found him in his room, standing beside the bed and staring into the shoebox. He looked at me. 'Did you know about this?'

'What are you talking about?'

He tilted the box. It was empty.

I reeled back. 'What are you suggesting?'

My heart was pounding. I was frightened for Nic, and where this moment might lead. Had she let herself into the house and taken the money?

'You told Nic. That's what I'm suggesting.'

I didn't respond. He hurled the box aside and strode out. I hurried down the steps after him. 'Don't go over there like this.'

He climbed into the Commodore. I tried to open the passenger door, but it was locked. He turned the ignition.

I thumped on the window. 'Wes!'

There was a wild look in his eyes. The car screeched off.

I sprinted back into the house, grabbed the car keys and my mobile, and ran out again. 'Shit, shit, shit.' After cranking the Ford to life, I rattled down Yardley Street as I fumbled Martin's card out of my wallet, held up the phone and dialled. 'Shit, shit, shit.' Why hadn't I taken Nic's advice and stored his number?

Martin answered after a few rings, while I was caught at the first traffic light.

'Wes is driving to Nic's. He's mad as hell. I'm chasing after him.'

'I'll be there in five,' Martin said, and hung up.

I threw my phone onto the passenger seat and accelerated through the red light.

A couple of minutes later I pulled into the driveway behind Wes's car. The front door was open. I charged into the house.

They were in the dining room, Wes circling the table as Nic steered away from him on the other side.

'So,' he said, 'we've reached a point where it's okay to steal from me?'

Hayden was standing in the doorway to the living room. 'Don't touch her.'

'Go back to bed,' Wes said, his eyes locked on Nic.

I edged into the dining room. 'Wes, come outside. Martin's on his way.'

His face reddened. 'Will everyone please stay the fuck out of my marriage?'

'Wes,' I said, 'this is my fault. I told Nic where the money was. This is because of me.'

He made a small dart around the table, but Nic was quick to react and managed to keep the distance between them. They slowed down to a shuffle, their hands brushing along the edge of the table. Wes smiled. Nic's eyes darted towards Wes, then me.

'I work hard for us,' he said.

'You'd rather see Hayden and me suffer.'

'I love you and Hayden. We're family.'

She scoffed. 'This is your idea of a family?'

'You deny me the right to live in my own house. Then you steal from me. This is the point we've reached?'

Hayden's voice rose. 'If you touch Mum I'll never forgive you.'

The threat didn't give Wes pause, and in the next moment he picked up a plate of spaghetti and flung it at Nic. The plate missed her by an inch, shattering against the wall behind her. She crumpled to the floor, conceding.

Wes ran around the table. I dived forward, trying to tackle him, but he was too strong. Nic curled into a ball, her head buried in her arms. Wes yanked at her elbows. I came at him again, this time with an added weight at my side – Hayden had rushed in. But together we made little difference. I concentrated on Wes's right arm, trying to pin it down.

Martin burst into the room. 'Stop!' he shouted, and rushed forward. Within seconds, Wes was separated from Nic. Martin slapped him across the face, sobering him. 'Let's get you some-place where you can sleep this off,' he said, pushing him towards the door.

Nic, Hayden and I watched from the floor.

'Fuck you,' Wes said to me or Nic, or both of us.

'Out you go, partner,' Martin said.

They disappeared outside.

#

We sat at the dining table, the wall behind Nic smeared with bolognese. Although the plate had missed her, a shard of porcelain had struck her cheek when it shattered, leaving a thin cut. She held an ice cube wrapped in a dishcloth to the wound.

Hayden was watchful, his attention on his mother. 'This wasn't the first time,' he said.

Nic didn't say anything, and started shaking. Hayden rose and went to put an arm around her.

'All we want is to start over,' she said. 'The house isn't safe with him in it.'

'You don't need his permission,' I said.

'But we need him to accept it first. Or he'll never let us go.' She patted Hayden's hand. 'Will you get me a glass of water?'

He went into the kitchen.

I leaned forward and whispered, 'You can get a restraining order. You must report this. Tonight. I'll go with you. Martin will help us.'

'I don't know.'

'What's stopping you?'

She glanced into the kitchen. 'If he can't get to me, he'll do it through Hayden.'

I pulled a face. 'Wes loves Hayden. He doesn't know how to express it, but he'd never use him that way.'

'He loves me,' she said.

There wasn't anything I could say to that.

Hayden came back with a glass of water and handed it to her. 'Can I change the subject?'

'God, please do,' Nic said, taking a sip.

'How did the audition go?' he asked me.

Nic frowned. 'That was today?'

I held up eight fingers.

Hayden scrunched his face.

'Eight seconds.' I nodded. 'That's how long before they told me to stop.'

'Oh, Geo,' Nic said.

Hayden's eyes widened. 'How can they do that?'

I shrugged.

'That's bullshit!' he said.

'Watch your mouth, mister – you've been amazing tonight, but that doesn't mean you have an open book on your language.' To me, she said, 'Did they at least give you feedback?'

'"Thank you." A voice said "thank you" after eight seconds.'

'That's bullshit.' She glanced at Hayden. 'Excuse me.'

'I don't know how to take this one.' I shook my head. 'Usually it's a month or two before I recover from a rejection. But eight seconds … I mean, was it even a rejection?'

'They found their person and were going through the motions. It's the only explanation.'

'Then phone and tell you not to come,' Hayden said. 'Or tell you there and then, "Sorry, but the person before you got it." Or let you play the full repertoire and say "no". There are ten better ways to reject a musician.'

'I'm just not good enough?' I shrugged.

'Cut that out,' Nic said. 'You know your talent. There's nothing to understand here. The only way to deal with this is to move on to the next one.'

'You're right.'

'Why does it have to be a symphony orchestra?' Hayden asked.

'What do you mean?'

'Why can't it be a string quartet, or a postmodern quartet, or a duo? Why can't it be composing? I loved the music you wrote.'

This was the question I hated being asked, because in the black well of my soul I knew the answer. 'It's a good question, mate.'

'I always wondered.'

'I don't know. It's like ... it's like if you were a talented soccer player, your dream might be to play for Juventus. If you then got picked up by Melbourne Victory, that would be wonderful. You'd have made it – but it wouldn't be how you imagined it in your dreams. The fantasy is usually larger than reality, larger than your talent, even.'

'I have a dream,' he said.

'I know. And you have the qualities to match it.'

'I just love playing. And I love getting better. If I can do it as my job, it doesn't matter how or where. If I were a soccer player my ambition would be to be a professional soccer player. To wake up and practise every day. If I could do that, I'd love life. All I know is I don't want a job like Dad's. Dad doesn't love life.'

'He's good at what he does,' I said.

'Well,' said Hayden, 'I've never watched him do detective work ... but I can tell you he was a better violinist than he is a detective.'

'He hasn't played since before you were born. How can you be sure?'

'Because I have his talent.' It was a comment made without arrogance.

'Do you think things would be different if he'd pursued a career in music?' I asked.

'If Dad was a violinist, we'd still be a family,' he said.

#

Back at Yardley Street I sat on the studio deck, speaking to Alessia on the phone. Nobody else was home. I presumed Paco and Camille were still at work, and that Sten was out ghost train hunting.

'No one should have to go through that,' Alessia said.

'I'm starting to think it's not meant to happen for me.'

'This is your dream, Geo. Do you know how lucky you are? Many people live without knowing their passion. But you found yours at the beginning, and you can spend your whole life expressing it. You are blessed.'

'I hadn't thought about it like that.'

'It is true. And if you want to know what I believe … I believe chasing the dream is more important than the dream. I am not saying this because of your experience today – I am saying it because I believe chasing something is what makes a person grow. And having everything is the beginning of dying. It is impossible to know your passion too quickly. But it is possible to have your dream too quickly.'

'There may be truth in what you're saying. I need to think about that.'

'You are a strong violist, Geo. You are becoming an excellent violist. And you have a special gift to compose. I would not allow you to stop playing. I could not love you if you stopped playing. I could not love anyone who knew their heart and did not show it.'

'I wish you were here. Not to see where I'm from, and not to meet my family – I don't think that would help you understand me any more than you already do. I just want to be next to you.'

'Are you going to be okay?'

'I'll be fine. I need to get the house on the market now.'

The kitchen light switched on. My heart leapt. 'Someone's home.' I peered through the window, and relaxed when I saw it was Paco. He was startled when he caught sight of me on the patio. He laughed and came to the door.

'It's Paco,' I said. 'He's coming outside.'

'I will let you go. I need to go too. We are playing at Fonclea tonight.'

Paco opened the door and started speaking, but when he saw I was on the phone he nodded and came quietly outside.

'Be safe,' I said to Alessia, walking down from the studio to the house. 'Who's driving?'

'Elena.'

'Good. We'll speak later.'

'Ciao,' she said. The line went dead.

'Italy?' Paco said, lighting a smoke.

I nodded.

'You are lucky to have someone.'

'You have someone. You have Camille.'

He shook his head and stuck out his thumb. 'She's talking about hitching to the West Coast, through Queenstown. She's serious. I'm trying to change her mind. But she could go any moment. Tomorrow. Saturday. It's out of my control.'

'You won't go with her?'

'She didn't ask me.' He took a drag and exhaled. 'Life is such an asshole.'

'Shit.'

He shrugged.

'I'm sorry,' I said.

'She is following her heart. I am following mine. Our hearts beat differently.'

'You seem, I don't know ... philosophical.'

'When I go into my room there will be tears, but I will not show her. I don't want her to feel bad. We came together for a purpose. We experienced great joy. But now we are being steered in other directions. This is life. Life the asshole.'

'Do you love her?'

'Of course. What else? I love you. I love Sten. I love her in other ways too. I don't spend time with people I do not love.'

'Do you love Wes?' It was a genuine question. I was family; I had to feel something for him.

'With Wes it's harder. Love must be let in.'

'I feel like that about him too.'

'I was talking with Sten before. I asked him if he thought it was possible to live fully without love. I asked him because I knew he had sacrificed love. Do you know what he said? He said, "I didn't come here to live. I came here to die for a dream."'

'Shit.'

He nodded. 'I was very moved.'

I lit a smoke.

'Where is everyone?' he asked.

'I don't know. The house feels different tonight.'

#

I woke to the sound of Audrey's voice, and gingerly pulled myself into a sitting position on the sofa. My focus landed on Wes in the kitchen. It took me a few seconds to register that he was listening to a voice message on our parents' answering machine.

He replayed it, and watched for my reaction. 'Geo, I'm sorry about the audition. Nic told me. Please don't return my call, we've … I just wanted you to know I'm thinking of you.' The message ended.

'You left a woman like that?' Wes said.

I held out my palm. 'Not today. Please.'

'This woman, who even after you abandoned her cares enough to tell you she's thinking of you when you fail … this is the woman you left?'

I went to take a shower, and when I came back into the kitchen he was arranging white roses in a vase.

'What are you doing?'

He didn't respond.

'Wes, you're not going over there. It's absolutely the wrong thing to do.'

The kettle whistled, and he poured himself a coffee.

'Sten still hasn't come home,' I said.

What if he'd actually done the impossible, and boarded his train? I knew I should be happy for him, but it felt like I'd lost something.

'This isn't his home,' Wes said.

'Do you think he's on it?'

'We need to start working our way back to reality with this train situation. Since Sten turned up a lot of things have become blurred that shouldn't be blurred.'

'Camille's leaving,' I said. 'That's a black-and-white fact. Paco will stay.'

'Good.'

He left with the roses, and I called Nic to warn her she had three minutes to vacate.

#

That Friday was a peculiar day. I had no music to rehearse, no chores to do, nobody to see. I felt emptied of all feeling. Sten still hadn't returned, the bare kitchen table a sharp reminder of his absence. Camille too seemed intent upon leaving, but thankfully Paco ensured a continuation of some life in the house. He worked quietly and diligently in the background, putting in the hours of three people now that he was the only one painting. But even he was less than two weeks from departing. The previous night he'd told me he was working towards a deadline, having booked a flight out of Tassie for early February. He hoped to kick around the music scene in Melbourne before heading on to Asia. I'd told him the prospects in Victoria were promising for all instruments except viola.

At sundown I poured a whisky and went into my father's study. Other than the night when I'd fetched the lamp, I hadn't stepped foot in the study since my return. Our father had spent most of his time in this space – writing reports, making calls, smoking his pipe while reading or staring out the window. My overriding memory was of him leaning back in his chair to look at me when I knocked on the door. The rich scent of tobacco wafted down the various channels of the house, and even now, two-and-a-half years after his death, the dominant aspect of the room was that musky, stale aroma.

I sat in his chair. It was the first time I'd done that. I wanted to occupy his aspect. The desk was longer than I recalled, stretching the width of the two windows that overlooked Yardley Street. I put down my glass and saw a couple of bottles of Scotch at the edge of the desk, one half-finished, the other unopened. I reached for the opened bottle and topped up my drink. To the right a bookcase with deep shelving was replete with literature encompassing topics such as criminology, psychology, crime culture, punishment and social control, and the criminal justice system. There were no books on music; I may have forgiven him for every wrong he'd done had there been even one.

A sheaf of papers protruding from the top shelf caught my attention. I had to stand on the study chair to fetch them down. When I saw what they were, my throat burned. But I refused to cry. Not for that bastard soul. The corners of the sheets were rendered black, and the suppressed memories from that night flooded back in one thrashing swoop.

It was the surviving sheet music of the compositions I'd written in my late teens and early twenties. I'd thought they had all been destroyed.

I downed my drink and refilled it. Within minutes I'd finished that one and poured myself a third. I sat in the chair with the music sheets spread before me. On one of the shelves was a record player. I found the vinyl of his favourite album, Bruce Springsteen's *Nebraska*, and lowered the needle to track five, 'Highway Patrolman'. I poured a fourth drink.

At some point Paco came to the door; he immediately retreated when he saw my state.

I don't remember much else, but I remember the thoughts: *That bastard. And Wes too. Bastard. Fuck this family.* I stared at the burnt remnants of my compositions as I drank, only getting up to start the record again from the beginning of side A.

#

A hand shook my shoulder. 'Wake up.'

I fought to open my eyes, and Wes drew into focus. He was holding out a glass of water. With effort I pushed myself off the desk and took the glass.

'Finish it,' he said.

I gulped it down.

He refilled the glass from a jug and handed me two Panadol. 'Take these, and drink down the whole glass.'

I did as instructed.

He filled it a third time. 'Take your time with that one.'

The headache was blinding, but clearly he was trying to pull me into a state where he could tell me something. I glanced at the whisky bottles on the table. Only one half of the two bottles was left.

'What time is it?' I said.

'Three.'

'In the morning?'

He shook his head.

'Did you give Nic the flowers?'

'Sten's in trouble,' a voice blurted out.

At that I sat up, and saw Labuschagne standing behind Wes. I moaned, my head aching.

'You don't know that,' Wes said to him.

Labuschagne held up Sten's Gladstone bag. 'I know something happened.'

'Where did you get that?' I asked.

'New Norfolk station.'

'When?'

'Last night. The train appeared, but Sten wasn't there. After it vanished I found his bag on the platform.'

'You saw the train?' I didn't think I could handle Sten boarding his train in the same week I was rejected in eight seconds.

'What the fuck am I supposed to do with this information?' Wes said.

Labuschagne jabbed a finger at Wes. 'He would never get on without his bag. Something's happened. He's in trouble.'

CHAPTER TEN

Wes, labuschagne and I stepped down from the footbridge onto the platform at New Norfolk station. Situated along a stretch of line no longer in use, the station's platform was a wild garden. Weeds covered the crushed stones between the wooden cross ties, and grass sprouted from the cracks along the concrete landing. The decrepit island platform ran for sixty metres, with a red-brick stationmaster's office situated at the far end.

Labuschagne placed the Gladstone bag on its side. 'This is where I found it.' He continued walking along the platform. Wes and I trailed after him.

'Which track leads into town?' Wes asked.

Labuschagne pointed to his left. 'It's the same rule as for the road.'

I glanced through a broken window in the stationmaster's office and caught sight of a homeless man curled up on the floor. I was about to say something to the others, but Labuschagne turned at the weathered green bench a few metres behind the building.

'This is where I was sitting. I arrived after nine, an hour later than planned. I had to speed to get here. When I ran onto the platform and didn't see Sten, I was shocked. My only fear was that he'd boarded the train and I'd missed it. Not for one moment did I think I had come to the wrong place.'

Wes rolled his eyes. 'You believed this because of that crystal trick?'

'It's a technique.'

'Your signal was obviously strong,' I remarked.

Labuschagne nodded. 'Like helicopter blades.'

'If you were so sure, why were you running late?' Wes asked.

'Because of you.'

He frowned, confused.

'I was locking up the bookstore when two police officers arrived. You let it be known I've been living there.'

'That's what you get for leaving cryptic messages under the windscreen-wipers of unmarked police vehicles.'

'The most important moment of my life, and I have to sit through an hour of questioning by two imbeciles whose only goal was to make me uncomfortable.'

Wes was unmoved. 'You got here, didn't you?'

Labuschagne indicated the bench. 'Anyway ... I was sitting there all hot and bothered, thinking I'd lost my opportunity, but at the same time feeling something wasn't quite right. It was this feeling that stopped me from leaving – a sensation in my belly that the train hadn't yet arrived.'

Wes arched an eyebrow. 'You're a man of many talents.'

'In my field, instincts are critical. I know when to be watchful and silent, and when to walk away.'

Wes snorted.

Labuschagne turned his attention to me. 'I don't know how long I waited – maybe thirty minutes – when I saw a light bearing down from that direction.' He pointed west. 'It appeared like a dim sun or a bright moon. My heart leapt. This was it. I thought, *The line is out of use, the crystal foretold it ... what else could the light be but the ghost train?* And then my feeling changed: *Where's Sten? Oh my god. The train is here and Sten is nowhere.*'

'Why didn't you call him beforehand?' Wes asked. 'I mean, if the crystal's a lock?'

'Sten tolerates me. That's the best way to describe our relationship. In fact, I would say for him it's more like a game. He never invites me, and I never ask. In twenty-two years we've only come together in three locations. What separates us are our motives. He wants to board the train, and I want to record him boarding the train. As connected as we are by fate and timing, we are as different as a wildlife photographer and an eagle that is hunting.'

'You found his bag,' I said. 'He was clearly here.'

'That's what worries me. I never caught sight of him. When the ghost train arrived I forgot about Sten. I was transfixed. It wasn't like anything I'd ever seen before in my life. Black and imposing, steam billowing from its body. And big. And I say this truly ... it felt to me like it was alive. That it was a beast breathing in the night. I'm convinced it was watching me.'

'Were you standing in line with it?' I said.

'I was facing it head on. It terrified me so that I retreated around the back of this building.' He went to stand behind the stationmaster's office, and pointed along the platform towards the footbridge. 'From this position I lost view of the locomotive, which is what I wanted, but I could still see the carriages.'

'And that's when you saw the bag?' Wes asked.

'That's when I noticed the end carriage door was open – the only carriage with the light on, just as Sten described. But still there was no sign of him. Then the train whistled, and I remembered that I needed to record it. Can you believe it? In the moment the train appeared, I forgot my objective. I grabbed my phone and opened the camera app.'

'I suppose the app froze, or something equally convenient?' Wes said.

'Oh, I recorded it,' Labuschagne said, taking out his mobile. 'Equipment dysfunction is a UFO phenomenon. Ghost trains apparently not so much.'

'You got footage?' I said.

'My success in capturing fifteen seconds is the most important accomplishment of my life.'

Wes and I huddled around him as he opened the video file. The recording started, and there it was, beastly and imposing, a vintage steam train standing at this unused railway station in New Norfolk. From the recording, nobody could question its physicality. Heat rising into the night, it looked as serious as a bull in a ring.

Its final movement was heart-stopping to watch. The big wheels chugged forward, the camera swivelling as Labuschagne tracked the train sweeping away from the platform – then, as it gained speed in the near distance, disappearing into the air with the grace of a ghost.

After it vanished, the camera swept back along the platform, and there by the footbridge was Sten's Gladstone bag. Labuschagne lowered the phone, and we peered over at the bag as it lay there now, glinting in the afternoon sun.

'Can you understand my concern?' Labuschagne said.

'Clearly he boarded it, but in his hurry dropped the bag,' Wes said. 'You were looking down at your phone. You said so yourself.'

'I agree that's a likely explanation – coincidental, but plausible. Another explanation might be he was already on the train.'

'You think he threw his bag onto the platform?' I said.

'Why not? He sees me standing here and runs to the back carriage to throw it out before the train departs.'

'Why would he do that?' I asked.

'Maybe he wants to tell us something, and the answer's in one of the journals.'

'Now you're reaching,' Wes said.

'Well, whatever happened here wasn't planned. My gut's telling me something's wrong.' He eyeballed Wes. 'And I trust my gut. I'm a well-tuned professional when it comes to paranormal gut-feel.'

'I hope you're including this in your report,' I said to Wes.

'It's not a report,' he huffed.

Labuschagne's eyes darted from Wes to me. 'Report?'

'I'm putting together an explanation,' Wes said. 'Would you mind flicking me the recording? It would be very helpful.'

'Me too,' I said. 'As a reminder of what a dream becoming reality looks like.'

Labuschagne shrugged. 'No problem.'

We made our way back along the platform, and as we passed the stationmaster's building I glanced through the window. The man was still asleep on the floor. Wes and Labuschagne hadn't noticed him, and I didn't point him out.

#

Wes dropped off Labuschagne and me at Phantom Time Books.

I pointed to the sign above the door as Labuschagne rummaged through his pockets for his keys. 'What's the story behind the name?'

'Phantom time?'

'Yeah.'

He scooped up the mail that had been slipped under the door, and stepped down into the shop. 'The idea that the Middle Ages either didn't happen, or they occurred in a different era.' He went behind the counter to turn on the hard drive and monitors.

'You believe that?'

'Naturally.'

'You believe everything.' I meant it as a compliment, but it sounded like a criticism. 'What I mean is … you believe in ghosts. You believe my father is communicating through a lamp, and my mother is communicating through an ouija board. You believe in Sten's train.'

'You're looking at it through the wrong filter. I don't believe in things – I believe in the people who believe in things.'

'You're exactly like Sten.'

His expression softened. 'That's the highest compliment anyone has given me.'

He disappeared into the aisle cordoned off with a sheet, and came back out with a tin kettle. He filled it at a little basin I hadn't noticed before. Opening a bar fridge, he took out a carton of milk. I hadn't noticed the fridge either. Speaking of things unnoticed, there were many items blended into the shelves that were easily missed if you weren't looking for them: a plate, a bowl, cutlery, two mugs, a vegetable knife, a frying pan, a small pot and a single gas burner. The bed was propped up by a mattress of books.

Labuschagne said, 'I recently read an article about people who live in tiny spaces. When I say *tiny*, don't think of a room the size of a study, think of the area under a large desk.'

'Japan?' I once spent a week in Kobe sharing a six tatami mat room with a Canadian contrabassoonist. It made me feel claustrophobic just thinking about it.

'Hong Kong,' Labuschagne said, spooning instant coffee into a couple of mugs. 'The article had a tragic tone, but to me the images were liberating. As I clicked through them I thought, *I could do it. I could actually live in a space that small.* And then I thought, *Wait ... I'm already doing it.*'

'If you tell that to Paco, he'll burst an artery.'

Labuschagne smiled, and splashed a dash of milk into each mug.

'Those police officers who dropped by earlier,' I said, 'are you worried?'

With the flick of a hand, he dismissed the question. 'I dealt with them.'

'Sounds like you're marked.'

He scoffed. 'Police are naturally interested in me. I'm in contact with influential entities.'

'I'd tread carefully if I were you.'

The kettle boiled. He filled the two mugs and handed me one. 'Let me show you my system for tracking paranormal activity.'

'I thought you relied on crystal and instinct?'

'The crystal is for confirmation; my instinct is for self-preservation. I use other avenues to generate leads.'

'Interesting.'

He ushered me into the aisle that was his room, and pointed out the portable hardware on the shelf at the head of his bed.

There was a three-legged stool positioned before it. 'GPS enabled, 9000 channels,' he said. 'Critical for my operation.'

'Impressive.'

'This is where I spend my nights. If there's an anomalous event in Kempton, I can be on the Brooker Highway in three minutes.'

I found it easy to visualise the intensely concentrated South African, headset on, crouched on the little stool as call-ins flew through the airwaves.

He gestured to the computers at the counter. 'That's my other source.'

'Google?'

'The dark web.'

I was holding the mug to my chest, as this seemed like a mug-to-chest kind of subject. 'I don't know anything about the dark web.'

'It's nothing complicated. Basically a part of the internet you can't find with a search engine.'

'But what you're doing isn't illegal.'

'True. But us anomalous practitioners like to interact without scrutiny.'

'Cool.' I had a sip of coffee.

'Different channels for different subject areas. It's here I learned of the ghost train's arrival in Hobart, and your brother's name and level of involvement. It's also here I broadcast a message to Sten to alert him of the train's location. Later I'll send out a notification to others that I have his bag, and that he's potentially boarded the train.'

'You think that's wise?'

'I have a duty.'

'To whom?'

'Sten's a celebrity. Thousands of people are invested in his story. What happened last night is the likely conclusion of a forty-year chase, and there will be vigorous debate over whether it's a comedy or a tragedy.'

'I had no idea.'

'Theories will surface like bats exiting a cave.'

'Did you see the homeless man?' I'd been waiting to mention this to Labuschagne. Wes was police, and police couldn't be trusted with people that didn't matter to them. *His* words.

'What homeless man?'

'In the red-brick building. He was sleeping on the floor.'

He pulled a face. 'At New Norfolk?'

'Yeah.'

'There's a witness and you didn't *say* anything?'

'He was sleeping or passed out or high. Probably he was passed out.'

'Oh my god. You must go back now immediately.'

'Why?' I expected him to say that.

'To find out if he saw anything. We need verification.'

'What about you?'

'I'll put some feelers out on the web. Also, I'll organise the journals.'

So this was what freedom was for Labuschagne? For him it was the chase.

That made me concerned for his well-being. 'You should move out until things cool down.'

'Don't worry about me.'

'They'll target you now. I know police. I come from police.'

He shrugged.

'Stay at the house,' I pressed. 'You can have Sten's sofa. You have nothing to lose by coming. But if things go south, you could lose a lot.'

'It's kind of you to offer.'

'Sten painted for board. Maybe you can resolve this lamp situation for us.'

My intentions weren't wholly pure: Labuschagne was Sten 2.0, which made him the perfect replacement buffer for Wes.

Labuschagne perked up at the suggestion. 'I'd be honoured. I'll come with you when you get back from New Norfolk.'

#

Paco and Camille were standing in the hallway when I strode into the house. Camille was her usual stoic self, backpack over a shoulder and ukulele in hand. Paco was holding a folded envelope.

'Pretend I'm not here,' I said, leaving the door ajar. 'I just need to grab the car keys.'

'I'm leaving,' Camille said.

'Oh.' I glanced at Paco. His eyes were red.

'Thank you,' she said. 'For picking us up. For letting us stay. For everything.'

I didn't know how to react, understanding the heart across from her was breaking. 'Thanks for helping Sten, and for making the house bearable.'

'Camille, let us give you a lift to the highway,' Paco said.

'Absolutely,' I said. 'I'm forgetting my manners. I'll just get the keys.'

'No, no. I can walk. I want to walk.' She moved towards the door.

'You're getting everything you want,' Paco said. 'Let me have this one thing. Let us give you a lift down the road.'

Camille conceded, and we filed out of the house in silence. They both climbed in the back, but sat away from each other on the short drive to the end of Federal Street.

'This is the only place to hitch on the Brooker,' I said, pulling over.

Paco got out, before Camille could protest, and walked her to the corner. It was a brief farewell, and he came to the car without looking back.

He climbed into the passenger seat. 'Let's go.'

We pulled off.

'Are you okay?'

'She is stronger than me. That is why I love her.' He wound down the window and stuck out his arm. 'I had to pretend I wanted to stay. I don't want to stay. My heart is like smashed glass.'

'What did you say in that letter you tried to give her?' I waved my hand. 'Sorry. It's none of my business.'

'What? The envelope?'

I nodded.

'A plane ticket. For the flight I'm catching on the sixth of February.' He took the envelope out of his pocket and dropped it on the dashboard.

'Come for a drive,' I said. 'I'll show you where Sten boarded his train.'

'Sten got on his train?'

I'd forgotten Paco didn't know. 'Yeah, it looks like it. Labuschagne saw the whole thing, sort of. We need to confirm the details.'

'Sten boarded his train.' Paco let out a sigh. 'Normally I'd be so pumped.'

I pulled into the Big Bargain Bottleshop on Federal Street and bought a bottle of red wine.

#

Thirty-five minutes later we pushed open the gate at New Norfolk station and cautiously made our way down the ramp. The dipping sun cast a gloomy shadow across the platform, making it difficult for us to pick out the discarded syringes. With Paco a half step behind, we edged towards the stationmaster's office.

I wanted to see the homeless man before he saw us. As fearful as I was at causing surprise, I was more concerned about being surprised. We came in line with the red-brick building and saw the man lying on the bench Labuschagne had been sitting on when he'd encountered the ghost train.

I raised an open hand, signalling for Paco to stop. 'Excuse me,' I said from a distance of five metres.

He didn't respond.

Oh god, I'm going to have to walk over and prod this man.

'Mister,' I said, louder this time.

He stirred, and settled back into his sleep or high.

On the drive over, I'd brought Paco up to speed on the objective of the mission and told him he needed to go with the flow. He said he liked the phrase 'go with the flow' a lot.

Now he watched in horror as I bent down to collect a small stone, and took aim. I meant for it to land nearby, to catch the man's attention, but it hit him squarely on the forehead.

'Wazzat!' he said, swatting at fresh air, a wild look in his eyes.

'Sorry. I didn't mean to hit you.'

'What the ... the fuck, man!'

'I apologise. It was a mistake. Can I talk to you?'

'Huh?'

'I came here to speak to you. I didn't mean to scare you awake.'

He pulled himself into a sitting position. 'What you want?'

I stepped towards him but quickly backed off when he reached down and came out holding the neck of a broken bottle, the jagged edges pointed at us.

'Now wait a minute. You need to calm down. I don't mean you harm.'

'We're fucked,' Paco said. 'Or he's bluffing. There is no middle ground.'

The sensible thing would have been to retreat to the car. But I didn't feel we were terribly threatened, as the man's condition suggested at the very least we'd break even in an exchange – and should the situation escalate, a smart jog would outrun any attempt he might make to chase us down.

'Stay cool,' I said to Paco. 'Focus on the flow.'

By his expression I could tell he was no longer ecstatic about the flow.

'Who are you?' the man said, feigning a jab.

'Detective Warrant Officer Cliff Wilson.' I opened my wallet and flashed my old student card. I didn't know where I'd got the name, or if such a rank even existed.

'I saw fuck-all,' he said.

'I didn't ask you anything yet.'

'Well if you ask, I'm telling you ... diddly squat.'

'I appreciate your time and effort in helping the force.' *Where was this language coming from?*

'Shit, man, what you want with me?'

'I need to clarify one or two things about what you didn't see.'
I held out the bottle of wine. 'For your cooperation and allegiance
to the flag, please accept this cabernet shiraz merlot blend.'
Who spoke like this? And what flag?

He became interested. 'I suppose as my train's late anyhows.'

I smiled, then said in a serious tone, 'I want to know about
a man who got on the train last night. Did you see anyone?'

'A sip from that bottle might loosen my memory.'

I handed Paco the wine. Giving me a pissed-off look, he
stepped forward to hastily pass the man the bottle.

He unscrewed the cap and took a swig. 'I saw a man.'

'Can you describe him?' I asked.

'He wasn't short or tall.' The man shrugged. 'Just normal.'

'What about his face? Or something else that stood out ...
something that might help me identify him in a line-up.'
Very un-Geo. But very Wes. Interesting.

He squinted. 'This bro wanted?'

'That's not important. I believe I know this person, I just
need to know he's who you saw. Can you remember any details
about him?'

'Shit, I don't know, man.' He took another sip. 'Truth is I didn't
notice him until the train arrived. I thought I was alone.'

'Were you sitting here?'

He pointed at the stationmaster's building. 'In there. Sleeping.'

'And then what? It arrived and woke you?'

'Like a grumbling bull. It woke me alright. Made me shit
bricks. Trains don't pass this line no more.'

'How can you be sure it was a train? I mean, how certain are
you —?'

'You mean, was I drunk? Was I high?'

'How can you be sure?'

'I muthafucking started back-peddling, is how I'm sure.'

'You're making rock-solid points.' *'Rock-solid' was the best adjective that had ever exited my mouth. But it was completely un-Geo.*

''Cept, and this is the thing ... 'cept I look out the window, and this bro comes out the shadows, running. The train's about to leave because the whistle just sounded, and this bro's running. He's running and his bag's swinging.'

'A swinging bag. Good. Specific.'

'He's going for the back door. That's the other thing. The back door's the only one that's open.'

Ghost train confirmed. 'And he got on ... that's what you saw?'

'God's my witness. But he paid a price. That door started closing, so he jumped. But the door closed on his arm. He had to let go of the bag to pull in his arm. This bro had balls, man.'

This was the detail. Labuschagne would be pleased. 'Did you get a look at the windows? Notice any passengers?'

'Yeah, a boy, staring out. I remember him because he had a mark on his cheek.'

I nodded. 'Very good. Remarkably specific. Did the train seem real to you?'

'It was real, alright. Real when it arrived. Real when the bro jumped on. Real when the door closed behind him. Real right up until the thing muthafucking vanished in front of my eyes. And that's the truth.'

Paco said in a low voice, 'I'm so pumped I think I *am* flow.'

I said to the man, 'What happened to the bag?'

'After the train disappeared, this other bro came from behind the building and took it.'

'He left with the bag?'

'Far as I could tell.'

'You've been very helpful.'

He didn't say anything.

'On behalf of the Queen, I'd like to thank you for your time and service.' *What the fuck?*

He raised the cabernet shiraz merlot blend. 'The Queen.'

Paco and I made our exit. I'd secured the information Labuschagne required. At the car, Paco said, 'It's unbelievable the experiences I'm having at such a young age.'

#

A *closed* sign hung from the door of Phantom Time Books when Paco and I got back to Elizabeth Street. After a few knocks, Labuschagne came out of the aisle with a headset around his neck. He let us in, and we followed him down onto the landing.

'Sten boarded the train,' I said.

'I know.'

'He lunged onto the carriage, and the door closed on his —'

'I'm up to speed.' He swivelled around the larger of the two monitors on the counter. The screen showed the footage of the train from the previous night, paused at the point before it departed from the platform. 'I ran the recording through some sophisticated editing software.' He grabbed a book to use as a mousepad. 'One of the forum moderators hooked me up with super-resolution filter enhancers. What I saw stunned me.'

'Wait. Before you play it, can I ask a question?' Paco had his hand raised like a student in a classroom.

Labuschagne looked at him.

'Is this the video of the ghost train from last night?' Paco asked.

'Yes.'

Paco shook his head in wonderment.

Labuschagne pressed *play*.

Paco's hand shot up again.

Labuschagne pressed *pause*.

'This bookstore … this is where you sleep?' Paco said.

Labuschagne nodded.

'This is where you perform your duties as president of your organisation?'

'Commission,' Labuschagne corrected him.

Paco's cheeks flushed.

Labuschagne pressed *play*.

Paco said, 'Can I just say, my blood is bubbling with elation right now.'

Labuschagne pressed *pause*. 'Are you finished?'

Paco was staring at the screen with glazed eyes. 'I don't know why we are waiting? I am so excited.'

The video played uninterrupted. The quality was unremarkable, being the same footage Labuschagne had shown Wes and me earlier that evening. Yet the sequence where the train vanished, as if slipping through a paper cut into a different dimension, was stunning on second viewing.

'That's the unedited recording,' Labuschagne said. He closed the interface and opened a new file. 'Now watch the footage where I de-interlaced the video to reduce the noise.'

He played it in slow motion from the point where the train left the platform. With the colour levels balanced and the highlights and shadows enhanced, the clarity was exceptional. The train shifted off, and in this footage the passengers in the window seats were easy to discern. The majority were staring forward, and of the female passengers I wondered which was Sten's mother. I caught sight of the boy with the birthmark on his cheek, the only passenger looking out the window. It sent a shiver up my arm.

The final carriage drew into view. This one held a lone passenger, and in the frames that followed, the occupant banged violently on the window. It was Sten.

Labuschagne rewound the recording and paused on the precise frame in which Sten's face was pin-sharp. The Swede seemed startled, his pounding fist frozen in midair. He was staring directly at the camera.

My eyes welled. 'That's one of the saddest things I've seen.'

'Why is he panicking?' Paco said. 'He is finally on his train.'

'I agree,' I said. 'If I won a place on a major orchestra, I'd be doing cartwheels across the stage.'

Labuschagne rewound a few seconds and played it again. 'His focus should've been on reuniting with his mother.'

'That's what I think,' Paco said.

'He was clearly trying to catch your attention,' I said to Labuschagne. 'Maybe he wanted you to get his bag so some random didn't get their hands on it?'

'I don't know. Nothing about it makes sense.'

Paco wandered off. 'Do you have a toilet?'

'No,' Labuschagne said.

'That's okay. I'll pee in the basin.'

'Boet, you absolutely aren't pissing in the basin.'

'Oh,' Paco said, surprised. 'I can probably hold it.' He pulled back the sheet to the aisle that was Labuschagne's living quarters. He turned to Labuschagne. 'You sleep on books?'

Labuschagne nodded.

'It reminds me of the capsule hotels in Japan,' Paco commented. 'Kapuseru hoteru. I've never slept in one, but I will before I die.' He slipped behind the sheet into the aisle.

Labuschagne watched after him. 'The guy literally exists on the signal line. Very rare.'

Paco re-emerged. 'It's my ambition to be confined in a space this small at least once in my life. Three months would be the perfect length of time. The smaller the space the faster the spirit grows. This is what I believe. World record holders for sitting in a cage with venomous snakes are the most enlightened people on earth. I'm only twenty-two, and already I've experienced so much. Can you imagine my spirit if I lived in a space such as this?' He shuddered at the thought. 'I'd combust from wisdom.'

I noticed Sten's journals on the floor in one of the aisles. They'd been arranged into a grid of eight rows of four. Atop each journal was a system card. I crouched down to read a few: *Seville, 1979*; *Caracas, 1985*; *Vladivostok, 2011*; *Tromsø, 1997*.

Labuschagne and Paco came up behind me.

'How many cities?' I asked.

'I've only scratched the surface,' Labuschagne said. 'But after forty years, you can imagine.'

'His energy is overwhelming.' There was a crackle in Paco's voice.

'Are you crying?' Labuschagne said.

Paco ran a forearm across his eyes. 'I thought we were the same spirits in different bodies, but we couldn't be more different. I am moving to be still, and he is moving to catch something … I miss him so much.'

Labuschagne pointed at the journal labelled *Hobart, 2018*. 'Check out the last entry.'

The page showed a sketch, the product of a remote viewing session. In the foreground were parked cars, and in the background a spread of yachts. The notation read: *Bellerive, Monday, 25 January.*

'It's the wharf at Kangaroo Bay,' I said.

'The Sorrell line,' he said, nodding. 'It ran out of Bellerive from 1892 until 1926.'

'Sten told me he almost boarded his train there in 1987. The year I was born.'

'Well ... he predicted it's coming there next Monday.'

'Good,' Paco declared. 'I will be waiting.'

I was less sure. 'What will this accomplish? I mean, even if we see him?'

'Let's first intercept the train,' Labuschagne said. 'After that we'll worry about what to do. Maybe he'll have forgotten about his bag and be talking to his mother. That would be the perfect scenario. But if he's still in a state of panic, perhaps he'll signal to us what he needs. Or maybe he'll get off.'

I shook my head. 'He's not getting off. He chased it for too long.'

I picked out a different journal and opened it to a random page. It showed the sketch of a train and was titled, *Boston, October 2012.* Another journal page detailed the dimensions of a platform in Bratislava, accompanied by a top-view sketch of the sighting. A scan through a selection of others referenced Buenos Aires, New Orleans, Jakarta, Kobe, Tel Aviv, Bogotá and Moscow.

I wondered if thirty years from now the footprints of my pursuit would have the same crisscrossing reach as Sten's. It was a staggering record of a dream. It said, *This person went where they needed to go.* It said, *It doesn't matter the cost, I go.* It said a mountain about sacrifice. It said the heart wins against reason. It said everything about readiness, about departing on command. It said, *Clinical.* It told of the relentless drive to get somewhere. It said, *There is nothing I'm not prepared to leave behind.* Even more than this, it said, *To be in motion I must be free of connection.* It said, *This is what it means to go alone.* And now that he'd realised his dream, this archive was the only evidence of his sacrifice. Because he had nothing. It said, *Nobody will miss me. Nobody will come looking for me.* It said, *Nobody will share in this with me.*

'I'll be there,' I said.

CHAPTER ELEVEN

O N SUNDAY MORNING Paco costed the materials needed to finish the house. 'If I also do the studio, and I believe I have the time, we'll need five litres of primer, twenty litres of white dove, four litres of pure white, and two litres of cottage green.'

I emptied the contents of my wallet onto the coffee table and counted a shade over $300. It was all I had until I flew out. My return ticket to Italy was booked, and I had €2000 banked away in Rome, my seed money for the next audition opportunity. I was prepared to dip into it, but I needed to be practical. If Wes continued to fight me on the house it might be months before I capitalised on my inheritance.

Within the hour I was standing above my viola case in Elizabeth Street Mall, playing Berlioz's *Harold in Italy*. It was slow for a Sunday, and after Bach's *Chaconne* I'd only amassed one dollar and twenty cents. I went over to one of the benches to have a smoke, and as I lit up Giacomo Pedroni approached me.

'Bellissimo,' the mayor of Orvieto said. 'You play with a true spirit.'

'Grazie, Giacomo. Come vanno le cose?'

'Va bene. We are leaving soon. So … no complaints.'

'They have given you a date?'

'They have given us a promise. We are waiting for temporary passports.'

'It must be a testing time.'

'È tollerabile … Besides, I am able to walk through your quaint town every day.' He pointed to my viola. 'Mi piace *Harolde en Italia*. Did you know Berlioz only wrote it because Paganini had a big Stradivari and asked him to create a concerto for him? But Paganini did not like it and would not play it. Later, of course, he changed his mind.'

'I never knew that.'

'È vero. A work of genius is often the suggestion of some-one else.' Before I could comment, he bid me farewell. 'Buona giornata, amico.'

He meandered off, and when he disappeared around the corner I went to pack away my viola. As I closed the lid a business card slipped out from the inside sleeve.

I dialled the number on the card.

The voice that answered was wary. 'Yes?'

'Hello. Is that Matthew?'

'I don't know a Matthew?'

His response caught me off guard. 'Uh … you introduced yourself as Matthew when we met. Your card says Matthew but doesn't have a surname.'

'I think you have the wrong number.'

'No, you're the person. I recognise your voice.' I squinted at the card. 'It says you're a truth-seeking journalist-slash-watchdog. "Slash" is written as a word, not a character.'

'Where was this?'

'Where what …? That you gave me your card?'

'Yes.'

'Royal Hobart Hospital. Two-and-a-half weeks ago.'

There was a pause. 'Are you the detective or the other person?'

'The other person. So you are Matthew?'

'I prefer Robert. Call me Robert.'

'Okay … Robert. Are you still interested in the situation involving the Italians who arrived here by train?'

Another pause. 'Where are you now?'

'Elizabeth Street Mall.'

'Are you alone?'

'Yeah. I have a proposition for you. I was wondering —'

'You're not speaking under the instructions of the detective, are you?'

'No … I —'

'I am interested. But people are listening.'

Very cliché-like – very Geo, in fact – I scanned the crowd in the mall to see if anyone was watching. It felt like everyone was watching.

'Do you know the Blue Dog Body Mod Studio?' he asked.

'No. Um … when you say "people", who do you mean exactly?'

'You should be able to see it from where you're standing. Across from Target, next to the shoe repair shop.'

I turned around. 'I see it.'

'It's a friendly place. Speak to the person behind the counter. But before you do … the card with Mason on it —'

'You mean Matthew?'

'Put it in your mouth and chew it for a bit. Then discard it in one of the receptacles.'

I pulled a face. 'I'm not putting your business card in my mouth.'

'In that case, keep it secure. I'll dispose of it when we connect.'

The line went dead. I picked up my viola and crossed the concourse with a bowed head, not wanting to draw eye contact from anyone.

A narrow staircase between the shoe repair shop and a record shop led up to the studio on the first floor. Three identical prints of a greyhound at full stretch decorated the Persian blue walls. Philip Glass played softly in the background. Two women seated in the waiting area, faces full of piercings, spoke in whispers as they thumbed through well-worn portfolios.

The man behind the counter was on the phone. He had an infinity symbol scarred into the skin above his left cheekbone, and the tip of a black tattoo at the bottom of his neck suggested something ominous lurking beneath his shirt. I waited at a respectful distance, pretending to admire the body modification photographs on the walls. I sensed his eyes on me as he spoke, and it took me a few moments to realise he was talking about me.

'Uh-huh,' he said. 'No, alone.'

I turned around.

He didn't blink. 'Nondescript hair. Five ten. Nondescript clothes. Violin.'

I stepped up to the counter.

'No problem,' he said, and replaced the receiver.

I waited for him to say something, but he just looked at me for a while.

Finally, he asked, 'Are you any good?'

I glanced at my viola case. Very un-Geo, very confident, I said, 'I'm excellent.'

'How much for half an hour?'

'It depends on the setting.'

'I have a corset body piercing on Wednesday. Stressful procedure. I'll pay you thirty dollars to play while I do the work.'

'Music can make a difference?'

'I don't know – it's what I'd like to know.'

'I wouldn't do it for less than fifty.'

'Be here at eleven. Now this other business.' He held out his hand. 'Your phone.'

'No chance.'

'You don't go past this point with your phone.'

His determination was so complete I fetched my mobile from my pocket and handed it to him.

He motioned for me to follow him down a narrow corridor. We passed five cubicles with artists at work, and after glancing into the first and seeing an artist splitting a man's tongue with a heated blade, I trained my eyes forward.

The end cubicle had a tattoo bed on one side, and on the other a sofa and a low table. The man with the infinity symbol went over to a safe in the corner and locked away my mobile. 'Your phone is more secure here than in a bank safety deposit box. When you come back, ask for me.'

'What's your name?'

'Just describe my face.'

'Okay.'

'Now … you go to Comicopia. Do you know it?'

'The comic shop in the Cat and Fiddle Arcade.'

'You'll receive your next instructions there.'

I crossed the Elizabeth Street Mall and went into the Cat and Fiddle. Comicopia was the first store on the other side of the food court, across from Just Jeans. I walked in, fully expecting someone to lock eyes onto me as they spoke into a phone. The counter was vacant. As I scanned the people perusing the aisles, I couldn't distinguish the customers from staff.

I lingered at the counter, knowing this would signal my arrival to whomever was charged with sighting me. A woman in her late twenties came over and slapped down a ream of comics on the glass countertop. She glared outside the store with a *what are you doing?* expression. I followed her gaze and found my mark.

Outside the entrance, leaning against the window of Just Jeans, was an early twenties man clad in a flat cap and a T-shirt that read: *Sarcasm is my Super Power.* He sucked on a toothpick as he watched me.

I sauntered over, and he held out a comic to me: *The Eyes of the Cat.* He spoke with the toothpick still in his mouth. 'Centrepoint parking, level four. Take the stairs by the toilets. Keep the comic visible. You're looking for a green Volkswagen Beetle.'

I stared at him.

He brushed past me. 'Go now.'

'Fuck's sake, Donnie, I'm supposed to be on my break,' the woman at the counter said.

The narrow lanes of the Centrepoint car park spiralled in tight turns for seven floors above the shopping centre. I stepped out onto level four but found no green Volkswagen parked within the vicinity of the door. I held the comic to my chest on the assumption a pair of eyes were trained on me through binoculars.

I needed the money, but this had gone beyond money. My return home had flung me into the company of people whose strange objectives boiled with an intention that made them seem more tangible than my own. It was, in fact, a lesson in dreams: people only needed to take themselves seriously in order for others to believe in what they were trying to do. Whether the dream itself was realistic, was irrelevant.

The first car to sweep around onto level four was the target vehicle. A more defining descriptor than its colour would have been its condition – it chugged around like it was limping away from a fight, a strange *click-click-click* exiting its engine. I held the comic in an unnatural pose beside my head. The Volkswagen jerked to a halt, and the driver, whom I presumed to be Robert, formerly Matthew, forced open the passenger door.

I climbed in, and we lurched off.

'Rupert,' he said, extending his hand.

'On the phone you said Robert?'

'That's right. Robert. I appreciate your patience in being vetted. I'm very interested in what you have to say.'

I reached for the seatbelt, but there was none. 'You have interesting friends.'

'They're allies. That's the first thing you learn in my field: a person has allies and enemies. There's no such thing as a friend.'

'What exactly is it you do?'

'What it says on my card.'

'So you're a journo.'

'Don't compare me to those fools. News organisations are propaganda mouthpieces. That's another thing you learn.' He held out an open palm. 'Speaking of my card.'

I took it from my shirt pocket and dropped it into his hand. In a move redolent of Camille and the pademelon bones, he folded it in half, and in one sweet movement placed it on his tongue and started chewing it. I stared at Rupert or Robert and thought, *This man is a hero.*

Three other cars were parked on the open top level. We pulled into a bay at the far end and got out. Rupert or Robert went to the corner and emptied the ball of pulp from his mouth into a drain. He came back with his hands in his pockets. 'Speak.'

I wished I had a toothpick for my mouth. It seemed like that kind of occasion.

'I know everything about the train,' I said.

'So there's no confusion, we're talking about the Italians?'

'There isn't one fact about the situation I don't have.'

'Give me a number. I can tell you have a specific number in mind.'

'One thousand.'

He raised an eyebrow. 'Did you not notice my car? Do I look like someone who pays their sources well?'

'I was hoping that wasn't another thing about your field.' My boldness was un-Geo and very Wes.

He searched my face for a weakness; I didn't flinch. 'It will depend on the quality of the evidence ... I'm assuming the evidence is exceptional.'

'Three things: access to the journals of the person who's been chasing the train for forty years; video footage of the train disappearing at an abandoned station in New Norfolk; and the date and location of the train's next appearance in Hobart.'

His eyes widened, but he was still difficult to read. He scratched his chin, and as he looked about to give his verdict, his mobile rang. 'Yes, it's Kyle,' he said, turning from me. 'I'm in the middle of something.' He shook his head. 'I'm meeting Bertrand at five. Are you free after eight?' He nodded. 'Something about the Saudis exporting camels to the outback.' He hung up, and turned back to me. 'This is my offer.' He opened an old leather wallet devoid of plastic cards and took out a strip of crisp fifty-dollar notes. He peeled off ten. 'Five hundred now, for the story. The balance you get when you deliver the three pieces of evidence.'

I took the money, and he opened the Dictaphone app on his mobile.

I gave him the whole gambit, from the twenty-seven Italians to Wes, Labuschagne, Sten, the body and the backpackers, and Sten vanishing. I told him the backpackers' testimony was on record at Hobart Police Station. What might not be on record, I told him, was the identity of the victim, a one Wayne Barnes. I asked that he be recognised, as everyone's truth mattered equally. I told him how Sten had been chasing the train for four decades, and that he'd recorded everything in his journals. He asked when he might see them, and I said we'd schedule something that suited him and Labuschagne. I told him Labuschagne was the president of an organisation that investigated anomalous incidents, and he said he and Labuschagne were aware of each other, and that the organisation was actually a commission. I detailed the night Sten had boarded the train, and he asked after the footage; I said I'd swing it his way in due course. I made it clear there wasn't a police cover-up, but that they were reluctant to investigate the situation, because really, what was the situation? I told him the police were treating the Italians as a 'sweep-it-under-the-carpet situation' – Inspector Henry Sutter's words. I told him the Italians were presently awaiting temporary passports so they could return home, and that he'd find them passing time in the lobby of Hadley's Orient Hotel. I informed him that Detective Wes Rosenberger was compiling a theory – an unofficial explanation, not a report – and that it may or may not be submitted to Wes's superiors. I gave him the context for the final appearance, and told him I'd provide the date and location after the next instalment of fifty-dollar notes was slapped into my hand.

Kyle stopped the recording. 'Let me just say, I love the story … because it isn't a story, it's history. Let me also say, I'm eager to complete the transaction.'

#

A light drizzle began to fall as I walked up Elizabeth Street. It reminded me of an early gig with the quartet at Fanfulla in the Pigneto Quarter. Unable to find parking near the venue, we'd traipsed more than a kilometre with our instruments to get there. In such instances you're thankful you're not the cellist. It was a wonderful night at my favourite setting in Rome, the thirty-something hipster crowd giving our music generous attention from the corner bar, football tables and cushy sofas. Because it was our last gig of the year, we were in good spirits as we made our way back to the van. Then the skies opened like sluice gates. One moment we were dry, the next we were wet as the sea. Our immediate reaction was to start running, but we quickly accepted our fate and retreated into a walk. So drenched were we that we began to dawdle; it then became a competition to see who could walk the slowest. We started laughing. Alessia, Lisa, Elena and me, walking and laughing in the rain. I wanted to be back there. With Alessia, with my friends, where I belonged.

I passed the State Cinema and recalled the night with Sten on the bus bench, waiting for his ghost train. I imagined him at a window seat, thinking, *I am on my train.* Perhaps he was in conversation with his mother, too consumed in their reunion to feel any satisfaction. Or had he become one of the black-and-white passengers, bored and staring, stuck in a loop? How would I feel in the week after I'd won a place in an orchestra? I imagined being giddy with excitement, but realised I might be so overwhelmed that accomplishing my dream wouldn't be celebrated. You didn't win a place on an orchestra; you won an opportunity to play with the company for a period to see if you were a good fit.

I pictured Sten and his parents caught in the emotions of reuniting. There was a lot to feel, but what was there to tell? In all this time, Sten had achieved nothing apart from finding them again. Would they be proud of him, or would they be disappointed there wasn't more news? A wife. Children. He'd sacrificed life's experiences so he might one day look at them and say, 'I am here.'

I turned onto Yardley Street, eager for a warm shower. I hopped up the steps to the front door, and lo and behold, sitting on the porch with a violin case and a small suitcase, was Alessia. She rose with a smile. 'Geo.'

'Oh my God! Less!' I put down my viola and rushed into her arms. 'I want to say something to you right now – I've been thinking about the words all day. I love you so much!'

'I love you too.'

I kissed her, and leaned back. 'What are you doing here?'

'I wanted to be with you.'

'You're truly wonderful. When did you arrive?'

'About two hours ago.'

I hugged her again. 'I'm in shock. I'm so happy to see you.'

#

Alessia placed her violin on the cane chest in the hallway, then meandered into the sitting room. I winced as she registered my father's rubbish. She didn't say anything, and proceeded through the rest of the house with her arms crossed. In time we found our way back into the sitting room among the overflowing ashtrays, unwashed glasses and empty liquor bottles, and the recliner, armchair, and sofas that were our makeshift beds.

'This is the mess you put away?' she asked.

'Yes.'

She retreated into the hallway to collect her baggage, and stood before my bedroom. 'This is your room?'

'Actually, I've been sleeping in the sitting room.'

She turned around, and from her expression she didn't have to say anything for me to know she was disappointed. It wasn't for how I was living, or how far music had slipped in my priorities; it was that I hadn't confided in her.

'Come here,' I said, holding out my arms. She put down her bag and violin, and we hugged. 'I can't believe you came all this way.'

'I was heartbroken when you told me about the audition.' She pulled away. 'Where shall I put my things?'

'Leave them in the hallway. We'll sleep in my bedroom, but we'll let Paco clear out his things first. Let's go for a coffee. Are you hungry? Tired? Tell me what you need.'

'I'm all of those things. But first I would like to take a shower.'

'Of course.'

I gave Alessia a fresh towel, then made for the kitchen. I cleaned what I could, but it was futile – the place was a disaster.

When she came out, I showed her the backyard. 'It's lovely,' she said. 'Can I go into your mother's studio?'

I opened the door, and she stepped inside and out onto the deck. We looked across the garden down to the house.

'It has good energy,' she said.

'I definitely feel her spirit when I play here. God, my heart is racing, Less. I can't believe you're actually in Hobart.'

'I am in Australia for ten days only. That is all I can afford to take off with the quartet. On Saturday I will go to Sydney to visit Federico for a few days. I will come back on Tuesday. He is getting tickets for me to watch him at Cirque.'

'That's good. I'm glad you're seeing Federico.' I felt a bite of jealousy.

'You are welcome to come.'

'No. You've been talking about seeing him for a long time. It will give me a chance to finalise things here. If everything goes smoothly, perhaps I can change my ticket to the same flight as yours.'

'That would be nice.'

Alessia insisted on helping to clean the house. I pointed out the objects that couldn't be touched, and she accepted these caveats without judgement.

'You smoked too?' she asked, taking two overflowing ashtrays to the kitchen.

'I have been. I'll stop when we leave. I'll stop now.'

She returned to the sitting room and collected an empty bottle of Scotch and bourbon.

'How were the others with you coming out?' I asked.

'We were able to cancel some gigs, and there were a few gaps. Elena and Lisa will be happy to know you are coming back.'

'I'll be happy to play with them again. I've been doing a lot of thinking about that – things I'll share with you over the coming days.'

She kissed me on the cheek. 'We need music.'

'We only have my father's vinyl record player.'

She disappeared into the study, and a minute later Roberta Flack's *Chapter Two* swept through the house. Alessia did a breezy pirouette and scooped up a rubbish bag.

Within a couple of hours we'd restored the other living environments to a reasonable state. We changed the bedding in my room and put out two washes. By the time we were done, five garbage bags stood alongside the bins around the side of the house.

As tired as she was, Alessia wanted to stay awake to ward off jet lag. We left a note for Paco and went down the road for a meal.

#

Paco had cleared my bedroom of his things when Alessia and I arrived back from dinner. She turned in soon after, and I joined Paco and Wes in the sitting room. Labuschagne was at the kitchen table working through Sten's journals.

Wes waved his cigarette in the air. 'Let me make a prediction —'

'Please don't.'

He went over to fill his glass at the cabinet. 'Drink?'

'Thank you,' Paco said.

I shook my head.

He handed Paco a whisky and offered me a cigarette. I declined.

'I think I'll turn in,' I said, getting up. 'I thought I wasn't tired. I'm tired.'

Later that night, I became aware of someone calling my name. I believed I was in the throes of a nightmare, standing across a railway line, faced off against the pulsating yellow glow of the living, breathing ghost train. A silhouetted figure emerged at the side. Sten? Perhaps his father? As my eyes adjusted to the glaring light I saw that there were two people, one standing behind the other. They were staring at me.

It was Paco and Labuschagne.

'What are you doing?' I said.

'Geo. Wake up.'

I squinted towards the door. Paco was leaning in, Labuschagne standing off his shoulder. The light wasn't from Sten's train in a dream; it was from my father's lamp flickering from inside the bedroom cupboard.

'Shit.' I glanced at Alessia. She murmured, and turned over.

Paco said, 'Your door wasn't closed, and when I went to the bathroom I noticed the light flashing.'

I slipped from the bed. 'We need to get it out of here.'

Paco and Labuschagne waited at the door, probably thinking I would bring out the lamp. But they quickly realised I expected one of them to remove it. Paco stepped aside to allow Labuschagne through.

'Quietly,' I said.

Labuschagne opened the cupboard and retrieved the lamp. The light was going berserk again, flashing up to a full glow then dying out in a slow fizz before flashing again. The plug dragged along the carpet behind Labuschagne as we left the room.

Alessia stirred. 'What's happening?'

'Dad's lamp is flashing again,' I said. 'Don't get up.'

'No, I want to see. I will come out.'

Paco placed the lamp on the coffee table in the living room, and we stood around it.

'Wes?' I said, nodding in the direction of the sitting room.

'Sleeping,' Paco said.

Labuschagne shook his head, and pointed to his ear. 'Listening,' he mouthed.

We turned our attention to the flashing object. Alessia was wide awake. It was impossible not to be impressed by the flickering unplugged light, but she showed no fear. I don't think any of us were truly frightened by this point, although it wouldn't be accurate to say I was comfortable with the activity.

'How many times has it happened?' she asked.

'Five, including now.'

'This is my third time to see it,' Paco said.

'Me too,' Labuschagne said.

Alessia glanced at me. 'Which time was the one when I was speaking with you on the phone?'

'The last time. We put it in the studio that night. The first time was with me, Sten and Wes.' I pointed at the door to our father's study. 'In there. The second time was in here with all of us.'

'And Camille,' Paco said. 'She's gone to the West Coast now.'

'I tried to communicate with it,' Labuschagne said.

Alessia raised an eyebrow. 'With a lamp?'

'We think a spirit is speaking through it,' Paco said.

'We believe it's Geo's father,' Labuschagne added.

Alessia looked at me.

'"We" is a tricky word,' I said.

She said to Labuschagne, 'What do you think it is saying?'

He glanced at me. 'The third time we communicated was through an ouija board. That's when we realised there are two spirits. The father is communicating through the lamp; the mother communicated through the board. We asked her to translate what the father was trying to say through the lamp.'

'And what did she say?' Alessia's arms were crossed; her posture was demanding.

I shifted uneasily.

Labuschagne glanced at me. 'Geo asked us to say goodbye – to close the board.'

She maintained a blank expression, and I found it difficult to read her thoughts.

'I am going back to bed now,' she said.

'Me too,' I said.

Labuschagne indicated his silver case in the corner. 'Do you mind?'

I shook my head.

'Goodnight,' Paco said to us.

I followed Alessia back to the room, and it wasn't long before we were asleep again.

#

The following morning Alessia and I drove up to kunanyi / Mount Wellington. At the lookout we used the diagrams etched on the glass window to spot the landmarks below. There were a number of people out on the boardwalks, and it seemed everyone was appropriately dressed except for Alessia and me. It had been eighteen degrees when we'd left North Hobart, but at 1200 metres the temperature was below five.

'You live in a beautiful city,' Alessia remarked.

'I don't notice it anymore.'

We didn't stay long, and on the drive back down she said, 'You will be free of this. You already are, but soon you will know it.'

She was aware of the history with my father, but I hadn't told her about that final night. This felt like the moment. The only person who knew was Nic, and that was because she'd wandered into the aftermath.

Seeming to sense my unease, Alessia attempted to change the subject. 'I can help you style the house. We have time before Saturday. Then all you have to do is finish outside.'

'That's kind of you, Less. But I only have enough cash for the paintwork. A thorough clean will have to do.'

'It will not cost much to get a few second-hand pieces. I have a good eye. We can busk together for money.'

Her optimism encouraged me. 'Of course we can.' After driving a bit further, I said, 'You know how you're always telling me I should compose?'

'I believe it is your talent.'

'Something happened that made me stop. Something on my final night in Tasmania.'

She stared ahead.

'You said you want to know me completely. There's only one important thing about me you don't know. I want to share it with you now. You came all this way.'

'I love you.'

I squeezed her hand. 'After Mum's funeral I knew I had to get out of the house. I'd only moved back to take care of her, and there was no way I could last a week living with our father. Audrey was in Sydney with Opera Australia. I told her not to come back for the funeral – it would have meant missing her first solo performance. She'd been rehearsing for three months, and anyway, Mum would have forbidden it.

'The night after the funeral, my father and I got into it.

A real mongrel of a fight. With Mum gone there was no buffer. He called me a "nothing", told me I had no talent, that I should get a real job. He was drunk, of course. He was drunk throughout that final year, limping around the house, bumping into stuff.

'We were itching to say the things we'd wanted to say ever since that bullet had lodged in his leg. This was our chance. I'd soon be leaving. We both knew it. So I told him straight. I told him he was a different father to Wes than he was to me. He told me Wes was a man. I told him I didn't respect him or Wes. He told me I was a failed musician. I told him I didn't know how Mum could love someone like him. That's when he struck out at me. But with his leg, and in his drunkenness, it was like trying to snatch a fly. I told him he could never disappoint me, because how can you disappoint someone who doesn't love you.'

I shuddered at the honesty with which I was relaying the memory. I glanced at Alessia as I turned onto Huon Road; there were tears in her eyes.

'I had two fathers, Less. I loved the first one. I remember him. I don't think about him much, but I remember him. The second father I despise. A real swine. Wes never knew the second father – he'd already moved out. But that night three years ago, I told our father to his face what I thought of him, and on word stakes, I won. He stumbled back into the sitting room, and I went into my bedroom. The next day I was moving out. I'd made up my mind. I'd ask Audrey's parents if they'd help me out for a night or two while I found my own place. They understood my situation.

'I don't know how long I slept, but light piercing through the curtains woke me. The same moment I opened my eyes I realised my left hand was cuffed to the bedpost. My focus landed on my father standing at the foot of the bed, a cigarette dangling from his mouth. He was watching me with a smug look on his face, waiting for me to register the situation. I saw the bin at his feet, and the sheet music of my compositions in his hands. And I knew what was coming. He'd drunk through the night, and now he was going to win. I kicked out and shouted, trying to lunge at him. He smiled, and took the cigarette from his mouth and moved the cone to the edge of one of the papers. It felt like an eternity, but eventually the sheet caught alight. He held it up as it burned, and dropped it into the bin. He proceeded to burn one sheet at a time while I screamed. They were the only copies of the music I'd composed. Finally, after crying myself out, I was reduced to a whimper. I watched helplessly as he burned the remaining sheets. Everything I'd ever written. The look of satisfaction on his face was terrifying. When it was done, I watched as he left the room, closing the door behind him.

'And there I lay, the loser. I tried to pull myself free of the handcuffs, but clearly it was pointless. I don't know how much time passed – possibly I fell asleep again. Sometime later, the door opened. I braced myself, but it was Nic. She'd brought over some cooked food, and when she heard me calling, she rushed in. The keys for the handcuffs were in the sitting room. She released me. I was weeping. We hugged. But then I went into action mode. I threw clothes into a bag. I packed my viola. I called a travel agency, booked a one-way ticket to Rome. Why Rome? Probably because Mum's home town was in the region. There was a flight departing that night from Melbourne. I had an Italian passport, and the flight from Hobart to Melbourne left in two hours. I booked it, emptying my bank account in the process. Nic watched in silence. I called a taxi. Of course, as luck would have it our father arrived

back before the taxi. There were some final exchanges. I told him
I'd never forgive him, that I wasn't ever coming back. He told me
I wasn't welcome back. And that was how I left Hobart.'

I took a deep breath.

'Pull over,' she said.

I glanced at her.

'Pull over. Please.'

I slid into an open bay on Macquarie Street. We got out,
and on the side of the street, with cars sweeping past, we held
each other.

#

We parked in the cul-de-sac by the wharf that was once the goods
yard for the Bellerive–Sorrell line. From there, Alessia, Paco and I
made our way up the narrow path to the footbridge that crossed
Cambridge Road.

As dusk was turning to night, we found Labuschagne on
the footpath beneath the bridge, triangulating the ghost train's
arrival with his pendulum. Not wanting to interrupt him,
we waited back. He had a faster technique than Sten: whereas
Sten allowed the circling crystal to use up its energy before he
released it, Labuschagne dropped the pendant into his palm at
the slightest movement that revealed a clockwise or anticlockwise
direction. With this speed he tested various points on the footpath on either side of the bridge, then ascended the ramp onto the
bridge to take a reading above each of the four lanes that served
Cambridge Road.

He came back down near to where we were standing, and
unbuckled a small backpack. Alongside it was Sten's Gladstone bag.

'The train is definitely coming tonight, and it's coming here,' he said.

I watched the traffic funnel in both directions between the Tasman Highway and Bellerive's one-street CBD.

'We should probably call Wes,' I said. 'If a train materialises here there will be casualties.'

'The only thing that might result in casualties is this.' Labuschagne rose with a metal instrument in each hand – they looked like divining rods – and strode out into the road. He took a position between the two lanes on our side, drawing to a standstill the stream of cars approaching from the Clarence Street lights. The sound of tooting horns filled the air. Ignoring the commotion, Labuschagne held the rods out like an Aussie Rules footy umpire signalling a goal. The metal arms crossed sharply. Apparently satisfied, he came back over to the footpath. The traffic moved again, someone shouting from one of the vehicles, 'Knob.'

Labuschagne was unperturbed. 'Everything is confirmed. Now we wait.'

We went up onto the footbridge and leaned over the railing above the two lanes that led out of Bellerive.

Labuschagne passed me his pendulum. 'I'll handle the rods. You take the pendant.'

'Uh ... sure.'

'Please also take responsibility for the case.' He passed me Sten's Gladstone bag. 'If the train appears while I'm working the rods, sprint to the back carriage and throw it on board.'

'Okay.'

'What's the difference between the rods and the pendant?' Paco asked.

'Not much – they both rely upon the ideomotor effect.'

'I know about this effect ... the body reacts reflexively without the person consciously making the action.'

Labuschagne looked impressed. 'That's high-level knowledge.'

'How is it possible you know so many facts?' I said to Paco.

He shrugged. 'It's surprising even to me. I'm very young.'

'It's the same principle as the ouija board,' Labuschagne said. 'These methods are all tapping into paranormal forces. I mostly use my mother's pendant, as it's less obtrusive and easier to carry out quick readings in public without people noticing. But divining rods are where my natural gifts lie.'

'I'm a pendant person myself,' I said.

Alessia frowned. 'What do you know about such things?'

'I tried a couple of times with Sten.'

'Sten didn't use a pendant, he used a crystal,' Paco said. 'He let me try as well.'

'Even so,' Alessia said to me, 'did you do it with the rods yet? To know for certain what kind of person you are?'

'The rods look unwieldy – I wouldn't like the feel of them in my hands. The pendant takes a clean technique, which appeals to my sensibilities.'

'I'm a surface person,' Paco said. 'Ouija boards and table-turning. I suspected this for a long time, but when we did the ouija board with Sten and Camille, I was convinced.'

'This Sten sounds interesting,' Alessia said. 'I wish I could meet him.'

Paco bowed his head. 'Sten is my hero. I miss him so much.'

We were watching the road absentmindedly as we spoke. Every few minutes a fresh stream of cars was released from the Clarence Street intersection, throwing up gusts of wind as they swept beneath us.

Labuschagne peered at Alessia across from Paco and me. 'What kind of person are you?'

She didn't hesitate. 'I am more for my instincts. I get a feeling about people and things. And I trust my feelings above everything.'

'A clairsentient,' he nodded.

I frowned. 'What's that?'

'A guts person.'

'I have excellent guts,' Paco said. 'One time in Tenerife I was sleeping on a beach under a palm tree. An electric storm arrived suddenly during the night. The palm leaves gave me shelter, but my feeling was bad. I moved immediately because I recognised something wasn't right, and found a dry spot beneath another tree further along the beach. The next day I came back to that first place, and the tree had been struck by lightning.'

'Incredible,' I said.

He nodded. 'I am only alive because of my instincts. So yes, I would say I'm a guts person and a surface person equally.'

Labuschagne glanced at Alessia and pointed at the Clarence Street intersection. 'What do your feelings tell you about that man over there?'

We all squinted, and quickly found the target. Lying sniper-like atop the roof of the Abra Kebabra Kebab House on the far side of the intersection, wearing a Kangaroos footy cap and with one eye pressed to a telephoto camera lens aimed in our direction, was the journalist known as Matthew or Mason or Robert or Rupert or Kyle.

Alessia appraised the situation. 'My reaction is that there is a man interested in what we are doing here. My feeling is that his interest is friendly.'

'His name's Kyle,' I said.

Paco was alarmed. 'Someone tell me it's a lens for a camera and not a sight for a rifle.'

'He's a watchdog person,' I said. 'His passion is the truth. There's nothing to worry about.'

'That makes me relieved,' said Paco. 'In fact, it makes me pumped.'

'Message him to come over,' Labuschagne said.

I pulled a face. 'What makes you think I have his number?'

'He called today to schedule a time to look through the journals.'

'Oh yeah … I meant to give you a heads-up about that.'

Labuschagne turned to Alessia. 'Your instincts are impeccable. Mine are limited to hauntings, UFOs, cryptozoology, things of this nature. I'm envious of people who can perceive people.'

I messaged Kyle: *We see you. Join us.*

Kyle's head came away from the lens to look down at his mobile. He peered in our direction. I waved. He pushed himself to his knees and packed his camera into a bag.

Paco's eyes lit up as he watched Kyle slide down the side of the kebab shop to street level. 'For most of my life I was the most interesting person I knew. I searched the people around me, and I say this with complete modesty – there was no one more interesting than me. Only when I started travelling did I realise, *Yes, I am one of many.* Hobart is a supreme example … you, Sten, Labuschagne, Alessia, and now this Kyle. It's possibly the most interesting place on earth.'

'His name may not be Kyle,' I said.

Labuschagne said, 'He introduced himself as Cale when we spoke this afternoon.'

Paco held out his hands. 'When I say "pumped", I'm talking about facts like this.'

Kyle or Cale walked up onto the footbridge.

'Everyone … Kyle or Cale,' I said.

He shook Paco's hand. 'Call me Carl.'

After our introductions, Kyle or Cale or Carl said to Alessia, 'I know everyone but you.'

'She arrived from Rome three days ago,' I said.

'Plane or train?' he asked.

She shot me a quizzical look, and I shrugged. 'He's being serious.'

'Plane,' she said.

We wiled away the evening watching the traffic as we waited for the ghost train. Labuschagne had his divining rods in each hand, ready to go; Carl had his DSLR camera slung around his neck; and I had Labuschagne's pendant in my shirt pocket.

The highlight of the evening was when Labuschagne told us about the Silver Arrow.

'Who has been to Stockholm?' he asked.

Alessia raised her hand.

'Did you notice the colour of the metro trains?'

'Green,' she said.

'That's right. Except for one … Silverpilen. The only train out of a fleet of hundreds not painted. It was originally used as a back-up during rush hour.'

'I rode it,' Alessia said.

Labuschagne seemed disbelieving. 'You rode the Silver Arrow?'

'I didn't know it had a special name. All I knew is a silver train arrived at T-Centralen station, and my parents and I boarded it.'

'What year was this?'

'I was ten, so ... 1995.'

'You're very lucky. It was a rare sight even for locals.'

Carl took a photo of Alessia.

'I didn't feel lucky at all,' she said. 'The inside walls were covered with graffiti. The green trains were shining clean, but this silver train had a feeling of ...' She glanced at me. '"Distopico"?'

'Dystopian,' I said.

Labuschagne shook his head. 'What I mean is, you're lucky you experienced it when you did. It was decommissioned in 1996. If you'd boarded it one year later, you'd still be riding it.'

'Please tell me before I burst,' Paco said. 'Are you saying this train was normal before 1996, and afterwards it was a ghost?'

'The myth surrounding the train was there from the beginning. But it went to another level in 1996 when Silverpilen was pulled from service, as to see it was to conclusively experience the legend.'

'Which proves Alessia boarded a normal train,' I said.

Carl evidently thought we were devolving into a story in which we were the characters, and began taking photos of us from different angles.

'You could not be more wrong,' Paco said. 'If I buy a painting from a market and hang it on my wall, then years later I learn the painting is a Dalí ... what did I buy in that moment in the market? My point is —'

'I understand your point ... did it become a Dalí when you realised it was a Dalí, or was it always a Dalí? But your point is missing the point.'

Paco threw his hands in the air. 'The point is she got on a ghost train.'

I was as surprised by Paco's objection as I was unwilling to concede. 'The train had physical properties when she boarded it.

Those properties changed, which means we're dealing with two things. Just as life in a body is a human being, but separated from the body it is spirit, so there is the train and the ghost train.'

Paco waved his finger. 'The only reason I ask your forgiveness in disagreeing with you is because you've welcomed me into your home. But this is the opposite of logic.'

'You just said something completely illogical,' I said.

He pounded a fist on the railing. 'Of course a thing shouldn't be defined by its potential … but it also shouldn't only be defined by what it is.'

'What else is there?' I asked.

'What it is becoming.'

That's when I realised he was speaking about me.

'When did you first call yourself a musician?' he asked. 'When you started making money from music? No. I expect probably before you were ten. Labuschagne said the myth around this silver train was there from the beginning —'

'Silver Arrow,' Labuschagne said.

'Which means it was always ghost.'

A smile creased Carl's face as he decompressed the shutter on his camera.

I shrugged. 'I'm sorry. I just don't see it.'

Carl chose this moment to pass Alessia his card. 'I'd be inter- ested to write about your experience. I pay well. Ask your friend.' The name on the card was *Paul*.

'Uh … thank you,' she said.

Carl or Paul said to Labuschagne, 'Speak more to the legend of the train.'

Labuschagne perked up at this, and Paul changed his camera setting to a fast shutter speed and snapped away.

'What's interesting is that it meshes together two separate narratives. The locals were already afraid of Silverpilen – it wasn't unusual to see commuters wait for the next train if it arrived unannounced at their platform – as they believed anyone who boarded it would disembark weeks or years later. But it's when the train became connected to Kymlinge that the myth went to another level.'

'I've been to Kymlinge,' Alessia said.

'Where's Kymlinge?' I asked.

Labuschagne's eyes were fixed on Alessia. 'An uncompleted metro station that was said to be Silverpilen's home. You've been to Kymlinge?'

'I remember it clearly. My father told me it was a ghost station as we passed through.'

'How can you possibly remember such a detail if you were only ten?' I said.

'I remember *because* I was ten. It scared me.'

Paco shook his head. 'People are amazing.'

Paul raised his eye above the viewfinder. 'Speak to the narrative of connecting Silverpilen to Kymlinge. Speak about myth.'

Labuschagne said, 'The basic beats are a young woman getting on the aluminium train and noticing the other passengers are pallid in complexion. When Silverpilen doesn't stop at any of the stations, she panics. But the passengers don't react. The train eventually pulls into Kymlinge, and the passengers move right through the train's locked doors and disappear. Depending on which version you hear, the girl is either found dead or insane in the woods of Ursvik. As the saying goes, "Only the dead get off at Kymlinge."'

'You're lucky to be alive,' I said to Alessia.

Paco was dismayed. 'I see my first dead body – which catches me up to the rest of the world – and now I find out people are riding ghost trains? This is what I mean when I say life is the asshole.'

A glimmer of metal caught my attention. I glanced down to see the rods in Labuschagne's hands slanting inwards. He leaned away from the railing, and the rods whipped violently across one another. 'Pendant,' he said.

I took it out of my shirt pocket, and even as I fixed the clasp between my fingers I felt the energy surging though the chain up my arm. It circled above my palm like a fairground swing.

'Feelings?' Labuschagne said to Alessia and Paco.

Paco shook his head. 'I'm mainly a surface person.'

'I feel that it is coming through this lane,' Alessia said, pointing at the fast lane leading out of Bellerive.

'Bring the case,' Labuschagne commanded, and strode off the bridge.

I grabbed the Gladstone bag and hurried after him down to street level. Alessia and Paco remained on the bridge with Paul, who repositioned so he had a better angle of the fast lane.

Labuschagne tested his rods at the side of the road. A wave of cars passed us in both directions. I stood silently behind him.

'I feel this is the point,' he said. 'But I don't know if it will be the front or back of the train. Be ready to run if it's the front.'

Gripping the handle of the case, I felt the perspiration in my palm. How had the key action been passed into my hands?

Paco's panicked shout from above drew me to the present moment. 'Don't.'

Labuschagne strode into the road, horns blaring as the traffic came to a standstill. He stood in the centre lane and held out the rods. The front cars swerved to miss him, and in the next beat there was gridlock as a growing line of cars were backed up on each side of the road.

I crouched like a middle-distance runner at the start of a race, ready to dart out should the locomotive appear before me.

Above the blaring horns was a faint sound like rolling thunder. Labuschagne raised his arms like Christ the Redeemer, and as the roar reached a crescendo he tilted his head and closed his eyes. At once we were enveloped by a swirl of rushing air. It was the energy and sound of a passing train, but there was no train. There were only six lanes of stagnant cars cut by a lone figure in the centre of the road, still and serene, as ghostly as the locomotive that passed through him.

The whistling sound dissipated, and the disturbed air was replaced by the honking of horns up and down Cambridge Road. In the next moment two police officers in reflective vests stepped out from the traffic and apprehended the statuesque Labuschagne.

CHAPTER TWELVE

THE NEXT MORNING the front door banged open, and Labuschagne spilled into the hallway with Wes in tow. I was frying an omelette at the stove, and Alessia was sitting at the kitchen table with a mug of coffee. Outside the window Paco was setting up materials for the day's work.

'There's no need to treat me like this,' Labuschagne protested. 'I'm probably the most mild-mannered prisoner your station has known.'

Wes turned him around and roughly unlocked the handcuffs. 'You broke the law.'

'I embarrassed you by being me … there's a difference.'

It was a valid point. There was only one mode for Labuschagne, and that was very Labuschagne.

Free of the cuffs, he shot Wes a parting glance and came through the sitting room into the kitchen. 'Where's Sten's case?' He spotted it on the floor next to the table, and relaxed. 'Thank god.'

Paco popped his head inside, and when he saw Labuschagne his face lit up. 'You looked fucking amazing last night. Your head

241

back, your hair flying around as the ghost train passed through you. You looked like art.'

Labuschagne accepted the characterisation with Sten-like casualness. 'It felt like art. It felt like —'

'When is this going to end?' Wes pointed his finger at me. 'It's bad enough you've turned our home into an open house, but when these same people are dragged into my station I draw a line.'

We all stared at him.

His face reddened. 'It's not a rhetorical question. I want to know – how long before you're done screwing with my life?'

I opened my mouth to speak, but Paco beat me to it. 'I think I'll finish the second coat today. Tomorrow I'll do the window frames, and after that the studio.'

'The photographer's booked for Sunday,' I added.

Paco nodded. 'In that case I'll push to do the gutters too. Let's hope it doesn't rain.'

Wes glared at me. 'You've booked a photographer?'

'I told you this already. Alessia's helping me style the house. We're shopping for a few second-hand pieces this morning. We'll work around our father's rubbish for now, but I'll need to clean everything out by the weekend.'

Wes stormed off and slammed the front door behind him.

Our heads all turned to Labuschagne.

'What does it feel like to be art?' Alessia asked.

He was caught in a state of wonderment. 'I don't know. Miró's *The navigator's hope*? I've been attacked by a demon before, but a train passing through me is not like that. In fact, I highly recommend it.'

'*The navigator's hope*.' Alessia nodded. 'I understand perfectly.'

'Did the cops charge you?' I asked.

He shrugged. 'Seventy dollars for jaywalking.'

I shook my head in disgust.

'Weren't you afraid?' Paco asked. 'I believe you were a lot closer to dying than you think. I saw that body on the track three weeks ago. The train was a ghost probably up until less than a second before it hit the man. In the click of a finger it went from rushing wind to metal. I suspect you were a finger-click from death.'

'The train knew we were there for Sten,' Labuschagne said.

I squinted at him. 'How so?'

'I don't know.' He looked at me. 'It felt emotional. Like friends who are sad because they can't reach each other.'

'You would be very comfortable living in my parents' rainbow community,' Paco said. 'In fact, if you moved to Beneficio, within one year you would be fucking mayor.'

#

After breakfast Alessia and I went bargain hunting. We were looking for three or four well-appointed pieces that might give the house a lift. There was no furniture on the porch, and she felt that a bench was needed in the first zone buyers would pass through. In addition to bedding and towelling, we were also after a new lamp for my father's study, a reading chair for the living room, and a lampshade for the sitting room. I hadn't bothered asking Wes for a contribution, but the previous day Nic pledged $300 from the shoebox money. Her generosity meant we had $500 to work with, and if Alessia and I could generate a little extra through busking we might also afford a few plants.

At Bunnings we picked out the greenery we'd return for later. We set our hearts on a fern in a hanging basket, then identified another three plants for inside, and a larger one for out back. Thanks to Mum there were plenty of pots under the house, so we only needed potting mix. We calculated ninety dollars. 'We can make this busking?' Alessia said.

'Divide that number by five. On a good day.'

She was defiant. 'We can do it.'

At the Antique Dealers & Traders in Margate we found a bench and a lampshade, as well as a welcome mat at the Carpet Junction next door. By then we were famished, and the Margate Train came to our rescue. Set behind the antique store, the decommissioned carriages were home to a collection of handicraft stores and bookshops. We made for the Pancake Train Café and opted for the mixed berries.

'My only regret is that I didn't meet Sten,' Alessia said, when we were seated across from each other in one of the booths.

'He would've liked you,' I said.

'I feel he is still in the house. Not in the way your father is. But there is something about Sten's energy I cannot explain.'

'It's funny you say that – Paco thinks the same thing.'

'He feels that Sten is in the house?'

'No, just that ...' I struggled to convey his perception. 'Just that there was something unnatural about Sten. That he was a part of the train's story ... more inside it than in the reality of chasing it. Something along those lines. Ask Paco.'

'I understand what he means. I don't know Sten, but I feel this too.'

A waitress served our coffees.

'What about you?' Alessia said. 'You felt nothing strange?'

'The strangeness to me was his intensity. His absolute sacrifice, and the complete lack of balance in his life. It wasn't natural. Not because he's unnatural, but because so few people are capable of that. Sten was *there*. In my view, more *there* than any of us. Perhaps we are the strange ones.'

'Do you not think this is also true for music? I feel differently when I play for an audience, compared to when I play alone. When I play for an audience I am there for them; when I play alone, I am just *there*.'

'It's interesting you say that. The day I met Sten, I was busking. He told me I sounded how he felt when he chased his train. Maybe that's what he meant.'

We made our way back into town, and within a couple of hours had tagged the additional items we were after. We were forty-four dollars short.

By the time we began playing in Elizabeth Street Mall it was mid-afternoon. We started out with two pieces we performed with the quartet: Schubert's *Death and the Maiden*; and Tchaikovsky's Waltz from *The Sleeping Beauty* – but the foot traffic took little notice.

I suggested leaving.

'One more,' Alessia said. 'Then we go.'

We slipped into Beethoven's String Quartet No.14 in C-sharp Minor, Op. 131, and Alessia pulled away to move with the music. She performed with a feeling that was entrancing. This was how she performed with our quartet; it was the reason we were popular. She twirled then knelt before a child holding her mother's hand. Normally those seated at the outside café tables paid no attention to the buskers, but here they turned to watch. They applauded generously when we finished, and hands reached into their pockets. We counted fifty-one dollars.

After five, we arrived back at the house with the furniture and plants. Not far behind us was the owner of the Antique Dealers & Traders, who kindly delivered the bench on his trailer.

Paco came down to help me unload it. 'This is good. This is, in fact, perfect.'

Nic arrived soon after, and did well to ignore Wes observing from the porch with whisky in hand.

Alessia said, 'I'll pot everything in the morning before I go to Sydney.'

Nic was surprised. 'You're leaving us?'

'I'm coming back next Tuesday.'

'In that case you're having dinner with us tonight.' She pointed at Wes. 'Not you.' She gave me a kiss on the cheek. 'See you later.'

Wes took a glum gulp of whisky.

#

When Alessia and I got back to Yardley Street that evening, everyone was there. Paco smiled from the sofa that had been my bed, and was now his. He'd been dozing but tried not to show it. Wes was laid up in his recliner. And I was particularly happy to see Labuschagne at the kitchen table poring through Sten's journal. He didn't acknowledge us when we came into the living room.

'What's going on?' Wes asked, tilting his glass at the case in my hand.

'Nic asked me to bring it to you.'

It was his violin. Our eyes locked, as we both understood what it meant. Although Wes still had most of his possessions at their place, his violin was the one thing Nic wouldn't strip away without notice. This was her saying: *There is nothing more for you here.*

'Shall I put it in the corner?' I indicated the area where everyone's belongings were stashed. He said nothing, so I placed the violin next to the recliner. The hard-shell case was covered in dust and cobwebs. I stepped back and wiped my hands on my trousers.

'Do you mind if I look at it?' Alessia asked.

I was alarmed. I could handle Wes targeting his rudeness at me, but I knew I'd struggle to keep my composure if he turned on Alessia.

'I don't care,' he said.

She knelt beside the case, carefully unclipped the lock and lifted back the lid. Whereas the shell looked badly worn for not having being touched for a decade, the violin, suspended on a bed of thick cushioning, was pristine.

'It is beautiful,' she said.

Wes took a drag from his cigarette.

'Can I take it out?'

He shrugged. 'It's fine.'

She undid the leather neck ties and brought the violin into her lap. 'How old is it?'

'It's a 1932 Carlo Melloni,' I said. 'A gift from our mother.'

'I know this make.'

'You can play it if you like,' he said.

'You wouldn't mind?'

'It makes no difference.'

Alessia tuned the violin as Paco and I watched on. The strings were surprisingly responsive. With the humidifier and hygrometer long since ineffective, the Melloni showed durability; there were no signs of shrinkage in the wood, and no open seams and cracks.

Labuschagne came into the living room and sat in the armchair.

After it was tuned, Alessia offered the violin to Wes. 'The sound is bright and warm. But only you can truly wake it up.'

Paco raised his hands in praise. 'That is what I was trying to say when we were at dinner with your family.'

'Perhaps the three of you can play something together?' Labuschagne suggested.

It seemed as if we were ganging up on my brother, and I was certain he would baulk.

He took a drag from his cigarette and stubbed it out. 'Fuck it.'

My jaw dropped as Alessia handed him his violin and bounced to her feet. 'This is wonderful. This is going to be my favourite part of the trip.'

In somewhat of a daze I fetched my viola and pretended to absorb myself in the task of tuning as I watched Wes handle his instrument. If you didn't know the history, you'd have assumed he was a practising player, so at ease was he with it.

'I feel quite nervous,' he said, playing a few chords.

'I always feel nervous when I play,' Alessia said.

'What music do you have in mind?' He was perched at the edge of the recliner.

'How about Terzetto by Maria?' she said.

Wes must have known, as I did, that she'd nominated that piece because like his violin, the composer hailed from Bologna. The score, which had three movements, was created for two violins and viola.

'I'll get the book from Mum's studio,' I said.

I returned with the sheet music and the stand, and positioned them at a comfortable distance for Wes. We readied to play, Alessia led us in, and we came together rather well. For the first minute or so we watched one another, but it wasn't long before the music found its groove. Even within the development of this one movement, Wes's violin had its own level of beauty, and I knew his talent hadn't abandoned him.

We drew to a close after the first movement, and lowered our instruments. It had been a wonderful, spontaneous performance, but no sooner had we stopped than Wes lifted the violin to his chin and played a solo version of 'Shenandoah'. We watched spellbound, and I saw him as my brother. It was an exquisite rendition – technically rusty, but with an emotional depth heartbreaking to the ear. This was the beat stolen from his heart; the lifeblood that balanced his spirit, and which had been absent these many years. Hayden was right: when Wes surrendered to his art, there was no space for anger.

I glanced at the others. Alessia was in awe, and a tear streamed down Paco's face. I wished Hayden and Nic were here. This was what had been missing – music had been missing. You could see it transform him as he played.

He brought the piece to conclusion and lowered his violin. At first no one responded, but then Alessia, Paco and Labuschagne rose in unison to clap.

'Bravo,' Alessia said. 'I do not have the words, in any language.' She went over and kissed him on the cheek.

'Your gift is tremendous,' Labuschagne said.

Paco was so choked up, he couldn't speak.

Clearly embarrassed by the compliments, Wes laid the violin down in the case. 'I think that's enough for one evening.'

'Labuschagne's right,' I said.

He pushed himself to his feet. 'I need a drink.'

Later, as I climbed into bed with Alessia, I said, 'I've never met anyone like you.'

'How do you mean?'

'You change situations. You don't change people – Wes is what he is. The bastard. It's true. I haven't misunderstood him. He is exactly that to me. And yet he's also the violinist who plays with the spirit we saw tonight. To access that beauty, he needs to make himself completely vulnerable. That's what you brought out. If you weren't here, what happened tonight couldn't have happened. That's how I mean.'

#

At some point in the night, a tap on the door roused me awake. For a moment I thought I was caught in a recurring dream of the ghost train, but it wasn't a dream – it was happening again.

'Paco?' I said, peering at the silhouetted figure by the door.

'Yes, it's me. The lamp is speaking. There's no need to come out. But I thought I should tell you. Labuschagne is working the situation.'

I rubbed my eyes. Alessia was apparently asleep beside me. 'I don't know.'

'That's okay. I will leave you.' He quietly closed the door.

Alessia stirred. 'We should go.'

'I don't want to wake you.'

'Your father is trying to communicate. We should go.' She slipped out of bed and put on one of my old T-shirts. I no longer wore T-shirts, and it was strange to see Alessia walking around in clothing that belonged to a version of me I was trying to forget.

When we came into the living room, the unplugged lamp – again positioned on the side table in the centre of the room – burst into a frenzy of flashes.

Labuschagne was sitting on the sofa with his finger poised above the switch for the floor lamp. To Dad's lamp, he said, 'Yes,' and promptly turned the floor lamp on and off. He waited a beat, then said, 'No.' This time he turned the floor lamp on and off twice in quick succession. He waited another beat, and repeated the commands: *Yes*, one flash; *No*, two flashes. After taking a breath, he said to Dad's lamp, 'Is a spirit trying to speak through the lamp?'

We stared at it. I don't know why, but as the seconds ticked by I had a strong inkling Labuschagne's tactic was going to work. The moment I had that thought, the lamp flashed once.

Requesting permission, Labuschagne said, 'Can we continue to communicate with one flash meaning "Yes" and two flashes meaning "No"?'

After a beat, the lamp gave off one flash.

Labuschagne said to the lamp, 'Are you happy to communicate through me?' He was no longer asking for permission; the permission had been granted. He was building confidence with the spirit.

The lamp flashed once, brighter than on the previous occasions.

Labuschagne nodded at us, his expression saying 'breakthrough' – finally, he'd created a corridor through which to proceed with the spirit that was supposedly my father. And I knew then, just as I'd known with Sten when I had fronted the dismembered body in Campania, that Labuschagne was what he claimed to be.

'Are you trying to communicate with someone in particular?' he asked the lamp.

One flash.

'Are you trying to communicate with more than one person?'

Two flashes.

'Are you trying to communicate with someone in this house?'

One flash.

'Is it Wes?'

Two flashes.

Labuschagne's eyes were trained on the lamp, but I felt Paco and Alessia glancing over at me.

'Are you trying to communicate with someone in this room?'

One flash.

He paused. 'Is it Geo?'

One flash, the brightest yet.

Although Labuschagne seemed to understand what the next question should be, he leaned back, projecting the impression he didn't know how to proceed. But he knew, and Paco knew, and I knew. Alessia, however, did not know.

Yet unlike on the night with the ouija board, Labuschagne hadn't explained the rules that there should only be one mediator. So it wasn't any surprise that Alessia stepped forward and said to the lamp, 'My name is Alessia. May I ask a question?'

I was certain Labuschagne would interject and resume the speaker's role, but this was a lamp, not an ouija board – apparently the rules for speaking to lamps are undefined.

Dad's lamp didn't respond.

Alessia said, 'I love Geo. We met in Italy in your wife's home town. He has told me everything about your family. About the pain. But also about the love. He told me about that final night, too. I would like to ask a question. May I ask a question?'

There was a long pause, as if the spirit was processing this new presence. The lamp flashed once.

'Are you Geo's father?' she asked.

A beat, followed by one flash.

'Do you want to tell Geo that you are sorry?'

A beat, and this time not a flash, but the light coming on and staying on. As we watched, it grew brighter and brighter, emitting a faint burning smell, until the globe blew with a shotgun bang, glass exploding across the carpet. We jumped in fright.

Gathering myself, I stared at the lifeless lamp on the table. There was nothing more to it than its physical properties. An ordinary, unplugged lamp. The spirit had departed.

It was Alessia who broke away first. 'I'm going to bed now.'

Paco, Labuschagne and I remained unmoved, our eyes locked on the lamp. After a minute, I said, 'I'm going to bed too.' At the door I turned to Labuschagne. 'Thank you.'

#

After I dropped Alessia off at the airport, I made my way to Blue Dog Body Mod Studio in Elizabeth Street Mall. Viktor – the man with the infinity symbol scar – ushered me to studio three. I took out my viola and bow, and sat down on a stool in the corner. To the left was a tattoo bed, and behind it a bench on which sixteen captive bead rings had been neatly arranged in two lines on a sanitised towel. On a second towel was a scroll of black ribbon, and an assortment of surgical instruments.

'The client knows you're playing. Start as soon as she comes in. It's going to get intense pretty quickly. She's a regular, high pain threshold, but a corset piercing isn't fun.'

'How long?' I said.

'Thirty minutes. Only stop playing when she gets up. Do you get queasy easily? You strike me as the queasy type.'

'No, I … uh, actually, yes. Very.'

'Close your eyes or stare ahead. But don't stop playing. Afterwards I'll get her to rate the pain from one to ten. It's something
I've been wanting to explore for some time. If it works out, we can
discuss a more permanent arrangement?'

'Yeah, uh … sure.'

'What are you going to play?'

'Um … I thought I'd start with *Les Voix humaines* by Marais.'

'Excellent. I don't know it.'

'If ever a piece of music sounded like human breathing, this
is it.'

'Sounds perfect, brother.' He made to leave, but turned at the
door. 'Who was that woman you were playing with yesterday?
We all watched from the window.'

'My partner from Italy.'

He nodded. 'I believe if she played here, nobody would
feel pain.'

Soon he returned with the client. A slender woman with
straight black hair falling below her shoulders, she greeted me
with a smile. I lifted the viola to my chin, and ran the bow
across the strings. The woman started unbuttoning her blouse.
I swivelled on the stool to give her privacy.

A few moments later she was lying face down on the tattoo
bed. Viktor sat beside her, a ruler and marker in gloved hands
above her back.

I played the Marais piece, and watched as he marked eight
adjacent points in two concave lines on either side of her spine.
He put down the ruler and reached for an instrument that looked
like surgical tweezers. Very deliberately, he grabbed the skin above
one of the marks. Holding it taut, he ran a fat needle through

the skin and released the tweezers. I almost dry-retched, and the music dropped off as my fingers sagged. I quickly regathered, and found my way back to the tempo. The needle was only a place holder, and I watched Viktor take one of the bead rings from the towel on the bench and guide it through the skin punctures as he slipped out the needle. In spite of his obvious experience and skill, the procedure was traumatic to witness. My bow came away from the strings, and the room fell silent.

Viktor coughed, and I hastened back to the piece. This time I took his advice and closed my eyes. I tried to concentrate on the music, but images of the needle and ring plundering through the woman's back sat at the front of my mind. Her skin had the toughness of leather, but she was resilient. Her hair fell around her face, and though I couldn't see her expression as Viktor fluently inserted the rings, she was a model of stillness.

The piercing part of the procedure was over sooner than I'd expected. And whereas the first phase had caused my stomach to turn, the lacing of the ribbon was majestic to watch. As Viktor wove the corset, I couldn't help but think he was constructing a train track across the length of her spine. Only when she went over to the mirror to appraise the body art, did I stop playing.

Viktor paid me in cash, and we made a commitment to stay in touch. I didn't tell him I was leaving Hobart.

My phone beeped with a text message as I exited the studio: *Proceed to Phantom Time Books at your earliest convenience. Highly sensitive information has come to light regarding S. Your friend and theorist, C. Labuschagne.*

#

I stepped down onto the landing in Phantom Time Books. Labuschagne was serving a lady at the counter. Behind her a balding man browsed in one of the aisles.

'Would you like a bag?' Labuschagne asked the woman, who shook her head.

He handed her the receipt, and she scooped up her book, *The New World Order* by Pat Robertson, then brushed past me.

'Thanks for coming so promptly,' Labuschagne said in a low voice. He nodded at the balding man. 'Please look around until we're alone.'

'Just to be sure, you are staying at our place until I leave?' It stressed me out that I'd walk into the house to find Paco and Labuschagne departed, leaving only Wes and me.

'Yes. But tonight I'll be later than usual. This morning a ghost ship drifted to shore in Hokkaido. I have a virtual appointment with a contact in Sapporo at 8 p.m. The Japanese deal with situations like this about as delicately as a spider deals with a fly.'

I pulled a face. 'Sounds gruesome.'

'It comes with the territory.'

'In any case, treat the house like you would your home. Come and go as you please.'

His expression softened. 'Sten was right about you and your brother. You are very kind.' He indicated the aisle nearest us. 'Please help yourself to a book. A small gesture of my gratitude.'

Sensing his eagerness for me to separate from him, I turned away to peruse the shelves. After the customer left, I approached the counter with *The Mothman Prophecies* by John Keel.

'Fine choice,' Labuschagne said, recording the title in a ledger. 'It's not covered in the book, but there's a connection between the Mothman sightings and UFOs. I'll tell you about that some other time.'

He flipped the sign on the entrance door to *closed*, and pulled back the sheet that was the partition to his makeshift living quarters. What confronted me was so overwhelming, it took a full minute to digest.

'A shrine to Sten,' I said.

'A timeline of his pursuit,' Labuschagne said, nodding.

A countless number of system cards were Blu-Tacked at chest height to the shelving that surrounded Labuschagne's bed. Each card displayed a location and a date, the first and last of which read: *January 1978 – Rotterdam*; and *November, 2017 – Concepción*. Stapled to the header cards were more cards filled with detailed notes, so that they cascaded down like a ladder. From the journals, Labuschagne had compiled a chronological log of every trip Sten had taken in search of his train.

I was impressed by the detail in Labuschagne's research, but my thoughts immediately turned to the magnitude of the pursuit: five continents and tens of countries and cities. Sten boarding his ghost train was a phenomenal example of tenacity. He had achieved his dream not only because he'd developed skills to intercept the train, but also because he'd persevered long enough. I'd take that every time, I realised; I might not be the most talented violist on the audition circuit, but I would outlast anyone.

'What does the writing in red mean?' I asked.

'Red means he saw the train.'

'That's right,' I said. 'Eighteen times.'

'Assuming Stockholm was the only port of embarkation, we're talking 204 unique trips,' Labuschagne said.

'You've done an outstanding job collating it.'

'His commitment deserves recognition.'

'There aren't any other entries about another appearance in Hobart,' Labuschagne said. 'I've studied every page.'

'Maybe the train has left Tasmania?'

'Not according to the pendant.'

'How wide were the circles?'

'Helicopter wide. I did a dowsing session this afternoon to tune into the train's energy – the heaviest session I've ever done. The train's still in Tasmania, I'm sure of it. The other thing I'm sure of is the location and date of its final appearance.'

Surprised, I gave him a questioning look.

With a wry smile, he disappeared into his sleeping quarters and returned with a pillow. He dropped it at my feet and advanced into the adjacent aisle. I watched him place one of Sten's journals on a three-legged stool, and on top of this journal an empty glass that he filled with transparent liquid from a flask. He came back and picked up the pillow, and stuffed it beneath his shirt. 'Stand behind me. The method I use is very physical.'

'If you're about to communicate with a poltergeist, I'm leaving.'

'I'm opening a channel to a dimension where all consciousness exists. We're just fetching a few details about a specific event in our near future. It's not the kind of channel spirits pass through.'

'Why the pillow?'

'The method I'm using ... it's like a highway rather than a footpath. The pendant struggles to contain the energy when it comes into contact with the target.'

'Have you done it before?'

'I've only seen it in action. I was very nervous when I did it this afternoon, and what I experienced stunned me.'

'When did you learn the technique?'

'When I was thirteen. My mother's boyfriend, a white witch, showed me. He and my mother were arguing about the race of giants that used to roam the earth. They both agreed on the giants, but my mother was postulating they lived in the same time period as dragons. Her boyfriend thought this was ridiculous and used the highway pendant method to settle the disagreement. I suspect there's a bit of black magic involved.'

'What? Placing water on a journal and doing the pendant thing?'

'Not any journal … it's the last one Sten was using. If he was here, it would be the one in which he drew the location of the train's next appearance. It holds the energy of what happens next.'

'So the highway technique requires placing water on an object that contains the potential for a near-future event?'

'I like the way you describe it. But not any water … rainwater.'

'Interesting.'

'The purest form there is.'

'I'd have thought mountain stream water was the purest.'

'That's what most people think, but it's incorrect. Impurities and salts from water on earth are left behind during vaporisation. Remind me to tell Paco – this is exactly the kind of knowledge he's trying to accumulate.'

'It hasn't rained for days. Where the heck did you get rainwater?'

'Ah,' he said, raising a finger. 'This morning Saul called —'

'Who's Saul?'

'You know … Cale.'

'You mean Paul?'

'Yeah, that guy. He wanted to come around to look through the journals.'

'You let him?'

'Well … he paid you $500. What choice did I have?'

'I really should have consulted with you about that.'

'Never mind. After some toing and froing – because who the fuck is Saul? – I added a small fee of my own.'

'Rainwater.' I smiled.

'I told him a litre would give him two hours with the journals. It was a long shot, I know … but this guy has connections. Believe me, if I told you the names of his connections you'd shit yourself.'

'He obviously came through.'

'I was both surprised and unsurprised. I'm saving a glassful for Paco. I know how excited he will be to drink it.'

'That guy probably brought you tap water.'

'No, what I did this afternoon can only be done with fresh, unadulterated rainwater. Besides, Saul and I are useful to each other. He knows I'm in communication with some influential beings. A different kind to his connections. He wouldn't want to jeopardise me as a potential future ally.'

Labuschagne dipped the pendant in the rainwater. I gave a nervous laugh at the pillow under his shirt as he stepped back and took up a position in front of me. I was slightly concerned because he had yet to define exactly what the pillow was protecting us from.

I shuffled behind him as he faced the glass atop the journal, situated four metres from where we were standing. He held the pendant above his left palm. Unlike Sten, who asked his questions out loud, Labuschagne posed them as silent thoughts. Almost immediately the pendant began circling clockwise. The motion gathered speed and height, to the point Labuschagne had to raise his right elbow so the pendant could rotate unencumbered.

I suspected he was asking a sequence of questions, as the rotations continued to build in velocity, like blades coming up to flight speed. I now understood the pillow and why I needed to stand behind him; if he let go of the chain at the wrong moment, a chest hit would be ten times worse than a paintball hit from point-blank range. Eerily, the rainwater started lapping up the sides of the glass.

Very softly, he summarised his interrogative into one query. 'Will the ghost train appear outside the State Cinema on Monday the first of February at 8.05 p.m.?'

The glass exploded with a thunderous crack, rainwater spilling over the journal. In the same instant the chain came loose from his fingers and speared through the air, the pendant lodging in the wooden shelving beside our heads with a stinging thud.

To think that the pillow would have acted as a buffer was laughable. If the pendant had come back in the direction of Labuschagne, it would have sliced through the polyester filling and penetrated his chest.

I gazed at the pendant, sticking out of a shelf like a dart, then leaned forward to wrap my fingers around the metal.

'Don't,' Labuschagne warned.

I heard the hissing even before the pain seared through my fingertips. I recoiled, and when I looked down, my thumb, forefinger and index finger were blistering. Fortunately, it was my bow hand.

Labuschagne wrapped some ice blocks in a dishtowel, and after a few minutes my fingers were suitably numbed.

'First of February,' I said. 'I'll be there.'

'The need to get Sten his case with the journals is more urgent than I thought.'

'How do you mean?'

His expression fell. 'I've learned something else. This is why I asked you to come here.' He went behind his counter of books, returned with a printed newspaper excerpt and handed it to me. It was from the *Svenska Dagbladet*, a Swedish daily newspaper. 'I had it translated. It speaks of an incident where the chairman of the Anomalous Phenomena Research Commission of the Swedish Academy of Sciences was staking out a ghost train in Stockholm. The train appeared. He lunged onto it through the open door of the last carriage. There were several witnesses. The train, along with the chairman, vanished. He hasn't been seen since.'

I felt the warmth ebb from my face. 'When was this?'

'1999.'

'Sten?'

Labuschagne nodded. 'That's the name provided. I made some calls, checked a number of directories. There isn't any record of him after the ninth of June that year.'

'But what does it mean?'

Labuschagne pointed at the index card marked *March 1999*. 'This is the last entry before he boarded that year. It's interesting … when you read the journal entries they are very emotive, filled with angst. Like diary entries. If you don't mind me saying, like when you speak of your auditions. There is a desperation in the pursuit. But following this date, the entries are recorded in a very matter-of-fact style. Factual, and without emotion.'

'You're saying Sten's a ghost passenger?'

'No. I believe he pursued the train for the reason he declared. But I believe he boarded it in 1999 And every time he lands in a new place, he gets off – just like he got off with the Italians here in Hobart. And he searches to find it again as if he never boarded it before.'

'As though boarding it erases his memory of boarding it?'

'I don't understand the neurology. But yes, I believe he was searching genuinely while he was here. Unaware.'

'But this is tragic.'

'That's why we have to be there on the first of February. It's critical we return his bag to him. Without the bag, he won't find his way back onto the train when he next gets off.'

CHAPTER THIRTEEN

THE HOBART POLICE STATION was one block along from Phantom Time Books. I'd been to the fourth floor often as a child with our father, and also a handful of times since Wes had started working there. As I moved between the desks I felt the eyes of the officers on me. I knew what they were thinking: *Here's the son who didn't return for the funeral.*

I reached the end of the floor, and a plain-clothes officer seated at one of the desks glanced up. 'Can I help you?'

'I'm looking for Wes Rosenberger.'

His eyes lingered on me for a moment. 'You're his younger brother?'

I didn't respond.

He pointed his pen at an office with a glass partition, and I glanced across to see Wes and Martin talking to someone out of view.

'Thank you.' I approached the office and saw Inspector Henry Sutter standing behind a desk with his hands on his hips.

Embarrassing Wes wasn't my intention; letting him know I wasn't afraid of him was every bit my intention. I knocked on the glass door, and when he saw me a look of horror crossed his face. Henry considered me with a blank expression.

Martin stuck his head out the door. 'Geo, we're kind of in the middle of something.'

'It's urgent.'

He clearly hadn't expected me to say that.

With a raised voice, so everyone on the floor could hear, I said, 'I know where the ghost train's appearing next.'

Henry glared at Wes.

Through gritted teeth, Wes said to Martin, 'Get him out of here.'

Martin stepped out of the office and ushered me away by the arm. I said to Wes over Martin's shoulder, 'The first of February outside State. It'll tie up your explanation nicely.'

Wes's jaw tightened. Henry crossed his arms.

'Alright,' Martin said, leading me out, 'you've done what you came to do.'

#

I arrived at Nic's place midafternoon. With Hayden's rehearsal finishing at one, I figured there was a fair chance she'd be home. Alessia had been gone barely three hours, Sten and Camille were gone forever, Labuschagne wouldn't be back until late evening, and Paco wouldn't be in until after his shift at the Winston. The more time I spent in the house, the more I found myself craving the company of those who went against my normal instincts and routines. I was comfortable being alone. Really alone. To the extent

Alessia was frequently reminding me to live: 'You can't create from an empty pool of experiences.' Now I missed these people. Not only that, but I'd come to depend on them to neutralise Wes.

When Nic opened the door I could tell this was a bad time. In her trackies, T-shirt and wide-cut headband, she was in the midst of cleaning the house. She didn't pretend to be pleased to see me.

'Nobody's home.' I hoisted a thumb in the direction of town.

'You don't realise how good you have it.'

'Pardon?'

'Wes came by this morning.'

'Oh no. Did he —?'

'His reaction when he realised the locks had been changed brought out the neighbours.'

'Oh god.'

'I didn't bother calling Martin. I called the police.'

I shook my head. 'Nic —'

'So how can I help you, Geo? You need company?'

'I'm sorry, Nic. I didn't mean for —'

'I'd love to be alone. I'd love to have the choice of keeping or selling, of staying or getting on a plane and disappearing forever. You act like you're trapped. You have no idea.'

I didn't say anything.

Her eyes were red from crying. She looked away. 'He has no intention of letting me go.'

'You have the right to choose what your life will be.'

Her voice hardened. 'We have a son, Geo, not a house.'

'I appreciate there are other —'

'You don't know anything.'

'I'm sorry, I didn't mean to ...' My voice trailed off, and she closed the door behind me.

I drove to South Hobart. I felt awful for Nic, and guilty for feeling bad for myself. She was right: my trip home was entirely selfish.

I parked across from Audrey's parents' house on Denison Street. I could never repair the hurt I'd caused Audrey, and though I wasn't looking for forgiveness, there was a history between us that deserved acknowledgement.

Audrey's mother opened the door. Her face fell when she saw me. 'How dare you?'

I didn't know what to say.

She raised a finger. 'Don't ever knock on this door again.'

I turned back to the car, and skidded away as she stared from the doorway.

After swinging around the corner, I pulled over. The day was deteriorating fast. I'd brought the first action upon myself with Wes, and it had continued to fall from that low height. I took out my phone and called Alessia. Her flight had landed in Sydney at 2.30 p.m., and it was now 3.20. The call went through to voicemail.

I flung the phone onto the passenger seat and drove off. Five minutes later I parked back at the house and set off on foot for the Winston. It wasn't busy when I arrived, and I asked one of the waitstaff if I might have a word with Paco. I said I was a friend, and it was semi-urgent.

With a look of concern, Paco emerged from the kitchen in his white top and blue apron. 'Geo. What's wrong?'

'Can we talk? I only need a minute.'

'Sure. Sure.' We slid into an empty booth. He looked at me with full attention.

'I'm having a bad day.'

'Tell me everything.'

I shrugged. 'I dropped Alessia off at the airport. There was a situation with Wes at the police station. Then Nic. Then Audrey's mother. Then Alessia didn't answer her phone. Now I'm here. I just needed to see a face I know. I'm sorry. I don't want to cause you trouble.'

'If they don't like me helping a friend, they can go fuck themselves.' He said it loudly, and the bartender and a passing waiter glanced in our direction.

'I was wondering … how about later, after your shift, we go ghost train hunting? For old time's sake. I'll grab a bottle of something.'

'Oh man,' he said, 'I would love to. But a few of the kitchen staff are going to a bush party at Nicholls Rivulet.' His face lit up. 'You should come. It will be the perfect thing. We will take wine. I have ganja.'

'Thank you. But I'm not in the right frame of mind.'

'It's a full moon. There will be fire, people laughing, stories. It will make you pumped. I'm pumped just thinking about it.'

'I think I'll decline. But it's very kind of you.'

We slid out of the booth and faced each other. He was defiant. 'Then I will cancel. I see you need somebody. This is not a problem for me. I'll come to the house after my shift, and we will go ghost train hunting.'

I hugged him and kissed his cheek. 'Absolutely not. I forbid it. You're a real friend, Paco. Thank you. You've given me everything by being you. Have a great time tonight.'

'We leave at eleven. If you change your mind, come here and we will go together.'

'Thank you,' I said.

Back at Yardley Street I stepped into the eerily quiet house. I went into the sitting room and took in our father's rubbish, item by item. I sensed a presence in the room, and if I hadn't known any different I might have thought it was a ghost. But this evening I knew it was something worse: the regret from memories old and new.

I did a circuit of the house, wending my way through the kitchen and back up the corridor that ran alongside the three bedrooms and bathroom, before entering the living room and standing at the threshold of our father's study. From this position I could see the study while looking back through the living room, across the corridor and sitting room, and into the kitchen. The house contained our family story. I felt it now, and knew I couldn't spend the evening here alone. I also believed I had one final action in me. Something that would draw a line for the area we'd already crossed.

I went into the sitting room and forced open the liquor cabinet, and took out the thousand-dollar bottle of Lark.

#

I woke the following morning with a searing headache and an empty glass in my lap. My gaze sharpened and fell on Wes sitting across from me. That was when I realised I'd slept the night in the recliner – his chair, our father's chair. That was also when my eyes landed upon the empty bottle of Lark on the coffee table. The homeless man from New Norfolk station – I couldn't recall his name; Mike, perhaps – had spent the night. I'd driven out there with the intention of drinking with him on the platform, but when I'd arrived it was obvious he hadn't eaten in a couple of days.

So I'd brought him back and made him a meal, and afterwards we'd started drinking. I didn't know what time I had passed out, but evidently we'd got through my father's prized whisky without too much trouble.

I glanced at the sofa where Mike had slept, but it was vacant. Wes was sitting in the other sofa, cross-legged, smoking a cigarette.

'Is he …?' I indicated Mike's sofa.

'I let him out.'

I made to rise. 'How long have I been —?'

He held out his hand, far too calm for my liking. 'Relax.' He took a drag and leaned his hand across to flick away the ash. I didn't understand why he would ash on the sofa, and then, to my horror, I realised my viola was beside him. The ash dropped neatly onto the belly.

'Holy fucking hell,' I said, coming up, meaning to lunge at him. But no sooner had I risen than I was slapped back down, a sharp pain shooting through my hand and up my arm.

My left hand was cuffed to the wall gas heater.

'You handcuffed me?'

He sipped his Scotch and took a sequence of puffs until a long cone had formed at the tip of the cigarette. Releasing it from his lips, he carefully held it over the viola.

'Wes … I'm begging you.'

He tapped lightly, and the ash fell into the f-hole.

'Fuck you,' I said. 'Fuck you.' I pulled at the handcuffs.

'You caused this.'

'What are you talking about?' I knew what he was talking about.

'You come into my place of work. You embarrass me in front of my boss … in front of my colleagues. Then when I arrive at the station this morning I have this shoved in front of me.' He slid the *Sunday Mercury* across the coffee table.

The front-page headline read: *Ghost Train in Tasmania. Illegals. Body. Police Cover-Up.* It was Saul's article, picked up from *BorderlessTIMES*.

'Wes —'

'As if that weren't enough, a sheriff of the court hand-delivers this to me at my desk.' He set down the envelope that I knew was the motion to sell. 'Then I come home, thinking what more? What more could make my shit life crappier than it already is? And I find you and a bum passed out in my sitting room, having consumed the only other possession in the world that means anything to me.'

'Wes, however much you hate me right now, you need to release me from these cuffs.'

He took a drag. 'So I'm thinking … I'm thinking the viola is a fair exchange.'

I knew in that moment I'd lost everything.

'What right do you have selling Dad's house?' he asked.

'It's just as much mine as it is yours.'

'You're a fucking bastard.'

All this while he was flicking ash into the viola's f-hole.

'So you handcuffed me? Now what?'

He refilled his glass but kept his hand with the cigarette suspended over the viola.

He said, 'You file a motion to force a sale, then you come home and break open Dad's cabinet. I'd almost understand if you drank it yourself. I still wouldn't forgive you, but I could understand. I could even comprehend it if you'd poured it down the drain. But to give it to a bum? That's not hurting Dad's memory, that's glassing me. So yes … I take it personally. As stupid as it sounds, that bottle to me was what your viola is to you. And you knew it.'

'I needed to get your attention.'

He laughed. 'You got it.'

'I want you to take me seriously.'

'Nobody gives a shit about talentless dreamers.' He lowered the cigarette and, very slowly, stubbed it out on the wood.

My throat burned; it took all my strength not to burst into tears. 'Wes, un-cuff me now.'

'Drink?' He stood up and roughly filled the Scotch glass in my lap, alcohol splashing all over me.

I caught the glass with my free hand before it toppled. 'What now?'

'We sell the house is what now. You made sure of that.'

'I'll cancel the motion to sell if you'll discuss a compromise.'

'Fuck you.'

'I'm serious. You can buy me out. We can rent.'

He looked at me scornfully. 'And then you can happily disappear down that shithole dream of yours.'

'How can you not get that this mountain in front of us can be reduced to an anthill if only you'd be reasonable.'

He dropped the stub into the f-hole and raised the viola to his chin.

My heart lurched. 'Wes, put it down. Please.'

He was holding it in position, bowless, ready to play. 'Why did you choose the viola? Did Mum put the idea in your head because you were crap at the violin?'

'I chose it because Dad also played it. We come from a family of violists, not violinists.'

272

He thought about it a moment, and shrugged. 'It's possible I knew that.' He was speaking with an unlit cigarette in his mouth, the viola resting on his shoulder. He took out a match with his free hand and tried to light it by scratching it against the body. He struck it a few times without success, the match snapping in two. He frowned. 'Swear as fuck I thought that would work.'

'Wes,' I said, my voice shaking.

He dropped the viola onto the table, and it tumbled to the ground. I could see that it had a chip on the waist. He lit a cigarette and flicked it at me. It landed on my lap, and I hastily scooped it up. He lit another and placed it between his lips. He reached for the viola and held it by the neck.

I laid the cigarette on the coffee table. He had a swig of Scotch.

'Wes, I swear, if you destroy the viola —'

'What?' he said, walking about the sitting room, the instrument slung across his shoulder like an axe. 'What do you swear?'

'It will be the end of us.'

He burst out laughing. 'Brother, you and I are done.' He kicked at the letter from the lawyer. 'The only thing more certain is that this house will no longer be here for me. And this viola will no longer be here for you.'

A car screeched to a halt outside. Wes went to the window and pulled back the curtain. 'Shit,' he muttered. He checked the latch on the door, then pointed the viola at me. 'Keep your mouth shut.'

There was a rap on the door. 'Wes?'

It was Nic. He didn't respond.

She banged on the door. 'Wes.'

'He's standing right there,' I shouted. 'I'm handcuffed to the heater.'

'Wes, open the door.'

'Go home,' he told her. 'I'm talking with my brother. I'll come to you after —'

'Wes, are you out of your mind? Open the door.'

'Go the fuck away. This is none of your business.'

'He's destroying the viola,' I said. 'Call Martin. Don't come in.'

There was more pounding.

Wes said to me, 'What the fuck's wrong with you? It's not enough you steal away Dad's house. Now you want to put a wedge between me and my family.'

'What family? They don't want you anymore.'

'Wes, open now. Geo, shut up.'

Wes looked at me. 'What are you talking about?'

'Nic's divorcing you. How can you not know?'

He pointed the viola at me, but his voice faltered. 'Stay the fuck out of my marriage.'

Nic pounded on the door again. He opened it, and she came hurtling into the hallway. When she stepped into the sitting room, I saw her quickly assess the situation. 'Give me the keys,' she said to Wes.

'Is it true?'

'What?'

'Is it true?'

She teared up.

He shook his head. 'I don't believe it. Tell me it's not true.'

She didn't move towards him. A tear rolled down her cheek.

I'd never seen my brother cry before. 'You have no desire to reconcile?'

She shook her head.

'How can this —?' He turned to me, in a state of such distress I thought he would strike me with the instrument. 'You.'

He made to swing, but Nic lunged towards him. 'Wes, don't!'

He stopped, then turned to the wall with the viola raised.

'Wes,' Nic shouted through tears, 'you've hurt enough people.'

In that pause the energy within him was released. He flung the viola to the side. It struck the liquor cabinet with a blunt thud, and fell to the floor.

Nic approached him, but he pushed past her and walked out. She quickly locked the door behind him.

There was a set of keys on the kitchen table. She brought them over and unlocked the handcuffs; it took her a few attempts, as my hands were shaking.

I scrambled out of the sofa and went to my viola. There were two gashes in the wood. The neck seemed intact, but it was impossible to know the true damage.

'He destroyed it,' I said.

Nic slumped in the recliner, her head in her hands. 'I hate you.'

There was a knock on the door, and we looked at each other.

She went over to the door. 'Who is it?'

'Nathan Green. Photographer from Pearson Realty.'

I hastily placed the viola in its case and grabbed our father's car keys. I was in no condition to drive, but I didn't care. I opened the door, sidestepped Nathan and hurried down the steps.

#

I stopped at Campbell Town to fill up with petrol and call Jacob.

'It's Geo.'

'Geo, how are you?'

'The viola's damaged. I had a fight with Wes. I'm in Campbell Town. Can I bring it to you in the morning?'

'How bad?'

'I don't know. I'm scared to look. He threw it against a wall.'

'Bring it now.'

'I don't want to disturb your Sunday.'

'Bring it now. The instrument is my child.'

'I'll be there in forty minutes.'

The line went dead. I bought some tobacco, filters and a lighter from the Caltex shop; I was regressing already. I rolled three cigarettes, lit one up, and pulled back out onto the Midland Highway.

Three-quarters of an hour later, I parked outside Jacob's luthier shop on Charles Street. I knocked on the door, and Jacob emerged down the stairs to let me in. 'Show me.'

I handed him the case. He took it to the counter, carefully lifted out the viola and examined it.

I couldn't contain myself. 'Is it lost?'

'I don't think so. There will be some scars, but the sound won't be affected.'

'Thank god.'

He immediately set to work.

'Do you mind if I smoke?' I said.

'Go ahead.'

I sat in the corner and watched him work. It was like observing an artist. He wasn't the type who spoke while he worked, and I didn't initiate conversation.

This was it. Our family had ended. Soon the house would be gone, the last link between Wes and me severed. I was relieved – I was nervous, but I was relieved. Hadn't it been my intention all along to fly out of Hobart with no physical link between us?

After an hour Jacob handed me the viola. He'd restrung it with composite-core strings that had a synthetic core. I took it into my hands and studied the repairs. The chips were smoothed out, but the most important thing was the sound.

I tuned it, then played a range of notes. It was precisely as I knew it, and I replaced it carefully in the case. 'Jacob, you have saved my life.'

'It will continue to breathe music.'

'Thank you.' I went around the counter to hug him.

He poured us each a Scotch, and we toasted the viola. 'To sure hands.'

We drank the whisky down.

'Are you okay?' he asked.

'I'm okay.'

'After our last meeting, I was thinking a lot about the story you told me. How your mother came to be in possession of the viola.'

I nodded.

'It's a wonderful story,' he said. 'Sad, and tragic, and beautiful. It's a love story. Wherever your heart takes you, the music from this viola will carry the notes of that story. And the more you embrace it, the richer the music will be.'

CHAPTER FOURTEEN

JACOB LIVED IN a one-bedroom apartment above the luthier shop with his wife, Greta. It was late afternoon by the time he'd repaired the viola, and I intended to sleep either in the car or on a bench in Princes Square. But Jacob kindly offered for me to stay downstairs. He cobbled together a few blankets to act as a mattress, and that night I lay in the dark beneath the shadowy projection of violins, violas and cellos perched on the walls. I imagined Labuschagne falling asleep like this every night beneath the ghostly silhouettes of books.

The next morning, the first of February, Jacob came down early to open for business. I folded up the blankets and excused myself, using the public toilets in Princes Square to wash up. Suitably refreshed, I bought a French loaf and some cheese and salami at Coles, and went back into the square to feast. It had been thirty-six hours since I'd last eaten.

When I returned to the shop I was grateful to find a pot of coffee on the go. I sat on the stool across from Jacob's workbench and sipped at the brew as he readied his tools for the day's work. 'Are you driving back this morning?' he asked.

'I think I'll hang around town for the day. I only need to be in Hobart this evening.'

'If you don't have anywhere to go, you're welcome to help in the shop.'

'I'd love the company. But what could I possibly do?' For a Monday, I imagined a handful of walk-ins being a busy day.

'You can play for me while I work.'

It was a lovely proposition. And so I spent my last Monday in Tasmania playing for Jacob in the corner while he cut and sculpted the scroll for an alto viola he was building. Between pieces he'd make a comment or two, but for the most part he worked in silence. He was interested to hear about Mum's last year, and how she would nominate a piece of music for me to rehearse. He didn't ask about our father, but he was curious to know if Wes still played. I told him about the evening with Alessia the previous week, and that it had been Wes's first time in seventeen years.

Jacob was dismayed. 'His violin has been denied the opportunity to realise its full potential.'

I watched him use a palm tool to undercut the two channels up the back of the pegbox. His craftsmanship was mesmerising.

'What music did he play?' he asked.

'"Shenandoah".'

He nodded. 'That is good.'

After a home-cooked lunch with Greta, the afternoon passed quickly. I told Jacob about the eight-second audition rejection, and that I'd been grossly underprepared. He said no piece should ever be cut short, out of respect for the player, the music and the instrument. He asked if I might play it for him now, so that the music might achieve its destiny. I complied, and when I finished he thanked me.

A little before 5 p.m. I bid Jacob farewell. We both knew it was the last time we'd ever see each other. With a heavy heart, I climbed into the Ford and began the two-and-a-half hour drive back to Hobart.

#

I parked at the house on Yardley Street just after seven-thirty, and set off on foot for the State Cinema. According to Labuschagne's prediction I was comfortably on time.

The atmosphere outside State was typical for a weekday evening. A modest amount of foot traffic diverted into the cinema, and the road traffic ebbed and flowed along Elizabeth Street in both directions. I did a quick scan from the bus stop to see if anyone had come for the train's last appearance, but found only strangers. It didn't surprise me that Wes hadn't bothered, but I was expecting to see Labuschagne and, to a lesser degree, the digital journalist-slash-watchdog with many names.

The last shard of daylight retreated, and I settled on the bus bench with my hands in my pockets, eyes trained on the street. Every few minutes I glanced around to see if I could spot Labuschagne. It felt surreal to be sitting on the bench where I'd sat with Sten about a month ago – on my first ghost train hunt – chasing what seemed the impossible dream. And now I'd returned to witness it with my own eyes.

A bus pulled up, and the driver gave me a fierce look when I didn't move to board. The traffic was starting to thin out, and within time I stopped looking for company. I checked the time on my phone: 7.55 p.m. Labuschagne had predicted an 8.02 p.m. appearance. What if the ghost train actually came? I'd be terrified. I wasn't really expecting it, was I? I wasn't hoping for it to appear. I was here because in the future I needed to look back knowing there were no regrets.

I believed Sten wholeheartedly, but I believed it for him. I believed it because it was my nature to believe in anyone's dream, just as I hoped everyone would believe in mine. I hadn't known Sten long enough to call him a true friend, but he certainly stood before me as a mirror to my life. He'd arrived for a reason, and he had stayed in our house for a reason. I was here, waiting for his train, because of that.

I checked the time again: 8 p.m. I concentrated my thoughts on the ghost train hunter. He was the person to whom my focus should be directed: the target of my tribute. I remembered how he'd approached me in Argyle Street; how he'd won over Wes with a rolled joint; and I'd thought, *My god, this person is going to paint our house and do it well.* I remembered how he'd helped me clean the house, and then when I had put the rubbish back out, how he'd said nothing.

Once again I checked my watch: 8.02 p.m. If the train didn't come within the next minute, how long would I wait? I glanced up, and I was about to look back down to track the passing seconds when a beam of light appeared from behind a curve in the road, about a hundred metres away. It was yellow and brilliant, and penetrated the night-lit road like no car or bus could. A few people turned to look.

In the next moment, the light flashed in without a sound. Before I could register the situation it stood before me, a mountain of billowing steam, shimmering and black, Sten's ghost train, outside the State Cinema.

Pedestrians shrieked. Some people scuttled away to watch from the safety of distance, while others hustled towards the train to see it more clearly. Behind me patrons within the cinema foyer stood pressed to the window, wide-eyed and speechless. Mobile devices were pointed at the phenomenon.

The train was huge and imposing. A breathing bull. And it hit me: *My god, the ghost train.* The front light was as stunning as I'd imagined from Bill Bright's account, large and pulsating like a full moon. The lead locomotive cast an ominous silhouette, and a thought flashed through my mind: *So this is what a dream looks like?*

I edged towards the front carriage, concentrated and alert, wanting to stamp the image in my memory so that years later I'd be able to retrieve every detail. Knowing the train was seconds from vanishing, I tiptoed as far forward as I dared, a white glow from the final carriage indicating the backmost door to be open.

To my astonishment a figure emerged from the crowd and strode purposefully towards the train. When I raised my hand to screen out the light, I recognised that the figure was Wes. At first I thought he was wanting to get a closer look, but from his demeanour I could quickly tell he was intent upon boarding the carriage with the open door.

I shouted and ran towards him. 'Wes.'

It was enough to make him pause, and in that moment I had time to reach him. His body was taut, but when I grabbed his shoulders he relaxed. A loud hiss emanated from the engine, and a puff of steam floated up towards the night sky.

I glanced along the front two carriages, and there in the window was Sten, looking back at us, ghostly pale. Sitting across from him was a woman, younger than him, whom I took to be his mother. He'd done it. Sten had boarded his train. Or as Labuschagne suggested, he'd been on and off the train for two decades, and had now found it again.

I sensed a second movement. Exiting the State Cinema, with snake-like urgency, was Labuschagne. He made for the open door on the back carriage. I truly believed he was going to clamber aboard, so certain were his steps, and there were gasps from the people on the street. One person shouted, 'Don't do it!' but Labuschagne didn't falter.

He pulled up short of the door and slid Sten's Gladstone bag into the carriage. He stepped back. In the next instant, Sten walked from the second carriage into the last carriage, and collected his bag. He nodded at Labuschagne. I imagined the thought surfacing in his mind: *Boy, this man is good.*

I thought he might get off, but he stood there with his bag, earnest and content. His eyes found mine, and a smile crept onto his lips.

The carriage door closed, and the train rolled forward with a heavy chug. It advanced thirty metres and, all at once, carriage by carriage, vanished before our eyes. People gasped, a woman fainted, and the cars that had been backed up behind the train erupted into a cacophony of tooting. Then everyone began chattering, and those watching from behind the State foyer window pulled away.

Matthew or Mason or Robert or Rupert or Kyle or Cale or Carl or Paul or Saul emerged from the crowd, his DSLR slung around his neck. We watched him amble away.

Labuschagne patted Wes and me on the back. 'Thank you. Thank you both.' He walked off down Elizabeth Street in the direction of Phantom Time Books.

#

When Wes and I came into the sitting room, my eyes went immediately to the unopened bottle of Lark on top of the liquor cabinet. I wasn't surprised he'd replaced it; that in his heart there was a symbolic need to spend a thousand dollars to wrest back what the whisky represented.

He uncorked the Lark without ceremony, as if he were opening a five-dollar cleanskin. He poured two double shots, and handed me one. We sipped without clinking glasses. I had no memory of the Scotch from two nights before, but tasting it now, it was the smoothest liquid ever to pass my lips.

Wes made a questioning gesture towards the viola leaning against the wall. I nodded. Relief crossed his face.

He placed his glass on the cabinet. 'Look, I know it's late, but the house is a fucking pigsty. How about we do a quick clean?'

I tried to play it cool, but when he said that, I lost a lungful of air. 'Good call.'

He went into the kitchen and returned with a roll of garbage bags. Stripping off two pieces, he handed one to me. He scooped up the packet of beef jerky on the coffee table, and the two bottles of JD on the carpet. I followed behind, gathering up the Chivas Regal and the empty carton of cigarettes. After we were done with the sitting room, we moved on to the living room. I had to catch myself from tearing up as we went through the house. Wes couldn't have said more with words.

Within an hour we'd restored the house to its normal state. We put the bags out back, and when we came inside my brother poured us another round from the Lark. This time he raised his glass. 'To Sten.'

'To Sten.'

We clinked glasses.

'Man, this is a good drop,' Wes said.

I shook my head. 'Stunning.'

#

The following morning I picked up Alessia at Hobart Airport. The tension of the past few days fell away as we embraced.

'I love you,' I said. 'Did you have a good time?'

'Yes. I am glad I went.'

'What did you make of Sydney?'

'Wonderful. But I like Hobart better.'

'There's something I need to do on the way home,' I said. 'I'd like you to be with me when I do it.'

As we drove back to town, she filled me in on her time in Sydney. She'd watched Federico perform with Cirque. He'd taken her to Manly Beach for a walk, and to Bondi for breakfast. They had gone to the Royal Botanic Garden and the Museum of Contemporary Art, and climbed the Sydney Harbour Bridge. She'd done what you're supposed to do when you visit Sydney, and she was glad to have spent time with him. I didn't feel jealous or insecure. I was happy for her; I was happy that she was happy.

'How are things with your brother?' she asked.

I told her the story of that night.

'Oh, Geo. I am sorry I wasn't there.'

'We couldn't have brought it to this point if you were here. Things are okay. Whatever happens with the house, there's a sort of acceptance. Even if our relationship is finished. The viola got bruised and has some scars, but we're fine. That's why I'm going back with you on Saturday.'

'I am glad.'

'I was running from it before. Now, I just want to leave with you.'

We drove through the gates of Cornelian Bay Cemetery and followed the road to the Derwent River side. Alessia knew I hadn't come here since my return to Hobart.

I took out my viola, and we walked through the flowering gardens until we stood above the bronze plaque that contained Mum's cremated remains. The inscription read: *Norina Ilaria Rosenberger. 1947–2014. Beloved Wife and Mother. Music in her Soul.*

'I wouldn't be where I am if not for her. I wouldn't have met you. She put music in my heart. She's the reason I keep stepping in the direction of my dream.'

Alessia pressed her face to my shoulder. I kissed her lightly on the head.

I glanced at my father's plaque beside Mum's: *Herman Franz Rosenberger. 1946–2015. Husband of Norina and Father of Wesley and Geo.*

My heart stirred, and I raised the viola to my chin and ran the bow across the strings. I played *Shenandoah*. Alessia stepped back to give me space. I played for my parents. As the music surfaced, the emotions within me surfaced, and my eyes filled with tears. I knew my father loved me. He hadn't known how to show it, and for a period of time he'd forgotten that he loved me.

The injury had denied him his passion for his work, and his own father had denied him his passion for music. Twice his own dream had been taken from him. I played for him now. My brother had lost his dream just as our father had. And our mother, like me, had pursued one passion, expressed one dream. I felt Alessia at my back. The thought I'd risk our relationship had broken me further – this person who'd flown from Italy to be with me, who stood here now as I played for my family. The music came, the tears came, and the touch of her hand gave me the strength to finish the piece. I lowered the viola and dropped the bow. Alessia came to my side, and my arms fell around her.

#

The house was quiet when we arrived at Yardley Street. Paco was asleep on the sofa; Wes had already left for work. We deposited Alessia's baggage in my bedroom, and I put on a load of washing.

'Are you hungry?' I said. 'Let's make bruschetta.'

We tiptoed around the kitchen so as not to disturb Paco. It was only when we sat down to eat that I noticed the envelope on the table. The affixed sticky note read: *Signed. Wes.*

It was the action to sell, from Pearson Realty. For the second time that morning I struggled to fight back tears.

Paco walked into the kitchen, bleary-eyed.

I gathered my emotions. 'Join us.' I pushed back the chair and served him a plate. 'Enjoy. There's coffee on the counter.'

'You are a legend. Hello, Alessia.'

'Hello, Paco.'

He dug into the food. 'I will miss this house.'

'I won't,' I said, and regretted the comment.

'I will. I gave it my heart. All of it. I finished.'

I looked at him. 'It's finished?'

He nodded. 'The house and the studio. I did a good job. I'm happy. You will be happy, I am sure.'

'Paco, you're a treasure.'

'And now I will leave. On Saturday.'

'Us too. What time's your flight?'

'Two o'clock.'

'Ours leaves at one-thirty. We can get Wes to drop us off.'

'That would be nice.'

After breakfast Paco took a shower, and Alessia and I stepped outside to admire the finished paint job. I had something I wanted to say to her, but as we went up the stony path, Walter stuck his head over the fence.

'Hey, Walter. Is Charlotte sleeping better?'

'Like a dream.'

I wanted to be alone with Alessia, but Walter kept looking at me. 'Hey, Geo?'

'Yeah?'

'Is your friend still here? The one with the tattoo on his chest.'

'He's inside.'

'Tell him I'm ready to make another transaction. He'll know what I mean.'

'I'll tell him, Walter.'

He nodded, and his head disappeared from the fence.

'You have interesting neighbours,' Alessia said.

'The light from the lamp was scaring his daughter. We bribed him, and Paco's obviously ...' I shook myself out it. 'Forget it. What I want to tell you, what's on my mind ... is that I want you to know I love you. In the same way you love me. I'm coming back to Rome with you, if you'll have me. I won't ever put my dream before you. I swear it.'

We hugged, and went to sit up on the studio deck.

'This used to be my sky,' I said. 'The sun rising over there, moving across here in the afternoon. I'd look upon it and feel like it belonged to me. At night I'd search it for constellations. But I belong to a different section of sky now. My life is steered by different stars.'

'This is my first time in the Southern Hemisphere. It only occurred to me, as you described these feelings … that it is my first time below the equator.'

'My destiny lies in the north. Perhaps that's why we fit so well together.'

She kissed my cheek. 'This is what I believe.'

#

Alessia and I passed the afternoon walking around town. At some point we found ourselves at the Hobart Book Shop in Salamanca Square. I was hoping to get a book on the history of Tasmanian rail.

As we were leaving I sensed someone watching from one of the aisles. 'It's Audrey,' I said.

Alessia turned. 'Where?'

'There. I think she noticed us. We should say hello.'

We walked back inside, and it was Alessia who spoke first. 'You must be Audrey. Geo has told me so much about you. I'm Alessia.'

'Oh,' Audrey said, taken aback.

'Geo says your voice is so … I don't know the word … but he tells me you could sing with the birds.'

Audrey's cheeks flushed. 'He is being overly kind.'

'How are you, Audrey?' I said.

'Good. Fine.'

'Would you like to join us for an early dinner?' Alessia said. 'We are having fish and chips.'

'Thank you, but … I have somewhere to be.'

'We're leaving on Saturday,' I said.

Audrey nodded. 'I'm happy to meet you, Alessia.'

'Me too.'

We made to leave, and when I glanced back Audrey had reached to take a book from the shelf.

#

Nic invited Alessia and me to dinner on Thursday evening. It had been a hectic couple of days: Wednesday had been spent cleaning, and that afternoon Nathan Green from Pearson Realty had returned to complete the photography. With the house restored, Wes slept in his bedroom. Paco took our parents' room, and surprisingly Wes offered no protest. Paco was a godsend, helping with a number of runs down to Glenorchy Waste Disposal as I made a final push to clear out the hoarded goods from under the house.

We were exhausted by the time we arrived for dinner at Nic's, and I was relieved to see it was just the four of us. We had a lovely evening, though no music was played.

After Hayden went to bed I told Nic that Wes had signed the contract to sell. She went to her room and returned with a sheet of paper. It was a notice of divorce, from Wes.

#

Friday passed in a blur. After meeting with Terry in the morning, Alessia and I went to see a film at State. Wes didn't stay at the house that night, and my suspicion that he'd found a rental was confirmed when Nic called to say he'd picked up his clothes and personals when she and Hayden were out.

On Saturday Wes came around to take Paco, Alessia and me to the airport. I asked if he'd mind driving by Phantom Time Books on the way out.

'Do you want to go in?' he asked.

'Just drop a gear as we go past.' I wound down the window.

As we cruised by the store the door opened, and Labuschagne emerged onto the footpath with his mother's pendant in his hand. He tipped a finger to his forehead in casual salute.

Sten, Labuschagne, Paco and Camille: they were the surprise gifts.

At the airport we unloaded our baggage and bid Paco farewell. He veered off to the Jetstar side of the terminal.

I noticed Wes's violin in the boot.

'Don't get too excited,' he said. 'It's just for me.'

We were parked in the drop-off zone, and an airport worker in a hi-vis vest was looking our way.

'You better get going.' Wes motioned to me.

I leaned in to hug him but realised I'd misread his gesture. He was holding out an envelope.

'Oh,' I said.

'Your half from Dad's car.'

'Right.' I took it. 'Thanks.'

The man in the hi-vis vest was striding towards us.

A smile creased Wes's face. 'Until next time, I guess?'

I shrugged. 'I guess.'

He slapped me on the shoulder, then went around the car and climbed in. We watched him drive away.

Twenty minutes later we were checked in and moving with the queue through security. I had thought I'd left Hobart forever, and now I was sure of it. My track led away from this place. There was something hopeful about that, but it also carried a little sadness. I was glad I felt that way.

We collected our carry-on baggage and walked to the gate.

'It's good you came back,' Alessia said. 'Do you think so?'

'I do.' Our eyes met. 'But I'm happy to be going home.'

ACKNOWLEDGMENTS

I'D LIKE TO thank my wife, Yvonne, to whom this novel is dedicated. We are so very lucky to share a passion for creating stories. Not only is she my favourite writer, she's my most feared reader, wielding a red pen like others might a weapon! I need her for this, and much more. Our plot-chat walks, tea & coffee literary musings, and post-film deconstructions, are my treasured moments of living. To Rohan Wilson, my writing brother, I wouldn't have got here without you. To my reading crew: David Beaton; Adam Berkowitz; Dave Canavan; Gerard Kambeck; Marc Weinberg ... you added the heart to this project; the next Tasmanian whiskey is on me. The best advice I received was from an aspiring songwriter I had a fleeting conversation with over twenty years ago: it was his belief that every artist had someone out there who wanted *their* work; and it was the artist's responsibility to find them. To my publisher, Barry Scott, and the team at Transit Lounge ... I finally found you! Thank you for seeing something in my story that moved you to take a chance on me. To my agent, Martin Shaw, who ushered me in their direction, I send my gratitude. I owe a great deal to the University of Tasmania Prize (in the 2019 Premier Literary Awards), which cracked open the door. Much love to Jessy Lewis-Blackburn and Kaya Levin for Paco & Camille (for the names, and their spirit). For the Italian and Swedish words, thank you to Rami Gawdat and Jenny Wiklund (all mistakes are my own). Thank you to the wonderful editorial team at Griffith Review, who first published an extract of the manuscript in *Griffith Review 69: The European Exchange*. Thank you to Natasha Cica for being an advocate of my work. Thank you to my editor, Kate Goldsworthy, for her firm and skilled touch. She so quickly understood the story I was trying to tell; if there are failings in the novel, it's because I couldn't rise to meet the challenges of her queries. Ever since I found this dream, there's been not one conversation with my mother where she didn't ask after my writing, or want to know in detail the project I was working on. She's had my back from the beginning, and sharing the fruition of this with her has been a great joy. I've been writing for so long that I'd become content doing so for myself; and now, after all these years, a book finally arrives into the world, and it's because of the encouragement and belief of others (many of whom aren't mentioned here): thank you, thank you, thank you. We are nothing without *our* people. I appreciate you all.

Brendan Colley was born in South Africa. After graduating with a degree in education, he taught in the U.K. and Japan for eleven years before settling down in Australia in 2007. Winner of the University of Tasmania Prize for best new unpublished work in the 2019 Premier's Literary Prizes, *The Signal Line* is his first novel. He lives in Hobart with his wife.

@brendancolley